Warlord of the North

Warlord of the North

Book 8 in the Anarchy Series

By

Griff Hosker

Contents

Warlord of the North...i
Contents ii
Prologue...2
Scottish Invasion...4
Chapter 1...4
Chapter 2...18
Chapter 3...25
Chapter 4...33
Chapter 5...44
Chapter 6...56
Chapter 7...67
Chapter 8...80
Chapter 9...89
Chapter 10...100
Chapter 11...110
Chapter 12...123
Chapter 13...133
Chapter 14...146
Chapter 15...159
Chapter 16...172
Chapter 17...181
Chapter 18...197
Chapter 19...208
Chapter 20...224
Chapter 21...234
Epilogue...250
Glossary 251
Maps and Illustrations...253
Historical note...254
Other books by Griff Hosker .... **Error! Bookmark not defined.**

Warlord of the North

Published by Sword Books Ltd 2015
Copyright © Griff Hosker
The author has asserted their moral right under the Copyright, Designs and Patents Act, 1988, to be identified as the author of this work.

All Rights reserved. No part of this publication may be reproduced, copied, stored in a retrieval system, or transmitted, in any form or by any means, without the prior written consent of the copyright holder, nor be otherwise circulated in any form of binding or cover other than that in which it is published and without a similar condition being imposed on the subsequent purchaser.

A CIP catalogue record for this title is available from the British Library.

Cover by Design for Writers
Thanks to Simon Walpole for the Artwork.

Prologue

The German Sea December 1135

As we toiled up the east coast of England through the vilest gales I had ever experienced my mind was on one thing; the succession. King Henry of England, the Duke of Normandy, had been poisoned. History would say he ate too many lampreys. I knew different. I had been there when he was murdered. I had killed his killer. He had been poisoned on the orders of King Louis of France and with the complicity of King David of Scotland. The nobles of Normandy and England had sworn to support the claim of the King's daughter, Maud, but I knew that Stephen of Blois was already heading to London to claim the crown. I would have gone there to stop him; at the cost of my own life if needs be, but I had discovered that my castle and my people were threatened by the Scots. I might regret my decision but I had some chance to save my castle. Stephen of Blois had taken many of his knights with him and I was alone. I might be King Henry's Champion but I knew that I would die needlessly. I would save my home and then wrest the crown from the usurper. I had sworn an oath to Empress Matilda and I would die before I would be foresworn.

My mind tossed along with the ship I had hired. I had with me six men at arms I had hired in Normandy. I had sent already Wulfric and my men at arms and archers home to England. There was danger there too. I knew none of the men I had hired. They had, however, been recommended to me and would have to suffice until my ship docked on the Tees. I was not worried. They were only needed if we were attacked at sea.

The rest of my men were either at my manor on the Maine or on the Tees at Stockton. Until I reached my men I was vulnerable and I was helpless. And I had to get home and get home as quickly as this merchant ship could manage it. Although he had not been party to the murder of King

Henry, Stephen of Blois would benefit more than any other. As soon as he had heard of the death of King Henry he had sailed for England and his brother, Henry the Bishop of Winchester. He had been quick. I just prayed that there would be barons in England who would remember the oath they made to make Matilda the Queen of England. I hoped that there would be others such as myself who would oppose his anointment.

I was not hopeful. I had met too many who looked for themselves before their country. I would have to fight to regain the throne for my Queen. Henry, the son of Maud would become king. I had promised myself that my son would rule and I was never foresworn.

Part 1

Scottish Invasion

Chapter 1

Walter, the captain of the *'Lion'*, the cog on which we sailed, was a nervous man. He knew the problems the death of the King of England and Duke of Normandy would create. The closer we came to England the more nervous he became. We had had a swift voyage and reached the Channel within a day of leaving Normandy. As we passed the Thames estuary he joined me as I looked westwards. "My lord, may I speak with you?"

"Yes Walter, what is the problem?"

"I have sailed the waters close to your home, my lord. I know them well."

"Which is why I hired you."

"I know, my lord, but with the King dead the Scots will flood from the north and who knows what we may find. What if your home is now under Scottish control?"

"It will stand and it will be defended." He looked fearfully north as though the Scots would appear over the horizon at any moment. "What is it you say? Speak plainly."

"My lord I would take you to York rather than Stockton. York is far from King David's clutches. I would feel happier and York is not far from Stockton along the road, is it not?" He smiled weakly, "I would give you half of your money for the voyage back, my lord. I beg you." He pointed to the scudding clouds. "And it will be safer too, my lord. The wind is coming from the north. At this time of year that brings snows and blizzards. We would be sheltered if we travelled the Humber."

"Walter you are a pathetic apology for a man. Perhaps I am used to fighting alongside my own men who have blood coursing through their veins and a backbone." My voice was filled with anger and he recoiled. Shaking my head I said, "It is fortunate for you that I am also a knight. Take us to York but I shall ne'er use your ship again."

He looked like a puppy which has just been rewarded. "Thank you, my lord! Thank you."

I waved over my men at arms. They were huddled beneath a cloak playing with dice. "There is a change of plans. We are to land at York and complete the last sixty miles on horseback."

The six of them were an unknown quantity. I had been forced to hire them by events beyond my control. As my son had gone to my manor in Maine with my remaining men at arms, servants and archers I had been left alone. Robert, Earl of Gloucester and King Henry's son. had advised me to hire swords to protect me. The six I had hired were the best that Caen had to offer.

Abelard, who regarded himself as their leader, nodded and smiled, " I, for one am, pleased that we will be off this ship. I fear it has the worm." He seemed as happy as the captain that we were heading for York. I was the only one who was not. "I have never been to England, my lord, but I have been told that the weather in December is oft times inclement. "

"Aye, that is true but we are men and we are hardy."

He nodded, "It is just that we have thin cloaks, my lord and no furs."

I was not used to such whining from my men. "I will get new cloaks for you at York but I confess, Abelard, I like not this attitude."

He smiled, "We are good warriors, my lord, and we will protect you. You can trust us to do as we were ordered."

I dismissed them and went to the stern where I could be alone with my thoughts. Abelard and his five companions were not my problem. Stephen of Blois and King David were. They were two separate problems and I was hurrying north because Walter was quite right, King David would not wait for a new King. Once he heard of the death of King Henry of England and Duke of Normandy he would seize the opportunity to grab as much land as he could. He would then negotiate with whoever took over from a position of strength. I had sworn an oath to support the claim of Matilda and her son Henry but I had also sworn an oath to protect the border. It was that oath which I would now honour.

As well as my six men at arms I had also hired a youth to look after my horses, Scout and Hunter. He came from a village close to Rouen and was the son of Guy of Tours who had been a man at arms. Guy had once served me and served me well. A slashed hamstring had cost him his livelihood and he now ran an inn close to Rouen. It was strange but I trusted Gilles, even though he was not yet a man, more than Abelard and my hired swords. I had already decided that I would pay them off once I reached Appleton Wiske. That was a mere twelve miles from home.

I descended below decks to speak with Gilles. I did so silently. I heard his voice before I saw him. He was grooming Hunter and speaking to him in Norman. "So, my friend, what is this England like? Although you, like me, are Norman, I know you have been there." Hunter stamped his foot and Scout whinnied. "I know, what is it our master calls you, Scout? You know England but I am speaking to this fine warhorse. My father says the Earl is an honourable man and a fine knight which a soldier can follow to hell and back, but England? I have heard that it is wild and there are naked warriors who paint their bodies blue and are savage. You are a noble horse what do you say?"

Hunter raised his head as though he was nodding.

"Ah, so you too have heard of these savages. Then I will keep my father's short sword by my side and sleep with one eye open."

I smiled. Many people would regard speaking thus with horses as madness. I knew it was not true. The more you spoke with a horse the closer you became. I had ridden Scout now for fifteen years. I had known him longer than any of my men at arms and archers. He was like an extension of me when I rode him. I spoke to him the way that Gilles spoke to both of my horses. Gilles' words to my horses comforted me. They told me much about his character.

I coughed as I descended.

"My lord."

"How are they, Gilles?"

"They would prefer to be running in the open, my lord, but they are calm in this floating coffin."

"You like not the ship?"

"To be truthful my lord, no. I cannot swim. I stay here, below decks, so that I do not have to look at the waves and the sea."

"Well, I came to tell you that we will be landing sooner, rather than later. The Captain will sail to York. We will be there in two or three days. The river runs high at this time of year. You will need to have our horses ready. I should warn you that horses take a day or two to regain their legs after a voyage at sea."

"My father told me. Thank you for the warning my lord." He continued grooming.

"Will you not miss your home, Gilles?"

"If I am to be truthful, my lord, no. At home I am the ostler and I stable and groom horses I see for one night and they are gone. It is dull."

"You crave adventure?"

"I do not know. I would not be a groom for my whole life." He suddenly seemed to realise what he had said. "I am sorry, my lord, I meant no disrespect."

"You will learn, young Gilles, that I value truth and honesty above all else." I could not help liking the earnest young man. "Have you any skills with that sword?"

He nodded, "My father may be crippled and cannot use his legs as he once could but he has trained me to use a sword and a buckler."

"Then when we get to Stockton I would continue your training. You will care for my horses but until I have a new squire then you will follow me to war. How say you?"

His eyes glowed, "It would be an honour, my lord."

"Good." I ascended the ladder to the deck. The King had knighted my son just before his death. My other two squires, John and Leofric were now also knights. For the present, I had no squire. It was a minor consideration. I had many doughty men at arms but a squire was a necessary tool for a knight. In battle, he would bring fresh weapons and horses and he could also guard a knight's back. I would see if any of my barons had sons who could fulfil that function.

As I stood looking west, to England, I wondered if I would have any barons left when I returned home. Stockton was a strong castle as was Durham but my other knights had wooden walls and not enough men to withstand an attack by the Scots. There were many rebels who had fled to Scotland and whom we had trounced who would take this opportunity for revenge. What would I find back in England?

The voyage became calmer once we reached the Humber. They had had rains and the Humber had swollen and burst its banks. It was like an inland sea as we sailed northwest towards the Ouse. I hoped that Walter knew his business. It was difficult to see the actual course of the river. He might have been a fearful man, a coward even, but he knew his craft and he navigated us unerringly to the Ouse and York. The towers of the cathedral and the Roman walls hove into view although I saw that many of the houses which were close to the river were now inundated and underwater.

When we disembarked I fretted for it was hard to see where the land began and the river ended. Gilles spoke to my horses calmly as he led them to more solid ground.

Walter came aft and knuckled his head, "I am sorry we had to land here, my lord. Perhaps Stockton will be as wet." I ignored his words and held out my hand. He nodded and handed me over a bag of coins. It was the half he had promised me.

"A word of advice, Walter of Dover, if you give your word then keep it. You will gain more business that way."

He nodded and I left the boat. I saw him nod to the men at arms as they came on deck. The six of them looked like drowned rats as they mounted their palfreys. None looked happy to be in England. I wondered, as we rode through the damp streets of York, what had made them take service with me. The unrest in Normandy would have ensured work for their swords. Perhaps they wished to serve me and despite the fact that I did not particularly like them they were all warriors and appeared to know their business. I put that from my mind. Thurstan, Archbishop of York, was someone in whom I could place my trust. He had been a loyal servant to King Henry. I desperately needed his advice and counsel.

There was a nervous edge to the guards and sentries as I approached the gates to the palace on the northern side of the city. Had I not been recognised I would have been viewed with suspicion. The Captain of the Guard took my men and Gilles to their quarters and I hurried to meet with the Archbishop.

He shook his head when he saw me, "A black day, Alfraed. That such an accident should befall King Henry..."

"It was no accident, your grace, it was murder."

"Murder?"

I told him all. He knew of Lavinia the murderess. She had killed one of his priests when she had made an assassination attempt on my life.

"That does not bode well." He looked at me. "Henry of Blois, the Bishop of Winchester, has written to me, my lord. I am invited to London. He wishes to crown his brother King of England."

I looked hard at the Archbishop. "Would you condone his coronation? What of Maud, Empress Matilda and young Henry? You know yourself the King's wishes. He wanted the crown and the duchy to be inherited by them."

He sighed, "Do not judge an old man, Alfraed. The Bishop of Winchester makes cogent arguments. King Henry wanted a stable England. Stephen of Blois would give such stability. He has the support of many lords."

I began to rise.

"Sit, I pray you and hear me out." I owed him that much, at least, and I complied. "Do not be so arrogant that you judge me harshly before you hear me out. The Archbishop of Canterbury also supports Stephen. He will be crowned whether I support him or not. However, I have written to them both arguing that we need debate and that King Henry's wishes should be honoured." I nodded, "The problem is that the roads south are impassable because of the rains. I cannot reach London soon. He will be crowned and then I must consider my position."

"We fight!"

"Who?"

"Why Stephen and his traitors, of course!"

"England has enemies closer to home than that." He sighed, "King David has taken Carlisle, the lands as far as Gainford as well as the New Castle. Had your castle not been as strong I fear that the whole of the north would have fallen to him. Balliol has shown his true colours and Barnard Castle is now in Scottish hands. The De Brus clan have claimed Hartness and Guisborough. Those who held lands in Scotland and England are now claiming their English lands and there is no one to gainsay them. I ask again, who do we fight?"

He was right of course and my decision to return home was justified. "We have lost Durham?"

"Geoffrey Rufus holds the castle and Sir Hugh Manningham holds Hexham but the lands of the Bishopric are now Scots. It is merely a matter of time before Durham falls."

"Then what do we do?"

He sighed, "We hold the line at the Tees. Until you return to the valley we are blind and we are impotent. You are the only one who can stir the barons into action. I believe that those who followed you before will be loyal but I fear for the likes of Sir Hugh Manningham. He is isolated close to the border. I am surprised he has held out this long. You must return to your castle as soon as possible."

"Can I expect support from you, your grace?"

Shaking his head he said, "You judge me yet! Of course, I will support you. I have sent letters to the barons. Should the Scots threaten the land south of the Tees we will meet them."

"But we give up the whole of the north to King David."

He ignored my words or at least appeared to. He poured us both a goblet of wine. "Until we have a ruler who can face King David with the full weight of our forces then my answer has to be yes." His voice became quiet, "You see now why I appeared to consider the request of the Bishop of Winchester. It is like a game of chess. The rook we have sacrificed is Durham. We have not lost the game but we have protected..."

"The King or the Queen?"

"Just so, Alfraed, just so."

I sipped my wine. "I will leave on the morrow."

"I am fortifying York. King David will discover that this is no juicy morsel to be swallowed with ease. It will prove most unpalatable I can assure you."

I now understood his position. My father had taught me that sometimes a leader had to make decisions he did not like for the good of all. The Archbishop was right. King David and his voracious Scots were taking advantage of the death of the King. I could not even blame Stephen of Blois. He was taking charge. I was disappointed that Empress Matilda had not taken ship and made her own claim to England. I put the crown from my mind and I vowed to fight King David with every ounce of my being.

We left just after dawn. I now reconsidered my decision to pay off my men at arms. It seemed that I might need them. If I was to fight the whole of Scotland then I would need men at arms no matter how surly they were.

We did not so much ride from York as paddled. Had I not travelled this road more times than enough I would have been lost but we rode, with water up to our horses' withers, along the Roman Road north. My seven companions looked at me as though I was mad but I knew the road. Soon the waters were not as deep and the road was clearer until ten miles north of York it rose from the waters and directed us home.

I pushed on hoping to reach Yarm before dark. It was in vain. The time of year, the weather and the condition of the roads conspired against me. We made it to the small castle of Osmotherley. Baron Ralph ruled here. It was a small motte and bailey castle. It was not a rich demesne but Ralph was a good knight. The walls looked to be bereft of sentries as we approached. The gates remained firmly closed. I crossed the ditch and used the hilt of my sword to bang upon the gate. A fearful face appeared above us.

"Oh my lord, it is you! I shall let you in. I am sorry."

I vaguely recognised the face. He had once been a man at arms and one of Sir Ralph's men.

The gate opened and he bowed, "Alan of Ingleby, my lord. Sir Ralph left me in command of his castle."

I dismounted and walked Scout into the castle. My men followed. I pointed to the stables. "Put the horses in there and meet me in the Great Hall." Great Hall was an exaggeration. It was a small and mean room above the stables but it would serve. As I walked across the bailey I asked, "Where is Sir Ralph?"

"His wife and child died of the plague in spring, my lord. He almost drowned in despair and then Father James convinced him to take the cross and make a pilgrimage to the Holy Land. It seemed to give him hope. I am old and he asked me and my family to stay here and watch his castle until he returned."

"How many are you?"

"My wife and my two sons, Alan and Alfred."

"We will stay the night. If you have not enough food then I will understand."

"We have food enough my lord. My sons are good hunters both. I will tell my wife that we have guests."

He hurried off. I went to the hall. There were two floors above the hall. The one closest was the baron's quarters. I went there and took off my cloak and surcoat. Both were wet. It was not raining but the air was damp. There was no fire. I shook my head. I was getting soft. I was too used to my own castle and the royal residences in which I had stayed.

Gilles came up the stairs with my bag. "You sleep here tonight, Gilles. My men can sleep in the stables."

He nodded, "They will not like that, my lord."

"I care not. They will be warmer there than we will. The horses will ensure that. See if you can light a fire in the brazier." A brazier, cold and empty, stood in the corner. It was little enough but its glow would give the illusion of warmth.

Alan's two sons helped to get a fire going in the Great Hall and Alan's wife, Ann, brought in mulled ale to warm us up. Despite Gilles' warnings, my men at arms seemed happy enough. Alan came to me. "Is all satisfactory, my lord?"

"It is. There are few of us. I would be honoured if your family would eat with us. I have been away from England for some months and I would know what goes on."

"It is we who would be honoured, my lord. We have all heard of the exploits of the Earl of Cleveland, King Henry's Champion and Knight of the Empress."

"Good." A sudden thought came to me. "Where do you and your family sleep?"

"We have a hut by the stable." He hesitated, "But I confess when the weather is as it is now we sleep here in the Great Hall."

"Good, then do so this night."

The food was well cooked. Norman food tasted different from that in England. I know not if it was my palate, having been brought up in the east, which allowed me to differentiate but I could. Mistress Ann presented fine fare which was well seasoned with herbs. The lack of pepper and spices showed me that Ralph of Osmotherley was not a rich knight. My men at arms were silent but the conversation around our end of the table was lively as Alan and his family told me of the effects of living without a lord. Their wariness was explained by the fact that brigands and bands of Scottish raiders plagued the dale. Many farms had been destroyed and the people enslaved. The Archbishop had been looking to heaven when he should have looked closer to home.

By the end of the meal, I knew more than I had before we had sat down to eat. There was worry, not about the next ruler of England, but the threat from the north. That was the people's priority. A ruler, no matter who it was, would tax them but the Sots would burn, plunder and enslave. When Gilles and I retired I had a mind filled with questions and worries. I had an even bigger job than I had anticipated.

There had been no wine and I had had too much ale. I was not drunk but I needed to relieve myself. It was cold as I stepped from the furs under which I was sleeping and made my way to the pot in which I would relieve myself. The cold woke me. The noise of my water woke Gilles. "My lord?"

"Go back to sleep, Gilles. I needed to make water."

"And now I need to, my lord."

When I finished I went to the brazier and put on another log. The flames began to lick at the seasoned wood and soon I felt a rush of heat. Perhaps the call of nature would, in the long run, keep us warmer. Gilles was just crawling beneath his fur when I heard a creak on the stairs. I am a warrior and I have senses which others do not have. I felt the hairs on my neck prickle and Alan's words of Scottish raiders and brigands came to mind. I drew my sword and hissed, "Gilles, arm yourself."

As he did so I took out my dagger too and moved towards the door. It was suddenly thrown open and two of my men at arms led by Abelard stood there with drawn weapons. Before I could speak Abelard had thrust his sword at my middle. I wore no mail and he did. I deflected the blade with my own sword and my dagger darted forward to pierce his throat. Warm blood spurted over my hand. I could hear the sounds of combat in the Great Hall but I had two enemies before me.

"Gilles, behind me!"

The two men at arms were no fools and they moved so that they could attack me from two sides at once. My lack of armour gave them the advantage. Kurt, who was on my left, stabbed at me first. I used my dagger to block his sword and then took the offensive. I did not wait for Stephan to attack my right. As I blocked Kurt's sword I stepped forward and spun to bring my sword around. It cracked into the back of Kurt's mail. It broke a few links but, more importantly, it cracked against his spine. Had he been my only foe it would have ended there but Gilles gave a cry. "My lord behind you!"

I continued my swing and barely managed to block the sword blow from Stephan with my dagger. Even so, the blade drew blood from my arm. Gilles only had a short sword but he brought it around as hard as he could into the back of Stephan's legs. He wore no chausses and the sword bit into his flesh. As Stephan crumpled I brought my sword from on high and tore it into his neck. I barely had time to bring up my left arm to block Kurt's strike as Stephan bled his life away on the floor. Emboldened by his first strike Gilles ran at Kurt and buried his short sword in the man at arms' middle. It was a mortal wound.

Below I could hear the sound of combat and I ran from the room. I saw Alan's son, Alfred, lying in a widening pool of blood. Alan of Osmotherley was fending off two attackers with a short sword and the leg of a chair. Even as I watched Alan was stuck in the arm. He continued to fight.

I moved down the stairs as quickly as I could taking them two at a time. It was not quick enough. As one of the men at arms lunged towards Alan of Osmotherley 's unprotected side, his mother, Ann, threw herself between them to take the sword intended for her son. It came all the way through her body. I brought my sword down on the spine of the killer. I had anger within me and I laid him open to the bone. Alan of Osmotherley ended the life of the other. Even as we turned his father, Alan, had his head taken by the last traitor. Gilles stabbed the man in the thigh. As the man shouted in pain I slashed my sword across his throat.

It was over.

We stood in silence and looked at each other then Alan of Osmotherley knelt next to his dying mother. She smiled up at him, a tendril of blood coming from her mouth. "I brought you into this world. I am glad that my last act was to save your life." Then her eyes became glazed and she died.

I ran back up the stairs. Kurt still lay with his guts spreading like a pool of worms across his middle. His eyes opened as I approached, "Who paid you to do this?"

He just stared at me and then said, "We were paid well, Englishman!"

"Who paid you?"

He tried to spit at me but the effort was too much and he coughed instead. The pain made tears spring into his eyes.

"Tell me and I will ease your passing into the next world. That wound will take many hours to kill you. I can end your suffering with one blow; one strike across your throat and all pain will be gone."

He remained silent but I saw the pain on his face. It was too much to bear, "You swear?"

"I have spoken. I am never foresworn."

He nodded and closed his eyes. "The Earl Gospatric sent money to us. He wanted you dead before he sacked your castle. The captain of the cog was in on it too. It is why we put in at York." He winced as pain raced through his body. "You swore!"

In answer, I drew my dagger across his throat. With a sigh, he died. Gilles was behind me. "I killed him!"

"Aye you did and for that I am indebted. Now go and search the bodies downstairs. He said they had been paid well. Look for coins and rings. I need evidence of this perfidy." He raced downstairs. I went to Abelard first. He had been the leader and it stood to reason that he would have the most gold and coins upon him. He did. Amongst the golden coins of King David, there were coins from Flanders and from France. I had many enemies. The other two bodies yield similar evidence. I gathered it together and descended. Alan was still holding his dead mother.

"I am sorry for your loss, Alan son of Alan. I brought death into your home and for that, I apologise most sincerely."

He shook his head, "These men were killers, lord. They were like rabid dogs. At least my father died as a warrior with a sword in his hand but my mother...."

"Your mother died protecting her son. She would not change the outcome, would she?"

He shook his head.

Gilles held out a handful of coins. "I have found coins, my lord. They were well paid."

"Give them to Alan as weregeld for his family."

Alan shook his head, "No my lord. My payment will be to serve you. When you came tonight my father said it was a sign. He wanted Alfred and me to serve you and saw this as a chance to do so. I will honour my father's wishes and follow your banner; if you will have it."

"I will be honoured."

I saw that dawn was not far off. I for one would not be able to sleep. "Alan, take the armour from these traitors' bodies. You two shall have the best of the six. Gilles, go to the bailey and find wood. We must burn their bodies else we attract carrion. I will dress and then we shall bury your family, Alan of Osmotherley. From this day forth you shall take the name Alan of Osmotherley and your father will live on through you and your deeds."

By the time the bodies had been stacked on the pyre and the graves dug it was morning. I lit the wood and kindling and the six traitors burned. I did not owe them that. They had betrayed me and taken innocent lives. They would rot in hell. We buried Alan's family and covered the graves with stones. Alan of Osmotherley was buried with his sword in his hands. He had been a warrior and he had died as such.

When that was done I said, "Your new lives begin this day. I swear that I will protect you whilst I live. You shall be my men and fight at my side." They both nodded.

"And I will serve you, lord, as my father served Sir. Ralph. I will become a man at arms."

"Pack the armour on the horses. Let us leave this place. We go from a place of danger to a place of death. We go to find Gospatric and end his life. It may take time but we shall do this for we are men and we have honour. He has neither honour nor manhood. A man would have killed me himself. He hired swords."

We packed the horses and left the castle at Osmotherley to the dead. Those who lived close by swore that it was haunted and none ever lived there again. Each time we rode south we had to pass it and it was a stark reminder for me. Sir Ralph never returned from the Holy Land and the castle at Osmotherley became a memory only, as the wind, the rain and the elements gradually took it apart until just the mound and the ditch remained. The dead remained untouched and the assassins unmourned.

Chapter 2

We headed up the road towards Yarm. I felt blind. I wanted to speak with at least one of my knights as soon as possible. If Durham was no longer a bastion and Carlisle had been taken then Stockton was the prize plum that King David would seize. I hoped that when I reached Yarm I would find that Sir Richard and his men had gone to Stockton. When I saw his banner fluttering from his castle my hopes were dashed. As we headed towards it I wondered if this was a good thing. Perhaps it meant that the Scots had not come south.

The bridge was up across the ditch. I had no banner and it was not until we closed with the wall that my shield was recognised. The sentry shouted, "Open the gate! It is the Earl of Cleveland!"

We clattered across the bridge and into the bailey. Sir Richard ran to greet me, "My lord, we thought you lost."

As I dismounted I said, "Lost?"

"We heard that your castle was surrounded by the Scots and you had perished. Some said the castle had fallen."

"From whom did you hear this?"

"Riders came from the north and told us."

"When was this?"

"Why a week since, It was just a day after we heard that the King had died."

We were in the open and it did not do to talk in such places. "Let us go into your hall and speak. I detect treachery in all of this." I turned to his sergeant at arms, "William these are my new men, Alan and Gilles. See to them if you would and prepare his lordship's men. We ride within the hour!"

William looked to Sir Richard for confirmation. Sir Richard nodded.

Once in the warmth of the hall, I turned, "Did you not investigate for yourself, Sir Richard?"

"Well, no, I ..."

"What of your son at Elton? Did you not think of him?"

His face fell, "We had thought him dead too. When the riders said the Scots were flooding south we feared for ourselves and prepared for a siege."

I closed my eyes. Sir Richard was a solid warrior and had been one of my foremost allies but he was not a great thinker. He was no strategist. If I told him to hold he would but he had little initiative. "Sir Richard, you know my castle. It is strong is it not?" He nodded. "John is a good castellan and you know that Wulfric is the staunchest of warriors. Did you think so little of my castle and, indeed, of me, that you thought it would fall so quickly? You have been duped."

"But the rider was English and wore a surcoat. I thought...."

"Think of those traitors and rebels who fought for King David. This is a trick. The castle stands yet."

"Have you been there, my lord?"

"I do not need to have been there. I know. Rouse yourself. Leave a garrison here but I want you and the majority of your men to come with me. We ride to Thornaby. Let us see if Sir Edward has been taken in too." I paused, "What surcoat?"

"Yellow and black stripes with a hawk on the breast." I did not recall that livery. I knew, in my heart, that it had been a Scottish trick.

As we headed along the south bank of the Tees I knew I had arrived home none too soon. The weather had helped me. Had the assassins struck on the road then we would have fallen. Six men at arms attacking when I least suspected would have but one outcome. I was grateful to Fate for making us stop at Osmotherley. We reached Thornaby towards dusk. The banner flew but the gate was barred.

"Open the gate! It is I, the Earl of Cleveland."

The gate opened and we trotted in. I saw Sir Edward stride towards me. His arm was in a sling. His face broke into a smile. "My lord! We heard you were dead! This is great news."

I dismounted and pointed towards his arm. "What happened?"

He led us within his hall. "When the news came about the King we were all shocked and then we heard of Scots rampaging north of the river. John, your castellan, and Wulfric sent the message that they had summoned Sir Tristan and Sir Harold from their castles to Stockton. I said I would check on those south of the river. I was about to ride to Sir Richard when a message came that Normanby was under siege. I led my conroi there with all haste. It was a trap and we were ambushed by the men of De Brus. They attacked us by the hamlet of Acklam." He shook his head. "I am getting old, my lord. I saw what I expected to see and the traitors came from all sides. I lost eight men and barely made it back here. I fear that Normanby has fallen."

It was not their fault. The fault lay with me. I was the one responsible for the protection of the north and I had been far from home. I had done nothing to save the King and now I had lost the north. We ate and I told them all that I knew. It took some time for the levels of deceit and treachery were manifold.

"So Stephen of Blois is now King?"

"I know not, Edward. I know he went to London and that his brother has put his name forward. We all know that the people of London feel they have the right to decide who shall be King. They are untrustworthy but they have the King's home within their walls."

"It is not right that such a small number of people may decide the fate of the realm."

"You are right, Sir Richard, but we must face facts. With us tied in the north and, I daresay, the Earl of Gloucester's knights doing the same in the Welsh Marches the future ruler of this country could be decided by a handful of grasping merchants who see a way to gain power."

"Gain power?"

"Think about it Sir Richard, Stephen of Blois is no fool. He will wish to make his position stronger and he will reward those who make him king and go against King Henry's wishes." I shook my head, "Even the Archbishop of York is powerless and may have to acknowledge Stephen as King."

Edward said, very quietly, "And you, my lord?"

I laughed, "I thought, Edward, that of all people you would know me and my mind. Do you think I would break an oath? I will not swear an oath of allegiance to Stephen even if he is anointed by the Archbishop."

"You would be a rebel?"

I looked at them both and spoke slowly so that my words would not be misinterpreted. "I will continue to fight for the rights of Empress Matilda and her son, Henry of Anjou. I will not rest until they have the throne as King Henry wished. You should know that if you are to follow me." They both nodded although Sir Richard's was less enthusiastic. "First I have to make this land safe from the Scots but be under no misapprehension, if Stephen tries to make me bow the knee then I will fight him. You have to make your own choices. I will not command either of you to join me in what may be a fruitless fight. If I have to fight alone then I shall do so."

Sir Edward raised his goblet with his good arm. "My lord all that I have I owe to you. I am your man. If I perish following you then that was meant to be and I will not regret it."

Sir Richard raised his goblet too, "And I know your worth too, my lord. Were it not for you then this land would have suffered many times before. I follow you too."

I nodded, "Then tomorrow we go to war. Is the ferry on the river yet?"

"It is my lord but it is moored south of the river. When we returned from the ambush I sent riders to Stockton to warn them of the danger but the Scots had encircled the castle and the town but the ferry was moored on the southern side. Ethelred's son, Harold is here within my castle. He took refuge."

"Send for him I would have news of my home."

Young Harold dropped to his knees and kissed the hem of my surcoat when he saw me, "My lord we heard that you were dead. When I heard you had returned I wondered if you were a ghost."

I raised him up, "You heard me dead?"

"Aye lord, riders brought news to the castle they said that you had perished in Normandy."

"Describe the surcoat of the knight who brought you the news."

"It was yellow and black stripes with a hawk on the breast."

I looked at Sir Richard, "Aye, that is the same rider who came to me."

"Did Wulfric believe I had died?"

Harold gave me a strange look, "No, lord, he said the messenger was wrong."

"Who else was within Stockton before the gates were barred?"

"Sir Tristan and Sir Harold brought their people within but that was all. My father told me to moor the ferry where the Scots could not use it and Sir Harold told me to seek help from Sir Edward."

"And Norton?"

"We had no word from Sir Henry, my lord. But your castle was prepared for a siege and the town walls are manned also."

I suddenly realised I had no idea of the times. "When did the messenger come?"

Sir Richard said, "Three days since."

"Your ambush, Sir Edward?"

"Three days since. I was not here when the messenger crossed on the ferry."

I looked at young Harold, "And the Scots?"

"Two days since."

Sir Edward and Sir Richard both had the look on their faces that one has when someone realises that they have been badly misled. "We were tricked!"

"Did you not think, Sir Richard, that the surcoat of this messenger is remarkably similar to that of the Earl of Gospatric?"

Sir Richard suddenly saw the connection, "Of course! Now it is clear."

"And is Stockton under siege?"

Sir Edward nodded, "We spied them. They are close to the river on the east. Your archers have made them be wary of approaching closer."

"And have they siege engines?"

"Not that we saw."

"Sir Edward fetch me a map!" He waved a hand and his squire disappeared. "We know now that we are in a parlous position. We must forget the machinations of Stephen of Blois. He will either be or not be the next King of England. I am powerless to stop him. We can, however, carry out the last orders the King gave to me. We can defend this land against the Scots." My glare left no one around that table in any doubt that I would fight on despite the apparently insurmountable odds.

Gille, Edward's squire, returned with the map. It was a piece of calfskin marked with the river and the manors of the valley. I jabbed a finger at Stockton. "All to the north, west and east is lost. I do not doubt that there will be pockets of resistance. Sir Hugh at Hexham will fight and I pray he will rouse his neighbours. Like me, he has the power to do so. I hope that the Bishop of Durham will fight but we have heard naught. Here we hold the southern bank of the river. Our fight begins here. Tomorrow we build a second ferry. We take over as many archers and men at arms as we can and leave the rest here at Thornaby. We have lost enough of our valley. Tomorrow we take it back. Inch by inch if we have to but we lose no more!"

I was exhausted by the time we had finished planning. Before I retired I sought out Gilles and Alan. "Tomorrow I go to war. Gilles, I will not be needing my horses but I want them cared for. You will remain here and watch over them for me."

"Aye my lord but I will fight by your side if you need."

I ruffled his hair, "That day will come but it is not tomorrow. Alan, you now have mail, a sword and a helm. Get yourself a shield and tomorrow you watch my back until we regain my home."

"My father taught me, my lord and I will guard you until your enemies prise the sword from my dead hand."

"I would prefer you to live so that you can join my men at arms."

I knelt next to my bed that night and held my sword before me, "Lord, I pray you to guide my arm and my mind. I know that you have set me a task and I hope that I am up to it. Protect my people from the ravages of these barbarians and protect my Empress and my son! I am ever your servant. Amen."

I kissed the pommel stone of Harold Godwinson. Tomorrow was a momentous day. Until either the Empress or her son was on the throne then I bowed my knee to no man. I was my own man and I would be Warlord of the North. I would carve out an enclave protected from all enemies or I would die trying.

Chapter 3

We rose before dawn and went down to the river. It was a misty morning and we could not see the northern bank. Some of Sir Edward's men were in the woods close by the river felling trees for the second ferry. I had all of the archers from Thornaby and Yarm as well as the remaining men at arms and Sir Richard. There were just forty of us. "Harold, take us across and drop us."

"My lord! The Scots!"

I smiled, "The Scots will believe the rumour that I am dead and that Sir Edward is no threat for he was ambushed and wounded. From what I have been told they are an arrow flight from the walls. Land us as close to the walls as you can manage. If we see heavy forces then we will return to Thornaby but if we have the chance then I will rejoin my men and Sir Edward will wait for news. You will need to watch for my signal."

"Aye my lord."

As we made our way across the Tees, hidden from view by the thick fog which blanketed us Sir Richard said, quietly, "Is this wise, my lord?"

"I know not Sir Richard but it is the right military decision. Up until now, everyone has danced to Gospatric's tune. All have done as he expected. He will not expect this." I turned to the others. I guessed we were halfway across. "Silence until I speak."

They nodded and drew their weapons. I saw the grey shape of Stockton castle appear before us. I began to hear voices to our right. It was the Scottish camp coming to life. I had four of the best archers we had at the bow of the ferry and they had arrows knocked. We peered into the gloom for targets. As I had expected they had two sentries on the jetty. I could smell their fire and the meat cooking on it. They had their backs to us. When I nodded, four arrows sped towards them and they fell. I heard a shout from my right and then the murmur of voices continued. It was not the cry of alarm.

As we closed with the shore I saw indistinct figures to my right. They would be out of bow range. That meant they would be well over a hundred paces from us. The ferry nudged gently into the wooden jetty and I heard a question shouted, "Angus, what goes on?"

I leapt ashore followed by Alan, Sir Richard, his squire and six of his men at arms. I pointed to the castle and waved the others towards it.

"Angus!"

The ten of us locked shields. The last of our men left the ferry and Harold began to pull in the rope which we had tethered to the southern bank. Others, under Sir Edward's supervision, would be pulling Harold back to safety. I said quietly, "Walk backwards towards the walls."

Walking through the fog which clung to the ground was weird. All that we could see, in the distance, was ghostly shadows moving around the Scottish camp by the river. I had no doubt that someone was investigating where Angus had got to but so far the alarm had not been given. That would not last. Sir Richard's men had fought with me before and, like their master, they were as dependable as any. We were ten paces from the dead sentries when the bodies were discovered.

We heard the voices, somewhat muffled by the fog, "Treachery! Sound the alarm. We are under attack!"

I smiled. The shout did more to add confusion rather than to present a threat to us. I could not see the men, just their shadows and we continued to move back.

"You four, search close to the castle!"

"What about those damned archers?"

"Fool! They can see nothing!"

I hissed, "Ready but keep moving back!"

The four men sent to find us came at us cautiously with swords before them. They wore no mail; even in the murk, I could see that. We were looking for them but they were scanning the skies for the arrows which never came. When they did see us it came as a shock. "We have them, my lord! Here hard by the castle!"

I knew we were closing with the drawbridge for the ground began to rise. The four came at us without any conviction. There were ten of us and all wore mail. We kept moving up the ramp. I wondered if the rest of my men had been granted entry to the castle. I had heard nothing but then the fog muffled all sound.

I heard the sound of metal on metal before us and a knight appeared behind the four scouts. He had many men at arms with him. "There is only a handful. At them!"

It was like running into a stone wall when they hurtled at me and my men. Our shields took the blows and we rammed our blades hard at the soft spots. Only a few had armour. Those fell quickly and we moved back leaving those pursuing us to fall over their fallen comrades. The Scottish knight took charge, "Shield wall behind me!"

We kept moving and I felt the wood beneath my feet. The drawbridge was down. I stopped, "Behind Sir Richard and me!" The drawbridge was only wide enough for four men and I knew that the ditch would be filled not only with water from the river but deadly stakes which would kill and maim any who fell within.

The Scots came at us and I stepped further back.

"The gate is open! Charge!"

It was what Dick and my archers within the walls were waiting for. A hail of arrows plunged down at such close range that mail afforded little protection. The knight and the first ten men fell with arrows sticking from them as though they were hedgehogs. We continued our retreat. Some hardy, perhaps even foolhardy, Scots thought the tempting target of the open gate was too much and a handful raced towards us. Two managed to evade the arrows by using their shields above their heads. They could not avoid our swords as they tore them open. The others vanished into the mist and we turned to walk into my castle.

When I stepped into the bailey a tumultuous cheer erupted all around. I saw that many of the townsfolk were within my walls. Wulfric and John, my castellan, strode over to me with huge grins on their faces. "I told them you were not dead, my lord! I knew it in my heart!"

"Thank you for holding out."

Wulfric snorted, "We could have chased them hence. They are a poorly led rabble."

Behind him, I saw Sir Tristan and Sir Harold. Sir Richard ran to embrace his son.

"Come, let us go to my hall. I have much to impart and there are decisions which need to be made. Ask Father Henry to join us. Much of what I say will concern him too."

It was reassuring to see my walls still standing and my people looking so elated. As we entered my hall, Alice, my housekeeper, burst into tears and kissed the hem of my surcoat, "My lord, our prayers have been answered."

"Rise Alice! It is good to be home. Fetch us some warmed ale to the Great Hall." I saw John my Steward and said, "Come with us, John. You need to know the situation too. Dick, Wulfric join us."

Once in the hall, I took off my helmet and sat at my table. The others took their places around me. I waited until Alice had brought the refreshments before I spoke. "You know that the King is dead?" They nodded. "He was murdered but the assassin is dead too." I took a drink of ale. "Stephen of Blois is, even now, in London claiming King Henry's throne." I let that sink in. The ones in the castle knew naught of that. I watched their faces for it meant different things to different people. What I would say next would be even more momentous.

"I will not swear allegiance to Stephen even if he is anointed in Westminster Abbey." That had an effect. I saw Father Henry make the sign of the cross. John, my Steward frowned; he saw his livelihood being removed. We would be rebels. His father had been a moneyer; they served the lawful king. My knights saw war before them and the risk of losing their manors. If they sided with me they gambled. Stephen, if he became King, would not view such disloyalty well. I would not hide my plans from them. If they followed me it would be because they knew the reality. This was not a romantic tale; this would be a brutal civil war.

"I will stay here in Stockton and I will fight to keep this valley safe from the Scots and others who would destroy what we have built. When that is done, " I paused, "I will take the fight to Stephen. I will not rest until either King Henry's wishes have been observed and either Empress Matilda or Henry rule or... I am dead. I will not break my oath." Surprisingly it was just Wulfric and Dick who did not seem put out by my words. Their faces remained impassive throughout.

"I have gathered you here for, with the exception of Sir Geoffrey and Sir Hugh of Gainford, you are the last of the valley knights. I do not doubt that Sir Hugh Manningham will have roused those knights north of the wall, but until I speak with the Bishop of Durham we are in God's hands." I saw Father Henry nod. "I release every one of you in this room from any oath you have taken. I will speak with the people of Stockton when this threat is gone and tell them the same. If you leave there will be no hard feelings. Each of you must look into his own heart and decide what to do. I cannot do that for you."

I stood, "I will not stand here to wait for the decisions you might make. I will go to my chambers and prepare for war. Regardless of what you decide know this. By tomorrow this Scottish threat will be gone from our gates. When they are gone and if we survive then tell me what is in your mind and, more importantly, your hearts."

I really wanted to go to my church and speak with my dead wife. Although the church was inside the walls of the town I needed to walk those walls and, when the fog had lifted, see where the enemy was and where we could attack.

I went to the east gate which overlooked the river. I received smiles and welcomes from my sentries. I was afforded space. Erre, my Varangian Guard, stood with his fellows on the gate wall. "Good to see you, my lord. Now we can send these barbarians back where they belong."

"How are they disposed?" I needed to know where the knights were camped. If we could destroy them then the battle would be over.

He pointed to the river. "There is a camp here with about sixty men." He chuckled, "There are fewer already. Dick and his archers have thinned their ranks. The main camp is north of here. That is where they have their knights. I fear they took Norton. They hurled the heads of Sir Henry and his men at arms at our walls. They have yet to try to breach the walls but we have heard them building siege engines. They will attack the town walls." He pointed, "Sir John placed men at arms there. We are the only ones here. The other sentries are archers. Perhaps they will hurry their preparations now that they know you are here."

"Perhaps. The women and children?"

"Sir John and Wulfric brought them within your walls. It is their men who guard the walls of the town. The Scots tried to attack the gate when they first came but they were repulsed."

"Good. Tonight we attack here and kill these close by the river. Sir Edward has reinforcements ready to join us."

"Men at arms, my lord?"

"No, but we need just numbers here."

I descended and walked over to the town gate. I spied Aiden and waved him over. "I have a task for you."

"Good my lord, I like not being confined."

"Tonight we will clear the river of our enemies. I want you to slip out and scout out the road to Durham. I would know where the Scots have a hold. Do not risk yourself and I care not how long it takes but I need to know what we face."

"I could slip out now, my lord."

"And you might get caught. Tonight will suffice. As soon as we attack the men by the river then you slip out by the west gate."

I left by the town gate. My town was eerily empty. The only ones within were on the walls. Had I led the Scots then I would have attacked already. The walls of my town were only founded on stone. The palisade was largely wood. Perhaps the ditch had defeated them. I climbed the walls to stand on the north gate. I joined Edgar and Wilfred. "Good to see you, my lord!"

"Have the Scots showed any sign of attacking today?"

Edgar pointed to the small rise on the Norton road. "They are building a ram and a mangonel. They had to go to Hartburn for the wood. When you arrived this morning there was confusion in their camp. Men came from the river and their leaders gathered to discuss it."

"Do you think they know it is me who has returned?"

"I do not know. Perhaps they thought it was just reinforcements."

"Tonight we clear them from the river. I will have you all replaced by archers so that you may rest."

"Good, we have taken enough of their insults."

Wilfred said as he pointed into the ditch, "They are not resolute my lord. See how few fell to their deaths in the ditch. They lost but fifteen. Your townsfolk are tough and they fight well. Alf your smith wields a mighty war hammer."

I saw him speaking with his sons. "I will speak with you all later. I have much to tell you."

Alf beamed when I saw him. "There, I told you that Wulfric was correct and it was a lie that our lord had perished. Go to the walls and spread the word!" His sons ran off to tell the others who had not left the walls since I had returned.

"It is good to see you, Alf."

"And you, lord."

Although I had said I would speak with the townspeople after we had cleared the Scots I owed it to Alf to speak with him first. He was the leader of the town and as good a friend as I could wish for despite his low birth. I told him, word for word, what I had said in my Great Hall. He took it as Wulfric and Dick had, stoically.

"I know not this Stephen of Blois and he may well be a good man but I know that you are a man of honour. Stockton would have nothing without you. We stand by you e'en though that makes us rebels and traitors."

"It is not a trivial matter, Alf, although we have to end the Scottish threat first. We are far from London and we may escape his notice but it will come. I intend to build up our army so that we can resist all foes." I smiled, "At least we shall not have to pay taxes eh?"

He laughed, "And that is a silver lining, lord, to this black cloud."

When I had walked the length of my walls I descended to my church and knelt by the grave of my wife and child. "Perhaps, Adela, you and our daughter are better off for your husband is about to become a traitor and a rebel. I never thought that it would come to this. I pray that I behave with honour and I hope that you and my father approve."

Father Henry's voice came from behind me, "You speak from the heart and God will understand."

I rose and turned to speak with the priest, "And you, Father Henry, what do you think?"

"I am just a priest, my lord. What I say has no bearing on any secular matters."

"You and I both know that is not true. My people look to you for guidance. I look to you for advice. Do I do what is right?"

"You swore an oath in a holy place upon a Bible. Stephen of Blois also swore such an oath. He is the one who has broken his oath and not you."

"But if the Archbishop orders you to obey the new King, what then?"

He smiled, "We both know Archbishop Thurstan, my lord. Do you think he will do that? Even if he appears to obey the new king he is a clever man who will find a way to support those he believes defend his land. You." He made the sign of the cross over me and said, "But think of the people too. They have little voice and are often trampled upon by the high and the mighty. If you think of them then God will approve."

As I returned to my castle I had food for thought. Was I doing the right thing? I knew, from our conversations in Normandy, that Stephen would heap rewards and titles upon me if I supported his claim to the throne. My people would benefit. My knights would benefit. Why could I not accept him as King? The Archbishop was right, it was good for England. It would give stability. Stephen of Blois was well respected and would rule from a position of power and yet... I could not. I was now set on a course that would bring me into direct conflict with Stephen of Blois. It would not be soon but it would come and it would be a fight to the death!

Chapter 4

My knights and my captains were still in the Great Hall. I had no doubt they had been speaking about my decisions. They were momentous ones. That I knew. I saw the anticipation on their faces as I entered. "Tonight, we attack the Scots by the river. I have walked the walls and observed the ones by the river. There are a small enough number of warriors for us to eliminate them. Dick, I want every archer on the walls of the town tonight. I wish you to rain fire arrows on their camp to the north. When it is ablaze and they attack then use your arrows to thin their numbers."

"And if we spur them to assault the walls, my lord?"

"The men of the town will be with you and you may retreat to my castle if they threaten to overwhelm you. If we lose the town walls then so be it. I want them to bleed. We can sacrifice the walls so long as they die to gain them. The men at arms and my knights will attack the camp by the river. Tomorrow we have reinforcements from Thornaby. The ones Sir Edward brings are the fyrd and we cannot afford to lose any of our men. We have too few as it is."

Wulfric nodded, "We attack without warning, my lord?"

"The warning will be the cries from those dying in the northern camp. I want them distracted by Dick's fire arrows. They will see them and their attention will be there. When we attack we use our small force of knights as a battering ram. When I was on the walls I saw that the men camped hereabouts had little mail. They will not stand."

Sir Harold asked, "When does the attack begin?"

"When the darkness is complete Dick will begin his firestorm. We make our way to the river then and we attack. Tell your men to rest. I want every man at arms here as soon as darkness falls."

I found Alan of Osmotherley and took him with me, "Where do we go, my lord?"

"To meet the man who will lead you and whose every word you will obey as though it was from my own lips."

Wulfric was sharpening his sword. "Wulfric, we have a new man at arms. He helped me at Osmotherley and his father served Ralph of Osmotherley. His mother, father and brother were all slain by the assassins who tried to kill me. He has armour and a sword. He needs a surcoat and a shield. I put him under your command."

Wulfric nodded. He could be intimidating but, at the same time, he could be the gentlest of men. He smiled, "Welcome Alan. You join the finest conroi of warriors that ride in England. You join men who are the equal of any knight I have ever seen, save his lordship. Can you ride?"

"A little."

"Not good enough. After we have scotched these Scots we will make you a rider. Come, the Earl has better things to occupy his mind than seeing to a new man at arms." As he led Alan off he nodded. He approved.

I took the opportunity to sharpen my own sword. Normally one of my squires would do that but I had none. I enjoyed the sound the blade made on the wheel. The sparks flew and illuminated the blade. When I struck it would slice through flesh. If it hit mail it would damage or destroy it. It was an extension of my arm and of me. When I was satisfied I did the same with my two daggers. I was ready.

I trusted Dick. He knew his business. I did not need to watch him begin his arrow storm and I joined my men at arms. With the knights and squires, we had fifty-three men. Our numbers would be the equal of the Scots but our quality exceeded theirs. I wanted a quick and decisive victory. I wanted those who were attacked by Dick to be shaken. I had not told my knights but I intended to use our victory to attack the main camp of the Scots. I wanted the scent of victory to be in their nostrils and use the energy that was created. There we would be outnumbered but we would have the taste of success in our nostrils. I was gambling!

We gathered behind my gate and waited. Dick would initiate the attack. When he began to loose fire arrows we would slip out of the gate and fall upon the Scots. The day which had begun foggy had ended with a cold hard frost. Indeed the river showed the faint sheen of ice upon it. I made my men draw their swords when they were within the castle. Sometimes a blade could stick in the cold; that could be fatal.

I had my knights at the fore. That was twofold. They were the best I had and I wanted our men to see that we were not afraid. We led and they would follow. I also wanted their weight of armour and weapons to decisively break our foes. The shouts from the north alerted me. The attack had begun. I nodded and the bar on the greased gate was slid back. It opened soundlessly and we walked, quietly out of my castle, across the bridge and down the ramp. The shouts from the north wall were now cries and screams. The smell of burning drifted on the crisp night air. Ahead I heard the alarm in the Scottish camp by the river. The smoke from their fire and its glow drew us on. They were not looking west, they were looking north and I heard strident voices as they debated what to do. Indecision was the worst state of mind; better a wrong decision than no decision. Their vacillation and procrastination enabled us to close with them. We were less than forty paces from them before we were seen and by then it was too late.

As one sentry shouted, "Alarm!" We raised our swords and fell upon them. I smashed my shield into the face of a man to my left as I gutted one to my right. The path and the jetty were narrow and I heard the splashes as men fell into the icy waters of the Tees. My river protected us too. If they fell in the icy waters they would last but moments. I became a killing machine. I blocked with my shield and swung my sword. Sometimes my blow was from above and at other times from below. Their eyes were still blinded by their own fires. Their defence was brief because we slew them so quickly. The ones we did not slay sought safety in the water. They died anyway. I daresay one or two hardier souls may have struggled ashore at the Tees mouth but they would not return.

I raised my sword, "Let us end this tonight. Follow me and we will fall upon the Scottish camp."

When I had been on the walls I had seen that they had the tents of their leaders to the east of the town. I headed for it.

The men who were dying at the hands of my archers were the ones who were on watch close to the walls. The leaders and the knights had been in their beds. Awoken by the clamour they now rose and gathered outside their tents. They watched as fire arrows fell into their camp. I saw a knot of them pointing and debating at this new lunacy. What were the men of Stockton up to?

It was now the time to strike. I began to run. With my shield held tightly against my chest, I held my sword above my head. To my right were Wulfric, Erre and the other Varangians. They spurned their shields, carrying them over their backs, and held their axes in two hands. The power which they generated when they swung their mighty axes was frightening. The nobles saw us and, like deer caught in the dark, stood almost petrified to the spot. It lasted but a heartbeat but we were moving so quickly that the heartbeat ended for some. I spied a knight with a gryphon on his surcoat. It was like that of the Senonche family. This must be a relative who lived in Scotland. Sir Guy had died at my hands but he had caused too much pain for me to be merciful. I brought my sword down from on high. It smashed into the knight's shield. He had failed to brace himself and the shield was driven down towards his chest. I had put my weight into the blow. I had been travelling at speed and the sword continued down. It bit into the mail of his coif and ventail. He began to fall backwards and I struggled to keep my feet. I had done this enough times to hold back a little and I stopped. My foe did not and he tumbled to the ground. As the breath was taken from him I raised my blade and plunged my sword into his mouth as he opened it to suck in air.

I pulled out the sword and sought my next foe. Wulfric and my Varangians were carving a path of death before them. No one was giving quarter. We were too few in number. These were largely men at arms who followed me and their reward would come when they searched the bodies of the dead. Until then they killed!

I had enough men behind me so that I did not worry about those who fell wounded. They would be despatched.

We ran on. Although we were spread out a little more we were approaching those men who were not as well armoured and were suffering from my archers' attack. I did not fear that we would be struck. Dick and the archers he commanded were too good for that. Some of the Scots had courage far beyond their skills. Some raced at me with bill hooks in an abortive attempt to slay me. I fended off their weapons and gutted them. Others had a small buckler and sword. None of the swords could match my well-made weapons and all were slain. When the gate opened and Dick led my archers and the townsfolk to complete our attack it was too much for the Scots who remained and they fled.

Dick and his archers led the fyrd to pursue and to hunt down the survivors. The Scots who had come south to claim Stockton left a trail of bodies and bones as they ran north across the frozen ground which led home. Dick and his archers halted only at Thorpe, seven miles up the road. By then it was daylight and the ones who could still run deserved to live.

None of the nobles had survived. My men had been ruthlessly efficient. The few wounded survivors were the low born and knew nothing of the plans of King David or the Earl Gospatric. They had been enticed to join the enterprise with the promise of Stockton's treasure. The only treasure they gained was a patch of earth. I had, however, achieved my objective. I had relieved the siege and halted the Scottish invasion.

As I took off my helmet and walked around the battlefield I was able to assess our position. There was no immediate danger. Aiden was looking for danger closer to Durham. Had he found any he would return quickly. We had breathing space. I would be able to think and plan. I joined my men as they cleared the ditches and the battlefield.

Alice and her women began preparing food. We would eat when we had made the town and castle secure once more. My men spent the late hours of the night and the early hours of the morning taking the treasure from the dead and stabling their horses. We now had fifteen war-horses and twenty palfreys. They had been captured intact. They were as valuable as gold. Then we piled the Scottish bodies together and began the task of burning them. For days the air was filled with the smell of burning flesh. It was an unpleasant task but it had to be done. Dead bodies would attract vermin.

As dawn broke I returned with my knights to my castle and we held a council of war.

While Alice served food, I spoke. "As long as the Scots are abroad we must ensure that your families are safe. I decree that until you decide your futures, then your families stay here. Stockton's walls are thick and they will hold."

Sir Harold said, "My decision is made already, lord. I will follow you even if it means my death. I would be nothing without you."

I waved my hand. "Do not be hasty Harold. I have asked Alf to gather those from the town to meet with me in the square. I will tell them what I told you. Make your decision then. I intend to tell the archers and men at arms the truth. They may be hired men but they deserve respect. I shall give them that."

By the time my hunters returned from the chase of the Scots it was gone noon. The pyre of bodies burned still. The graves for our dead had been dug and Father Henry would inter them after dark. The sentries on the river wall shouted, "My lord, the ferries from Thornaby come."

Ethelred had fretted about his son and his ferry all morning. His son now brought over our horses, Gilles, stable boys and Sir Edward. The rest of Sir Edward's men came on the second ferry. I went to the jetty to greet them. Blood still stained the grass where we had made our night attack upon the Scots. The air was still chill and the blackened blood stood starkly against the frost. As the ferry reached halfway Sir Edward shouted, "My lord, boats from the west!"

Could this be Scots? I was taking no chances. I turned and yelled, "To arms!"

Wulfric, Erre and my Varangians had not left my side since the battle had begun. Nor had Alan of Osmotherley. With drawn weapons, they stood in a circle behind me. The ferry bumped into the wooden jetty. "Gilles, get the horses into the castle and hurry." As they led Scout, Hunter and the rest up the ramp I asked, "Could you make out who was aboard?"

Sir Edward shook his head, "There was a canvas awning and they were using a sail."

I glanced up at my wall. Despite the fact that they had only recently returned Dick and his archers lined the river wall, arrows knocked. The three small river vessels had arrows protruding from the sides and the sails. They were heavily laden. They were riding low in the viscous, icy water. I drew my sword and prepared for combat.

Sir Hugh of Gainford's head appeared around the edge of the canvas awning, "My lord! You live!"

We sheathed our weapons and breathed a sigh of relief. Sir Edward said, somewhat testily, "The young fool could have flown his banner at the very least."

"And if the castle had been held by the Scots? What then, my friend? He was cautious and I applaud him for that. We have numbers which are too small for us to take unnecessary risks."

The first boat bumped into the jetty tied to the two ferries. Sir Hugh and his wife clambered out. I saw that there was a babe in a wet nurse's arms too. "Take your wife into the warmth of the castle, Sir Hugh. The air is too cold for women and babes."

"Aye, lord but it is good to see you. Our prayers have been answered."

That was the second time I had been told that. The first boat contained families and half a dozen men at arms. The second had another surprise for me as Wilfred, son of Geoffrey of Piercebridge, stepped ashore with his mother, Lady Hilda. "Where is your husband, Lady Hilda?"

"He perished with most of our men fighting the Scots. He held them until we could get to Gainford." She began to well up.

Wilfred, a youth of no more than fifteen years of age said, "He died well as did our men but their bodies were butchered and despoiled. Our enemies have no honour, my lord."

"Take your mother and your people to my Hall. I will join you there soon."

I stood to one side with Sir Edward and my men at arms. "Our army grows."

Wulfric said, "The numbers will not swell our own overmuch, my lord"

Sir Edward concurred, "Wulfric is right. It looks like they have suffered losses as grievous as my own. You have sent the Scots packing but they will return and now, my lord, we have enemies closer to home. The De Brus family control the land to the east. They can close the Tees any time they choose."

"And that is why we must improve the defences here on the river. I want ramparts erecting. We need total control and access across the river. When I have spoken with my people, Sir Edward, I want you to return with the men at arms and archers you sent over and fortify your castle and the ferry. I will send a rider to the Archbishop and tell him of our situation."

"You said he might be forced to side with Stephen."

"I did, Edward, but I do not think either man wishes us to lose the north and have the Scots control all the land north of the Tees. We must defeat our common enemy before we face each other."

Sir Hugh and the family of Geoffrey of Piercebridge gathered in the Great Hall. I told them my news, all of it and my decision. "I go now to speak with my people and when I return we will talk further."

Father Henry and Alf had gathered everyone in the town square by the water trough. I rode Scout so that all could see me. There was neither cheering nor shouting. This had been a narrow victory and everyone knew the danger still remained. "People of Stockton, King Henry is dead and Stephen of Blois claims the throne. King David has treacherously taken advantage of the death of King Henry to try to take our land. I swear that I will fight the Scots and bloody them until they find other lands to ravage."

That elicited a cheer.

"However, we are now on a war footing. Until we are safe I will be as a warlord. I will do all that I can to defeat the Scots and use every means at my disposal. From this time forth every male from the age of seven and up is to carry weapons with him at all times. When you are not working on your land you are practising with a slingshot, war bow, using a sword. We make arrows until we have enough to slaughter every Scotsman in Scotland!"

That elicited a second cheer.

I paused and glanced at Father Henry. He nodded. "When the Scots are defeated then I will fight for the rights of the rightful heir of England, Empress Matilda and her son, Henry. I will not swear allegiance to Stephen."

For the first time, I saw the doubt on the faces of my people and heard a murmur of conversation.

"I do not command any to follow my banner. This is a decision each man will make in the future but I was appointed your lord by King Henry and I will not lie to you. Each person must make their own decision." I waved a hand at the still smoking piles of bodies. "We have defeated one enemy. There are more. We make our walls stronger, while winter remains so that no one will try to breach them. We prepare weapons and we gather food. As Warlord I give each family permission to hunt game in my forests. What we hunt we share! The road south is still in English hands and I hope for allies and reinforcements but if we have to fight on alone then we will do so."

I turned to return to my hall and Alf shouted, "I know not about the rest of you but I follow the Earl of Cleveland. Him I know and the man from Blois I do not!"

There was a cheer which began small but grew until by the time I rode through my gate it was deafening."

Dick took my reins as I dismounted. He was grinning, "They have given you their decision." He nodded to his archers on the walls. "We have decided too. We follow you as Earl or as Warlord."

"It could mean a traitor's death."

"Aye, my lord it could but I think it will not and I also believe that what you do is right. King Henry would approve." He laughed, "I began life as an outlaw. It is but a small jump to traitor!"

"And Wulfric?"

"He will tell you himself, my lord, but he and his men at arms did not find it a hard decision to make."

I felt better as I entered my Great Hall. The gathered knights and their families almost filled it. They stood expectantly. I was not yet ready to ask the question for part of me feared the answer. If they did not follow me could I fight against them?

"Tell me, Sir Hugh, your story."

He looked tired and more than a little shaken.

"Sir Barnard sent a message to me to visit him at his castle. I was suspicious, my lord, and I used bad weather as an excuse not to attend. On the same day, Lady Hilda and her family fled to my castle, pursued by Scots. They barely made it. I sent a messenger to Sir Barnard asking for help. The messenger did not return. The three ships we brought were on the river. I thought it fortuitous that the river had not frozen and we were going to send our families to you for safety when a rider came from the east to tell us that you had been slain on the journey back from Normandy. We did not know what to do and the Scots then attacked my castle. Sir Barnard was with them, lord. You were right. He is a traitor."

I nodded, "Scottish and French kings hired six killers to end my life on the way back. They failed but their plan almost succeeded and Barnard Balliol will pay a price for his treachery."

"He came to our walls on the second day of the siege. He begged me to surrender and join with the forces of King David. He said he would fight under the Scottish banner; that was where his heart lay. We refused and he said there would be no quarter. They attacked." He shook his head, "My castle is made of wood and it is small. We could not hold out for long. When night came and we counted our dead I decided to chance that Sir Edward or Sir Richard lived yet and we might find sanctuary. We slipped out after dark, boarded the three boats and managed to escape. They chased us down the river for a while and showered us with arrows but they lost men and we did not. Now we are here."

"I will tell you now what I have told my people. From this day forth, until we have the rightful ruler on the throne I will rule as regent for Empress Matilda and the erstwhile Prince Henry. When I have spoken with the Bishop of Durham, who is Prince Bishop, I will know my position better. None need to make a quick decision. We have the Scottish pox to remove but once that is done then we have a decision to make."

They nodded. Some shouted, "I am for you now, Earl!" and the like. Others held their counsel.

"Sir Hugh, I am sure your father in law will care for your family until we have regained your home. Lady Hilda, use my castle as your own. Wilfred, until you are knighted, would you be my squire?"

"Aye, my lord. I would be honoured."

My banner stood in the corner. I went to get it and handed it to him. "Then on the morrow, we begin the fight back! We take what the Scots have captured and make this valley England once more!"

Chapter 5

I went to speak with Sir Richard and Sir Edward at first light. "I need you two to take your men and ensure that you are bastions protecting the river's southern bank. With Piercebridge gone and the mouth of the Tees closed we have to keep this vital artery to York open. If the road is cut then we will be helpless."

"But that leaves you perilous few men with which to defend the walls of Stockton, my lord."

"I know Edward but I am counting on the fact that there will be others who live and seek a lord behind whom they can fight. Train men. We have bows and spears aplenty. We use what we have."

"But we might be throwing their lives away."

"I rely on you to see that does not happen. I will use speed and the skill of my archers in the woods. My plan is to find those who are close to us and eliminate them first. We keep moving out until we are joined with Durham once more."

"And what of Durham? Surely the Prince Bishop should be fighting the Scots."

"Do not judge him yet, Richard. He may well be fighting. Until Aiden returns we are in the dark. Now go and keep me informed. Any information no matter how trivial should be sent to me."

I sought out William the Mason. "My old friend. I have need of your skills once more."

"Aye, my lord. I will do all that I can. This is my home and while I cannot wield a sword, I can, at least, wield a mallet and chisel."

"I need the northwest town gate improving. I would have it made of stone. My men will deepen the ditch. I wish the wall to continue to the river wall and gate."

"You intend to make a small enclosure between the town and the castle."

"I do. We can make daub and wattle huts. The castle is too crowded now and I do not wish it to become pestilential should we be besieged. We need somewhere for the people to live if we are attacked again."

"I will get my sons and we will start straight away. I have some stone which was intended for some houses in the town."

"Tell those for whom you would build that I will recompense them but the town takes priority!"

Alf was already hard at work making swords. His sons were making arrowheads and spearheads. I saw fletchers making arrows. "Alf, your work is all that I would wish it but I must tell you that I am using the stone that you and the others bought for your houses. I am making a stone gate and wall. If we are under siege then we can use it for the people. If any complain, tell them I, personally, will recompense them."

He spat into the fire and it hissed and sizzled, "If they complain they answer to me, my lord. You purge the land of these savages and I will bang heads here if needs be." I knew I could rely on Alf. He was the Wulfric of my town.

I gathered my men. "Erre I leave you and the Varangians with Sir John to protect and guard my river crossing. William will work on the new gate. Have the men deepen the ditch and use the wood the Scots gathered for their siege weapons and make a drawbridge. We ride to find Scots. We will return after dark. The password is Miklagård."

He laughed, "I like that. God speed my lord."

Young Gilles had brought Scout for me and he led his palfrey. I shook my head, "No Gilles, I need you here on my walls. You must defend my home. The others who work with the hawks and the stables will be here also and Sir John will command."

I led my men and we headed to Norton. All that we knew was Sir Henry and his men were dead. We knew nothing else. We went defensively towards Norton. I doubted it was still occupied but it did not do to take chances. Dick and the combined archers spread out and we moved along the Hartness Road. The burned walls had long since stopped smoking but they stood bleakly like the teeth in an old woman's mouth. The gate my father and his men had built was thrown down. The dead still lay where they fell. No one was left alive. Although they had not despoiled the church, even the Scots would not dare do that, they had killed the priests.

"Should we bury them, lord?"

I shook my head. "We will do that when we have scoured this side of the land of Scots." I did not like the decision and it was not taken lightly but I had to take it. We headed towards Hartness. We passed burnt out farms where the carrion had picked over the bodies. There had been no treasure to take. They were killing those who lived and then moving on.

We were approaching the hamlet of Cowpen when we saw our first sign of life. Dick rode up to us, "My lord, there is a band of Scots. They are attacking Cowpen. The large house is being assaulted. There are men within still fighting."

"Take your archers and cut them off. They will try to retreat to Hartness."

I knew what the village looked like. There was a circle of huts around a green. Although there was no lord of the manor, Aethelred, the headman, had been one of my father's men at arms and he knew how to fight.

I turned to my knights and men at arms. "We ride in hard with neither trumpet nor shout. We give no quarter. I want no ransom! I want them dead!"

I drew my sword and spurred Scout. Wilfred, my new squire, could barely keep up with me. Sir Harold and Sir Tristan flanked me. Both had been my squire and knew how to stay close. Sir Hugh was behind me so that we made a diamond and like a diamond, I hoped that we would be as sharp. As we burst between the first rude houses I saw flames licking at the large hut. I could hear the clamour of battle. Even as we charged I saw arrows loosed from within. Men defended their homes. The Scots were commanded by a knight and they had a ram to batter down the sturdy door.

I led the charge and I saw a Scot with his breeks around his knees as he tried to rape a woman. Two of his fellows held her down. I charged towards them and, at the last moment, lifted Scout's head as I swung my sword at the man on the right. He leapt over them. Scout's hooves smashed the skulls of the rapist and his accomplice. The woman was showered in brains and blood but she lived. I did not rein in my horse but I ploughed into the backs of those at the door. The four of us and our squires were a mass of mail and horseflesh. Even had we been without swords many would have died. With swords it was carnage.

Some of the Scots stood or tried to stand. They were the oathsworn of the knight who wielded a double-handed axe. I turned Scout's head to take on this knight. He did as I expected; he swung the axe at Scout's head. I anticipated the move and jerked Scout to the side. I almost miscalculated for the axe took some hair from Scout's mane. I brought my sword down and it bit into the arm of the knight. I broke through the mail and into his elbow. As soon as the tendons were severed the axe fell from his hand. Sir Harold took his head with a single stroke of his sword.

I heard a roar from my left as Aethelred rushed from the burning house with the remnants of the villagers. They fell upon the Scots; they hacked and chopped them apart. It was a wild fury I had rarely seen. My father had often spoken of berserkers who would fight with similar fury. I dismounted and handed my reins to Wilfred. The villagers were hacking at bodies already dead.

I sheathed my sword and put my arm on Aethelred's back, "Aethelred!"

He turned and there was a wildness in his eyes.

"It is me, the Earl. They are slain."

He began to breathe more slowly, "I am sorry, lord. They are savages." He pointed to the slaughtered children whose bodies lay in the track which ran through the village. "I was a soldier; there is no need for this."

I nodded, "The Scots have taken much, Hartness and Greatham belong to our enemies. Norton and Wulfestun have fallen. None remain. Believe it or not, you have been lucky." I took a deep breath. "It will be too dangerous for you to stay here."

I wondered if he had heard me for he said, "Is it true that the King is dead?"

"Aye, he is."

"Then who will drive the Scots hence?"

"I will."

"With these men only?"

"If I have to then yes but we will have more. Take your people to Stockton. There you will be safe. When we have reclaimed our land, you can farm here once more or take Norton for it is a graveyard now."

"And you, my lord, where do you go?"

"I go to leave a message at Greatham." I mounted my horse. "Aethelred, take the knight's head. That will speak for me. The weapons you should take for your people. This is a fight to the death. Let us make them pay dearly for each sod they stand upon."

He took the axe from the dead knight and swung it high. He took the helmet from the skull and handed it to me. I rammed the gory trophy in my saddlebag. "Keep together. We will escort you when we have done this."

Greatham was just a few miles up the road. Like Cowpen, there was no castle but there was a ditch as well as a wall. We found Dick and his archers. They had slain the ones who had escaped the wrath of the Cowpen villagers. "We have taken their weapons but they are poorly made."

"We need all the weapons we can muster. Beggars cannot be choosers."

We rode hard and reached Greatham quickly. The gate was barred and the standard of the De Brus family fluttered from its wall. Armed men appeared on the walls. I turned to Dick. "Clear the walls!"

"With pleasure." He dismounted. Dick had twenty-eight archers with him and they were all well trained. They pulled back, their war bows straining. Those on the walls, some one hundred and fifty paces away, looked and wondered. When the arrows fell my men released a second and a third volley. The arrows came down almost vertically. I saw one crossbowman pinned through his skull to the ramparts. Dick shouted, "Hold!"

I spurred Scout to the gate and threw over the skull. "De Brus! Whoever commands here know this. I will return and I will burn this manor to the ground and slaughter all who lie within. If you wish to live then go to Hartness and take ship for Hartness burns tomorrow too!"

I turned and rode away. Sir Hugh said, "Is that wise, lord, to warn them?"

"I intend to terrify them. Fear not, Sir Hugh. I will not waste men and both manors will be in our hands by the end of tomorrow. We return to Stockton merely to use Erre and his Varangians." I paused, "And now we can bury Norton's dead."

We caught up with Aethelred and his people at Norton. They helped us to bury the fallen and then we made our way home. It was just becoming dark when we reached the safety of my walls. My men had done well and the ditch had been deepened. In addition, they had finished an eight feet section of the wall in stone.

"Aethelred, you can build homes here. There is willow aplenty by the river and the people of Stockton will help." I turned and shouted, "These were driven from their homes in Cowpen. I would that you made them welcome. Here they will build homes and they will fight alongside us on these walls!"

Alf shouted, "Come on! You heard the Earl! We are English and know how to share!"

I dismounted and gave my reins to Gilles who had run up to me as soon as we had entered the town. I shouted to the walls, "Erre!"

"Aye lord." He made his way down to me.

"We ride again tonight. We leave at midnight and we go to Hartness. I need you and your Varangians. I want you to break down the gates of the town."

He rubbed his hands, "And then kill the Scots, my lord?"

"And then kill the Scots."

He rubbed his hands, "Good!"

"Dick, have your men rest. I want you to attack Greatham with fire arrows this night."

He nodded, "And drive them to Hartness, where you will be waiting."

"Exactly! I gave them a fair warning. I believe they will send a boat to Guisborough. They will want their women away from my wrath and they will summon help. Perhaps they too believe I am dead. When they return north I want them to see the blackened remains of the two manors they captured. If we cannot have them then no one shall."

It was but twelve miles to Hartness and even less to Greatham. We could be there in under two hours. We rested and we sharpened weapons. It was a sharp cold night and the moon rose early. That was unlucky. We would not be hidden by the dark. On the other hand, my archers would have easy targets. We parted close to Greatham and I headed for the dunes and the sand. We would approach the walls of Hartness from the sea. It would also enable us to catch any who fled Greatham.

Despite the temperature, our horses and our speed kept us warm. As I saw the buildings, rising above the sea, I thought about this town which was so close to my own. Hartness had always been the bane of my life. It was from here that Scottish knights had raided Norton and slain my father. When I had rid myself of the lord of the manor I had thought it secure but when my lord was killed it proved to be another weight about my neck and now I had lost it. I had meant what I said. I wanted the town rendered useless to the Scots. It would be one less thing for me to worry about.

What was on my mind as we headed along the track which bordered the sea was Aiden. Where was my scout? I had expected him back before we had left Stockton. Had I asked him to do too much? I now felt the weight of the world upon my shoulders. Things had happened so quickly that, since the King's death, I had just reacted to problems. Perhaps I needed to sit down and plan my strategy. I had not even given thought to my son, William, nor to my knight in Anjou, Leofric. I prayed that they were safe on the Angevin border, however, I was powerless to help them.

We had no archers to silence any guards on the town walls. They were all with Dick. I was just grateful that the walls were made of wood and, as such, easier to both scale and destroy. I had no idea of the garrison but I was gambling that my men were made of sterner stuff than the Scots. We dismounted just half a mile from the walls. We had not seen signs of a sentry but I would not take any chances. We led our horses. The gate on the southern corner of the town walls was relatively low. The sea almost lapped at its base. I think, for that reason, they had few guards there.

We stopped at a large dune and peered at the walls. I could see no one on them. I nodded to Wulfric. He sent forward four of our younger men at arms. We left the horses to the squires and we followed. Erre and his companions were happy to be back on foot. They were never comfortable horsemen. There was little breeze but what there was came from the north. That was good for it took our scent away from any dogs and, more importantly, the smell of a burning Greatham from Hartness. We waited while the four men formed a human pyramid and one of them clambered over the wall. Something made me turn and I saw, to the south, a glow in the sky. Dick had done as I asked and the manor of Greatham was burning.

I heard a noise from above us and a body was pitched over. It was a Scot. He had a second mouth beneath his chin. There were footsteps from within and then I heard the bar moving. Deep in the town, I heard the shouts as the alarm was given. They had not seen us but they had spied the fire in the south. The door opened and we slipped through.

Hartness rose from the gate to the south on a slowly rising piece of ground up to the church on the headland. There were walls on three sides but there was no castle. The cliffs protected the fourth side. The houses through which we passed were the low mean huts of those with the lowliest tasks and I doubted that they were Scots. We left them and ran towards the harbour. That was where we would do the most damage. We had half a mile to go before we reached it and we managed half of that before we met our first foe. Wulfric must have heard the clatter of horses for he waved us into the shadows. Horsemen galloped down towards the gate shouting for it to be opened. The gatekeepers lay dead and would heed no more orders.

We had thirty men at arms and we were spread out along both sides. When four of the ten horsemen had passed I yelled, "Now!" Our ambush from the dark was sprung.

I swung my sword at the mailed leg of the knight who rode by me. It sliced through the mail, flesh and finally bone before the leather stirrup stopped it. The rider tumbled over the other side of the horse. A horse reared and would have clattered my helmet had Wilfred not waved my banner before it. The flapping flag made the beast try to turn but there was nowhere to go and it fell, taking its rider with it. I used the fallen horse to jump up and plunge my sword into the rider's chest. Erre, Wulfric and the Varangians had fiercely sharp axes and they used them to good effect. The horses and the horsemen were ruthlessly dispatched by masters of the axe. The luckless horsemen had ridden to aid their comrades and been attacked in their own town. The garrison was in disarray. Five lay dead or wounded and two dying horses blocked their escape. The remaining three turned and galloped back to the harbour and the church.

We followed. In the narrow confines of the street, we could move as swiftly as they could. We ran so close to them that one of Sir Hugh's men managed to strike a blow on the rump of one of the horses. It reared and brought its hooves down on men at arms running to aid their lords.

The town was now wide awake but there was confusion. The cry had been that Greatham was afire and yet now men were dying in their streets. I have no doubt that we were outnumbered but it mattered not for we were mailed and we knew where they were. As far as the Scots were concerned I had a whole army with me. Panic set in. The darkness increased our numbers and our sudden appearance terrified all. Some Scots tried to slow us down. They used spears and swords to stop our advance and buy their last two knights time to organize. Their swords struck our shields. Our axes and swords found flesh. Within a few blows, they were gone and there was no one before us. Suddenly we emerged into the middle of the town.

"Harold and Hugh, take your men and capture the port. Burn any ships you find."

My two knights ran off with their men in close attendance. The Great Hall was next to the church of St. Hild and I shouted, "Wulfric, Tristan, to the manor house!"

We ran up the slope. It should have had a ditch here but it did not and that was a costly mistake. We were a long line of fifteen warriors and we were driving the survivors up to the manor house. They should have used the slope but they did not. There was little honour in striking at unprotected backs and hacking at their legs but we were not in a position to do any favours. We had to kill to survive.

Wulfric reached the door first. Someone just managed to shut it but they had not put the bar in place for Wulfric brought his axe over his head and the door shattered in two. Erre and Sven the Rus followed him into the hall yelling their wild war cries. They were all three in their element. With shields over the backs, they were willing to trade blows with whoever they found. The sword blows they took did not pierce their armour but their axes tore through mail, bone and flesh. The defenders retreated to the second floor and pulled up the ladder. When Sven received a spear thrust to the shoulder I yelled, "Enough! Fall back! Bring kindling. We burn this to the ground!"

As we backed out we dispatched the dead and took any weapons or treasure which lay on the bodies. Henry of Langdale had found some torches and he and Gurth went around setting light to anything which would burn. Richard of York raked out the burning wood and coals from the fire and they, too, began to burn. We had to back out hurriedly as a draft dragged the flames up and we heard the screams from those above as they realised that their place of refuge was, in fact, a trap. There were no windows or openings and, as we watched, we saw them hacking holes in the wall to escape. Only one succeeded although as he jumped he was enveloped in flames and he writhed in agony on the ground until Gurth put him out of his misery.

We saw more flames from the water and we ran to join Sir Harold. There was one cog along with ten fishing boats in the harbour. All were set alight by my men and they burned. Sir Hugh's men were finishing off the last resistance. Some men threw themselves into the water in an attempt to escape. Some may have made it but they would have had to shed their armour and survived water which was as cold as ice.

"Back to the gate!" The fire had spread from the manor house to the adjacent houses. The only ones which would not be burned were the ones by the gate. They belonged to the poor and the lowest. I would let them live. They were not Scots.

When we reached the gate I had my men mount. "Come we go to the aid of Dick."

Wulfric snorted, "If he needs any help then I am a Welshman!"

We were halfway to Greatham when we met Dick. He and his archers had been pursuing those who had fled the manor. He returned with us to the manor of Greatham. When we reached the manor we found that there were two wounded men who had not perished. One had lost a hand and the other had been hamstrung. Neither would pose a threat to me or my people.

"Who is your leader?"

The one who had lost a hand had cauterised himself but he was in pain. "Give me something for the pain and I will speak."

Dick picked up a jug that still had wine left in it. He found a discarded goblet and poured some. The man drank greedily. I doubted it would do much to ease his pain but we had obliged him.

"Now speak."

"It is Robert De Brus who is head of our family now. It was his nephew Richard whose head you threw over the wall. The Captain of the men at arms sent word to Hartness along with Sir Richard's wife."

I turned to Sir Harold, "Did you see any women in Hartness?"

Before he could answer the one-armed man said, "They sailed this afternoon for Normanby. Sir Robert has taken over the castle there. All the women left. We thought you were dead. We were bold then. All fear your name. It is said you have never been defeated."

I said nothing.

Wulfric said, "Should I end their miserable lives, my lord?"

"No. There is no need. Hartness is destroyed and all are dead or fled." I turned to the two men. "If my men see you after the next new moon then you will die. I would head back to Scotland and tell all there that the only piece of England they will claim is that which covers their body."

"I will lord and thank you for your mercy."

We mounted and headed home. Dawn was breaking in the east when we spied my walls. We had made a start and now I had the name of one of my enemies but it would be a long war and I had no doubt that there would be many more battles before it was over.

Chapter 6

John, my steward, woke me just before noon, "Sorry to wake you my lord but you said you wanted to be awakened as soon as Aiden arrived." I sat up. "He is here."

"Thank you, John. I will need to talk with you later about our finances. If we are to fund this war against the Scots then I need to know how to pay for it."

He looked shocked, "Surely the Bishop of Durham will provide funds!"

"Plan for us to pay and then if we are given any by the Palatinate it will be a pleasant surprise." As I strode downstairs I reflected that money was the least of my troubles.

Aiden was waiting patiently for me, "I was worried, Aiden. Did you have trouble?"

He looked puzzled, "I did as you asked, lord. I kept out of sight. I found the Scots and I scouted Durham."

"Sit, please. I am sorry. I should never doubt you. You are like the forest itself. Go on..."

"There are small bands of Scots between here and Durham but not enough to trouble you, my lord. Further west there is a large army. It is at Barnard Castle. I think I saw the Scottish Royal banner there. Durham is free from Scots and is on a war footing. I did not enter. The Bishop's standard flies yet."

"You have done well. Tomorrow we ride to Durham and scour the land of these brigands."

Sir John came to speak with me once Aiden had left us. I still saw him as my squire and yet he was now a knight in his own right. "Earl, may I speak?"

"Of course, John."

"Have I disappointed you in some way?"

"Disappointed?"

"You did not take me with you when you raided Hartness. I wondered if you thought less of me."

"Sit." He sat and I saw the young man in his eyes. This was another mistake on my part. Perhaps I had taken on too much. "John you are my castellan. Your job is to protect my castle. When I ride abroad I do so knowing that my castle is in safe hands; yours. I asked Sir Edward and Sir Richard to remain in their castles too and you know how much I value them."

"But I do nothing!"

"You are right in that I have not given you enough to do and for that, I apologise. The men you command are mine. You should have men, like Erre and the others who guard the castle but are your men. You need oathsworn of your own. I have told John that the priority now is defence and he will make funds available. There will be young men of Stockton who wish to become warriors. You and Leofric did a fine job of training William. Do the same for your own men at arms. There are archers too for Alf has everyone at archery after church each Sunday. Find those who wish to serve."

"I can do that?"

"You are a knight and you are my castellan. Remember your men at arms and archers need no horses. They will be static. They guard my castle. They guard you and your family."

"But I have no family yet."

I smiled. I had not told him all the trivial news from Maine and Normandy. "Leofric is taking a wife. Even now they may not only be married but have children. Tristan, Hugh, Harold all have wives and some have children. You will too. This Scottish incursion will end and peace will return."

"And yet if Stephen of Blois...."

"Ah, you are right. He is a boil that has yet to burst but we have time. I hope and believe that the Empress and the Earl of Gloucester will return to this land to claim the throne that is rightly hers. On that day I shall ride behind her as a Knight of the Empress."

"Thank you, my lord, for confiding in me."

"I should do this more often. This is your home as well as mine. When I am here then join me whenever you can. We need to speak. If we do not understand each other's minds then what chance do our warrior's stand?"

He rose, "I will begin to choose my men in the morning, lord."

"Oh, one thing; we must look to ourselves for everything. Find women of the town whom we can pay to make new surcoats. We need our enemies to know who we are."

I did not take all of my men with me when I headed north. I left Wulfric and Dick along with Sir Hugh and his men to help with the new gate and the wall. I took Sir Tristan and Sir Harold along with their retinues. Aiden came as a scout. He had told me the road to Durham was clear. If there were any small bands of Scots then the two conroi would be more than enough to deal with them. It was my tongue I expected to use and not my sword.

It was depressing to ride the Durham Road and see the burnt-out farms and the flocks of carrion birds feasting on the corpses of the dead. This was because I had been absent and the Bishop had procrastinated. Sir Harold and Sir Tristan flanked me. "Can we win, my lord? Can we beat the Scots and then take on Stephen of Blois and the might of England?"

I looked at Sir Tristan. "I believe we can but even if I thought we were doomed to failure then I would still fight on."

"Why, my lord?"

"Because a knight has to fight for that which he believes. He has to do what is right. It is what makes us different from our men at arms. Let me ask you a question. Are you happy for the Scots to ravage our land as they have done?"

"Of course not but in fighting the Scots we weaken ourselves and we will be in no position to fight Stephen of Blois."

I laughed, "One battle at a time, Tristan. But I take heart from your words. You fight with my banner still"

"Always, my lord but I have a family now and I fear for them."

"And that is why I have your families behind walls. I am improving my defences and I have told your father to do the same. The worst thing you can do, Tristan, is to give up hope."

We rode in silence and then Harold said, "Tell him of the Spartans, lord."

"Harold is right, the Spartans are a good example. When I studied in Constantinople, I read of three hundred Spartan warriors who defied and held up an army of ten thousand Persians. They did not give up hope."

"Did they win?"

"They died and yet they won for Greece remained free because of their sacrifice. That may be true of us. I believe we will win but I am no fool. We may all perish but if those who come after us can live under either the Empress or her son Henry then our deaths will have been worthwhile."

He nodded and reflected.

"However take heart from Harold."

"Harold?"

"Aye, he grew up an outlaw. He lived in the forest and the men of William the Bastard and William Rufus could not capture or subdue them. They used the forest and they used the land. That will yet be the most important ally. The land will help us drive these Scots hence. My father and my namesake took to the forests and fought as outlaws against the Normans when they came. They survived. Do not give up hope just yet."

The gates of Durham were barred but men still worked their fields. Their shouts of greeting gave me hope for they were pleased to see my banner. It was my standard that gained us entry to the mighty bastion. Our squires took our horses while the three of us hurried to meet with the Bishop. He was in his hall along with his clerk, William Cumin. I did not like that. He was related to the enemy and a papal spy. Why did the Bishop tolerate him?

The Bishop smiled and rose to greet me, "My lord this is the best news I have had in some time. We had heard that you were dead!"

I pointedly looked at the clerk, "The Scots tried to have me killed but as with all things Scottish it was badly managed and I live."

I saw Cumin colour.

"This is good news then. I pray you to sit. We have much to say to each other."

I drew my sword and put the point to the clerk's throat. "I will not speak while this Scottish spy sits here. I wonder he is not in the deepest dungeon in Durham!"

"My lord, sheath your sword in my hall!"

William Cumin was sweating. "I am waiting."

The clerk began to babble, "I have sworn to my lord that I am a loyal servant of Durham and owe no allegiance elsewhere!"

I looked in disbelief at the Prince Bishop, "And you believe this snake?"

"There is no need for such language, my lord. Yes, I do believe him. He swore on a bible."

I sheathed my sword. "He lies but it is your home. You, get out of my sight. I would not lose a moment's sleep if I ended your life so think about that. Do not let me see you again or you will die."

"My lord! It is my home!"

"Go! Worm!"

When he had gone I saw that the Bishop was shaken. "That was not well done."

I rounded on him, "And was it well done when you allowed the Scots to come to my valley and slaughter my people? Where are your armies? Where is the opposition to the Scots?"

"I was helpless. Some of my castles defected to the Scots when they came south. What could I do?"

"You should have been more of a Prince and less of a Bishop. You have a banner. Lead forth your men and others will flock to it."

"They did not attack my lands."

I pointed to the door through which the clerk had gone, "You have a spy in your home. Can you not see the plots and plans of King David and the earl Gospatric? Are you a fool?"

"How dare you! I am Prince Bishop and you owe allegiance and fealty to me!"

I said nothing at first. "You know that King Henry is dead?" he nodded, "And that Stephen of Blois claims the throne?"

"Aye, I do."

"How stand you with that? Do you not support the claim of Empress Matilda and her son Henry? Did you not swear an oath to King Henry?"

"King Stephen will bring stability to the land and he has a firm hand."

"King Stephen? Then you have joined his side. If he was such a strong leader he would have come north to rid our land of these Scots. Now I know your mind. What of Sir Hugh Manningham? He would not defect."

He shrugged, "I know not. We have had no word."

"Have you tried to contact him?"

"I cannot risk my men. I have few enough as it is."

I stood, "I once thought you brought hope to Durham, Geoffrey Rufus, I now see that I was wrong. You say I owe you allegiance and fealty; you are wrong. I owe you nothing! You lost those rights when you failed in your duty. I owe my allegiance to King Henry and his heirs."

"But the King is dead!"

I nodded, "And until the Empress and her son have a throne I have no one to whom I will bend the knee. Do not cross me Bishop or you shall be my enemy. I once captured this castle with a handful of men and I can do so again. You have few men who can stand up to my warriors. If you allow the Scots through your land again and do not fight them then you become my enemy and I will happily put my own Prince Bishop in Durham."

"You cannot do that!"

"I am a warlord and I do anything I choose!"

I strode out of the hall leaving a white face cleric who genuinely feared for his life. As we headed to our horses Sir Harold said, "Was that wise, my lord?"

We mounted our horses and I swept a hand around the waiting men at arms of Durham. "Do you think that the Bishop and these men will oppose the Scots? They will wait to pick up the morsels the Scots leave for them. We are better off without them for they are not to be trusted."

The grizzled Sergeant at Arms said, "My lord that is not fair! We would fight the Scots but we were told to stay within these walls."

I nodded, "Well, know this; I fight the Scots. If there are any men among you who wish to fight then go to Stockton. I can use men with spines." I saw the Bishop and his clerk as they came to the door of the hall, "For the rest; the spineless ones who follow a procrastinator, then stay here but there will come a time for vengeance and retribution and I am a good friend but a terrible foe! Remember that!"

We galloped out and headed across the Wear. I led them east and north. None said a word for they saw my anger. Eventually, Wilfred, my squire, asked, "Where do we go, my lord?"

I slowed Scout down. There was little point in thrashing our horses to death. "Hexham. I must speak with Sir Hugh. Aiden ride ahead and warn Sir Hugh that we are on our way."

"And if there are Scots there?"

"Then return to us, Aiden, but I believe he holds out yet."

As Aiden galloped off I spoke with my two knights. "I now see how the Scots succeeded. Their spy poisoned the mind of the Bishop. He is weaker than I thought. It allowed them to get close to Stockton unseen. I doubt not that Sir Hugh is free. They have captured the New Castle but Hexham will be a beacon. From now on expect enemies rather than friends." I looked up at the sky. "We have less than three hours before nightfall and we have forty miles to cover. We ride hard!"

We used the Roman Road. It had the advantage that an ambush was difficult and its surface suited our mounts. Even so, we did not reach Hexham in daylight. Darkness fell and riders loomed up out of the dark. We drew swords but I heard Sir Hugh Manningham's reassuring growl, "Thank the lord we have found you. There are Scottish raiders everywhere."

We rode in silence with drawn swords for the last three miles. We did not speak until our mounts were stabled and we were in the Great Hall whose fire took the chill from our faces and hands.

"We have little enough food but we shall share it."

"Until this is over, pay no taxes and I would allow your people to hunt in the forests and fish in the rivers. I delegate that power to you."

His servants poured us ale heated with a poker and I felt alive as the amber liquid filled us with warmth. "Tell me all, my lord. We are isolated here."

I gave him my news and held nothing back. When I spoke of the Bishop he shook his head. "A weak man! Now I know how the Scots were able to enter our land. There was collusion."

"Aye treachery at home and abroad. How stands the border?"

"Norham, Rothbury, Morpeth and Otterburn hold. There is a thin strip of England but we are surrounded by Scots. The New Castle and the crossing of the Tyne are in enemy hands. The west is Scotland now and the land twixt here and Durham is unknown." For the first time since I had known him, he did not look confident. Confusion filled his face.

"I intend to fight as my own master until the Empress or her son is on the throne. The first threat is Scotland and I will rally the men of the north to fight under my banner. The Bishop of Durham has abdicated his rights to rule by his vacillation."

"And after, my lord?"

"And after they are defeated then I oppose Stephen."

"I will fight alongside you against the Scots but after…"

I nodded, "I understand. You know it may mean I have to fight you if you side with Stephen?"

"Aye, my lord, and I would not have that for the world but if it is meant to be then so be it. It may not come to that. He may not be crowned."

I shook my head, "With the greedy grasping citizens of London eager to gain power he will. His brother is Bishop of

Winchester and he has influenced all of their clerics with his persuasive arguments."

We sat in silence as my words sank in. I was also deep in thought. I had thought Sir Hugh would have followed my banner. My allies against Stephen were shrinking.

Sir Hugh banged the table. "Why worry about something which may never happen. How do we drive the Scots hence?"

"There is a large army at Barnard Castle. Balliol has been given power by King David. We march against Balliol. When he is defeated then we retake the New Castle."

Sir Tristan said, "Why not take the New Castle first? It is closer?"

"Aiden told me that the army at Barnard is in the town and not the castle. It is a mighty host. We have more chance of destroying that army. When they are defeated, the garrison in the New Castle may well decide to surrender. A siege takes time and we are short of that commodity; we can hire men and make swords but we cannot buy time."

Sir Hugh nodded, "I will send for men from the loyal castles. We will have to leave garrisons."

"I know. I need to return to my castle and bring my army north. It is winter and they need not work in their fields. We can use those who are not warriors. This is a war of people against people. There can be no bystanders. Use the fyrd. It is the number we need. Our knights and men at arms have more skill."

Sir Harold said, "It is our archers who will win the day. None are as good as them."

"You are right. We meet at Auckland a week hence!"

We left the next morning and I called at Durham on the way back. I did not enter but spoke to the Bishop from his bridge over the Wear. "I have visited your knights in the north. Unlike you, Prince Bishop, they are defending this land from the Scots. I go now to gather my men and rid the land around Normanby and Guisborough of the Scottish invader. Then I will visit the Archbishop. I have much to tell him."

He said nothing in reply. As we headed south Sir Tristan said, "I thought we attacked Barnard Castle?"

"We do. The message I sent was for the Scottish spy. They will send word both to Barnard Castle and Guisborough of my intentions. The De Brus family will wait for an attack which does not come and Balliol will relax and, perhaps, even think about attacking me." I smiled at their faces. "King David and Gospatric are not the only ones who can be devious. I have plans and strategies."

I kept my counsel for I was still formulating my risky plan. Much of it depended upon my new squire and Sir Hugh of Gainford and just as much rested upon the weather. When I reached my castle I was pleased to see that the wall and the gate were higher. They were not complete yet but every brick and every course made us that little bit more secure. My knights and my men at arms toiled next to the townsfolk. We worked together.

Sir Hugh and Sir John came to speak with me as Gilles led Scout away. "Lord we have more men at arms." Sir Hugh pointed to a dozen men at arms I did not recognise. They were toiling with my men. "Some came from Durham while others were from Piercebridge and my estate. Our numbers grow."

"Good for we leave here in five days and go to war."

Sir Hugh pointed to the skies, "But my lord it is winter and soon there will be snow."

"And that is why we attack now. They will not expect it." I put my hand on his shoulder. "Tonight I will explain all and tell you my strategy but first I must visit with Sir Edward."

Ethelred and his sons had worked as hard as any and his ferry now had a protective wooden wall that was lined at the bottom with stones. I saw weapons ready there to repel enemies. He grinned when he saw me, "I will teach these Scots to try to take the bread from my bairns' mouths! You go to Thornaby, lord?"

"Aye. I will not be long. I would have you wait for me."

Edward had now built a tower on his wall which was but a hundred paces from the ferry. There, too, was a sally port.

He met me there having seen my approach. I saw that he no longer had his left arm in a sling. "How goes it, my lord?"

I smiled, "We know where we stand, old friend... alone. We cannot count on the Bishop and Sir Hugh has just five castles under his control. Our war begins small."

As he led me inside he said, "My arm is healing. My men and I can ride with you."

"I shook my head. I have much to tell you and I have a plan. It necessitates you waiting behind your walls. I tempt De Brus to attack you."

"In winter? Only a fool would do so."

"I will be attacking Barnard Castle so does that make me a fool?"

"You were never that my lord. I pray you to tell me in simple terms. I am just a soldier. I was never a strategos."

"Do not do yourself a disservice." I spent half an hour telling him my plans in detail.

He smiled when I had finished. "We have our own Caesar amongst us, my lord. I will hold here and we have more men trained to fight. When Spring comes we will be ready."

I headed back to my castle more confident than I had been. Perhaps that was born of desperation but when your back is against the wall you have nowhere left to retreat. The only way is forward.

As I stepped onto the ferry there was the clatter of hooves and we drew weapons. These were nervous times. It was a rider from the Archbishop. I recognised him. He had been one of the archers the Archbishop had loaned me when I escorted the King's gold to Normandy. He handed me a scroll. Leaning down he said quietly, "My lord, King Stephen has been crowned in London. The Archbishop wished you God speed. He says he will pray for you and he is ever your friend." He nodded towards the scroll. "None of that will be written down. He begs you to use trusted men. These are dark and treacherous times."

Chapter 7

We had a bigger host gathered at Auckland than I expected. We had more recruits and men at arms who wished to fight back. Dick had managed to train more archers too. As we left our camp in Auckland the snows blew even harder than when we had arrived two days earlier. The thirteen miles were along a road otherwise the task would have been impossible. We had fifty archers, ten knights and squires, a hundred men at arms and fifty men of the fyrd. Aiden had reported that Balliol had over two hundred and fifty men camped at his castle in addition to those within. We could expect to face three hundred men.

Wilfred of Piercebridge rode now as my standard-bearer with my banner. My standard remained in Stockton. It flew from my walls. Wilfred had one of his men at arms as a squire and rode with his father's standard. Sir Hugh of Gainford was with us. Our counsel of war ensured that all knew my plan. It involved splitting my army; that was always dangerous. We left my main force and headed towards the old Roman Road which led from the south. We had but ten horsemen, two mounted archers and what looked like forty men of the fyrd. In truth, there were just ten volunteers from the fyrd and the rest were Wulfric and other men at arms disguised in rude raiments. We were the bait. Sir Hugh Manningham commanded the bulk of my army. He would be the hammer.

As we rode along the virgin snow, for no one had passed this way in the blizzard, I stressed again to Sir Hugh of Gainford what our plan would be. "Remember that Balliol thinks I am at Normanby. He knows not that you escaped his men. When he sees us he will think you are both foolish young men trying to reclaim your land. He will not be surprised when we flee. His men will think to make sport with us. They have been camped by the castle for almost three weeks now. They will be eager to raid our lands."

Sir Hugh asked, "Why camp here in winter?"

"King David took advantage of the death of the King and my absence. Although not a perfect time of year to attack, by occupying this land he is ready to invade when the weather improves. The Tees is not his ultimate aim. He would, I believe, take the land as far as York, if he could."

We were not moving at the speed of the horses but that of Wulfric and the men on foot. I knew that Erre and his fellows were more than happy to be marching rather than riding. Their shields and axes were covered by cloaks and furs. In their hands they held spears. We would be an inviting plum to be picked by the Scots. Sir Hugh just had to tempt them.

The two roads met half a mile from the castle. There were houses and huts straddling the main road, the one we were on, closer to the castle and it was the area behind that which was occupied by the Scots. We could smell the roasting mutton from their camp. I had no doubt that their raiding parties were gathering sheep daily to be slaughtered. They were English animals and, as such, fair game.

We halted less than four hundred paces from the first house. We were spied as I knew we would be and ten riders galloped out. They were not knights. They halted twenty paces from us. Their leader was a man at arms. His livery suggested he was a follower of Gospatric.

"What do you wish, sir knight? You are Gainford are you not?" He laughed, "We have taken your land and your animals what else have you to offer us? Your women, yourself?" He thought he was a wit baiting a young knight. My face was hidden by the hood of my cloak. I was just another knight.

"Piercebridge and I come to tell you that the Earl of Cleveland has returned and he sends a message to Balliol to get back to Scotland before he comes and destroys him and his army!"

The smile was wiped from his face. "If that butcher comes within ten miles of here we shall gut him like a fish and watch him bleed his life away."

"I came here to deliver a message and not to be insulted. Deliver the message Scotsman!"

"Or?"

Sir Hugh nodded to the two mounted archers. At twenty paces they could not miss and the two men next to the man at arms fell dead.

"Treachery!"

The ten of us drew our swords and the man at arms whirled his horse around and galloped back yelling, "To arms! To arms!"

Sir Hugh nodded again and two more arrows flew and plucked a third Scot from his horse. "Well done, Sir Hugh, and now we leave!"

We headed up the old Roman Road which led to Auckland. This was a much smaller road. In fact, I doubted that it had been used much for the woods had reconquered the sides which had been cleared. In places, cobbles were missing and the ditches had long since filled up with leaves and the detritus of hundreds of years. As we turned to see if they pursued I said, "Remember Wulfric, you are playing a part. Appear as though you are frightened." Our ambush was waiting up this road. We just had to drag as many Scots behind it as we could.

"Aye, my lord! If I can pull this off I shall become a mummer!"

I was aware of trumpets sounding behind us. Osric son of Dale was at the rear and he shouted, "They are mounting, my lord."

"Good, then turn and begin to act agitated. Remember we appear to be surprised by their numbers. You men from the fyrd now is the time to run."

The ten volunteers laughed as they ran through us. They were in on the ruse and were confident despite the proximity of so many enemy warriors.

"I think, Sir Hugh that such a youth as yourself might ride a little harder."

We spurred our horses and our line lengthened. Had it been any other than my handpicked men at arms I might have feared for their safety but I did not. We looked over our shoulders. It fitted the part we were playing. I saw that their knights were leading the charge. They had grabbed spears and were eagerly racing after this sport. Not all had joined the chase but I saw a mob following. They had taken the bait.

"My lord! Now!" Osric's call was the signal.

"Run as though the devil himself was behind you. Knights, wheel!"

As Wulfric and his men ran through us we turned and lowered our lances. The knights would have seen it as a foolish gesture. It was merely a delaying tactic. We charged towards the horsemen. Although outnumbered the ten of us filled the narrow road in two ranks. Our sudden turn took those at the front by surprise. Sir Hugh was an accomplished knight and his squire was well trained. It was just Wilfred and his squire whom I did not know.

We did not meet at full tilt but Sir Hugh and I stood in our stirrups to punch our spears at our enemies. The knight who took my spear in the chest hit my shield. Sir Hugh's foe was speared in the thigh. As we struck their line and they recoiled Sir Hugh yelled, "Retreat!"

As we turned disaster struck. Wilfred had not killed his enemy and as he turned a spear was thrust at his face. His life was saved by his turn but the spear went through both cheeks. His squire managed to thrust his own spear into the side of the knight who fell backwards tearing the spear from his bloody mouth. "Take your master to the rear!"

The squire grabbed Wilfred's reins and spurred his horse. Wilfred was held by the cantle of his saddle else he would have fallen. Ahead, my men at arms had formed a shield wall. The ambush was about to be sprung. As we galloped towards Wulfric and my men they opened ranks to allow us through. That should have warned the Scots that they were not the fyrd. These were highly trained men at arms. As we wheeled around them the shields of Wulfric and my Varangians locked. The second and third ranks laid their shields over them and spears protruded like the spines of a hedgehog.

The Scots tried to stop. This was where the weather aided us. The snow was icy and, where we had trodden it had turned to an icy slush. The horses could not stop. They slithered and slipped. Some tumbled into the ditches and trees but most were impaled upon a barrier of spears. At the same time, the archers who were strategically placed around the sides began to loose arrows at a ridiculously short range. Even those with armour could do nothing as the deadly arrows flew from the dark recesses of the forest. The Scots were tightly packed and had nowhere to go.

While we still had the initiative I dismounted and, with Sir Hugh, joined my men at arms and we stood to push back the Scots. The ones on horses were at a disadvantage. The road was very narrow and they got in each other's way. Erre and Wulfric made a space for me and Wulfric grinned as he said, "Push! Now!"

The men behind us, all twenty of them pushed into our backs as we stepped forward swinging our swords and axes. The four axes alongside Sir Hugh and I were terrible to behold. They did not just cause minor wounds and cuts, they lopped limbs, hacked bodies and they tore mail. Sir Hugh and I stabbed, slashed and hacked along with them and we moved relentlessly forward.

Sir Hugh Manningham, meanwhile, led the rest of my knights and our mounted men at arms to charge the Scottish camp. Many Scots were caught wandering into the woods in the hope of finding some treasure or spoils of war. As the men of Hexham charged all that they received was an icy grave. While my archers and men at arms held the bulk of their men Sir Hugh Manningham tore through their camp slaughtering all. Those who were able fled into the castle but the gates were quickly slammed shut as my knights closed with the mighty stone walls of Barnard Castle.

My archers now began to slip amongst the Scots using their short swords and the packed ranks to kill all those at the edge of the forest. They were masters of such warfare. Any hope of a fightback ended as more spears prickled from our line as we spread out; my men speared and impaled the confused Scots. We were moving at walking speed. I wondered if I would either blunt my sword or tire before the slaughter ended and then we heard a collective wail as Sir Hugh Manningham brought his conroi into the rear of those in the woods. They were hemmed in from all sides. I know some escaped; some lay, feigning death. Some climbed trees and some just ran and were too quick to be caught. It took all night to finish the slaughter. As dawn broke my men were busy dispatching the wounded. I took my horse from Aiden and rode with my knights to the walls of the castle. My archers were gathering anything of value from the camp. The plunder they had taken was now ours. Their horses, weapons and mail belonged to us. Even the mutton they roasted was taken to be devoured on the way home.

We sat on our horses, out of bow range and I lifted my helmet so that Barnard de Balliol could see my face. He remained hidden but I knew he would be watching and listening. I shouted, "Barnard de Balliol you are a coward and man without honour. Your men have bled and died here yet you hide behind your walls. You send others out to attack your neighbours. Know this it is I who rule this valley. Not King David. I will hold this land until Empress Matilda or her son come to claim it. I give fair warning that neither Scot nor rebel will be safe. If I find you then you will die. Today you have had a taste of what we can do. Warn your master that he is not safe. I fear no king and no king is safe from my blade. The only king I swore allegiance to is now dead! Your master had a hand in his death and I will have vengeance."

I allowed the words to echo. I wanted his men to hear the implied challenge. I had insulted him and if he was a man who had any kind of honour then he would fight me. He did not.

"Gospatric, you bloated carcass, you pustule on the backside of Scotland, I swear this. You shall never rule one inch of Northumberland but shall have a piece of earth five paces by five paces. That should be big enough to bury the vastness that is your body!"

My knights and men at arms began banging their shields and cheering. I said nothing but continued to stare at the walls. Finally, I held up my sword and all went silent. "There is no one who will answer me? Then before I go I say this. If there are any Englishmen within Barnard who cannot stomach fighting for a man who is insulted and does nothing about it then join me. If you have joined Balliol and Gospatric for riches then you have chosen the wrong side. All that they will bring you is death!"

I turned my horse around and led my men away east. Sir Hugh Manningham rode next to me, "By God, Earl you make a bad enemy! Insulting them was a masterstroke. There will be many inside who wonder at their lack of courage."

I shook my head, "So long as King David backs them then they will survive. I wanted the Scottish King rousing. I hope I did so."

"Why rouse him?"

"I want him angry and hasty. I want him to make mistakes. When you return to Hexham send your spies to find out what goes on at Berwick and north of the border. Keep me informed. I want news, no matter how trivial. We have the upper hand and I do not intend to relinquish it." We spoke, as we rode, of my plans and I gave him instructions.

When we reached the road where we had ambushed the Scots he led his men towards Auckland and thence home. I led my men south and east along the Roman Road. Edgar sought me out. "Lord, we must get Wilfred to a healer. I have staunched the bleeding but it needs Father Henry."

I turned to Aiden, "Go with Edgar the falconer and ride as fast as you can to Stockton. You know the best ways to go. He is a brave youth. I would not have him die because of me."

Along with Wilfred's squire, the four of them sped off. They would not spare their horses and I prayed that Wilfred of Piercebridge's life would be saved. It took us all day but we reached home; we were frozen and wet but we brought great booty. The men at arms and fyrd who had walked to Auckland rode back. Every one of the fyrd who had volunteered had a new sword, helmet and, in some cases, mail. Aiden had beaten us back by some hours and my people gathered to cheer us through the gates. We had had a victory and it was close enough to home to mean something. It was the beginning of our fight back.

Wilfred had a heavily bandaged face and was asleep when I went to visit him in the quarters I had given to him and his mother. His mother stood over him. She was the wife of a knight and she shed no tears but I saw concern etched all over her face. Father Henry was there too. They both turned when I entered.

"Your son is brave and did well." She nodded, "Tell me, Father Henry, will he heal?"

He nodded, "Your healer, Edgar, saved his life. He stopped the bleeding. I have instructed Alice that he should be fed broth for I do not wish him using his jaw. It is just time to heal that he requires."

"Then tell him, to aid his healing, that when he is healed I shall knight him. He has all the virtues a knight needs and when we take back your manor he will be lord once more."

Lady Hilda impulsively took my hand, "Thank you, my lord." She hesitated, "You believe you will take back our home?"

"I have no doubt, my lady. Come the spring when our numbers are grown and our defences here are secure then we will begin the fight back."

"Thank you, my lord. My husband was ever your man and my son will be the same."

We did not rest on our laurels. The next day I left my men at arms to continue to work on the gate and walls while I went with Aiden, Dick and every archer. I had another message to send. We first went to speak with Sir Edward.

He was in his bailey practising, despite the snow, with his squire and men at arms.

"The arm is healing then?"

"Aye my lord but we both know that the best way to heal is to use. I will be ready the next time you fight. How went your raid?"

"There is no threat from the west, at least not until spring. I have bought us enough time to improve our defences. And the east?"

"My scouts have reported that Guisborough and Normanby have both begun to prepare defences. It seems your words to the spy worked!"

I smiled, "Good. The more his word is doubted the better. The Bishop has been duped by his clerk, what better than to dupe the clerk? I ride with my own archers to scout out the east. I need to send a message to Robert de Brus."

"And what of the New Castle?"

"Sir Hugh Manningham and his knights will call there and demand its surrender."

"Does he have enough men for a siege?"

"He needs them not. He will leave it a week and then take his men there. By then the word of our victory at Barnard Castle should have got out and the word of what I do here. We hope to deceive them into thinking we have more men than we actually have. They cannot know which of my knights remain. If it does not succeed then I will, indeed, take my men north but I wish to improve my defences. I want my castle to be a haven from the Scots."

The south bank of the Tees from Thornaby to Normanby was swampy and filled with small streams and rivulets. The safest way to reach Normanby and Guisborough was to head south and use the low line of hills some way south of the river. They were covered in trees for this was not farmland. A valley ran from the west to the sea and emerged at the scar which jutted out into the icy waters of the ocean. Had I so chosen I could have raided that valley. It was the granary for Normanby and Guisborough but I knew that most of those who farmed there were English.

The low hills separated Normanby from Guisborough and I intended to show Sir Robert just how vulnerable he was. Aiden led us by trails which only he knew. I had brought Gilles with me for I wanted him to watch Aiden. If he could learn to be another Aiden then I would be satisfied.

We emerged above the castle at Normanby. It was not a stone castle and I could have reduced it but there was little point so long as I had no lord. I also needed men to man the walls and defend against De Brus in Guisborough. I wanted De Brus on the defensive. I could not afford to have him and his men raiding the southern bank of the Tees. So long as he was isolated then he could not help King David. I was no fool and I knew that King David would have to deal with me sometime. He had the west of the land he claimed and I was the enclave in the east which he needed.

We dismounted and tied our horses to the trees while we went to the eaves of the forest to spy out the enemy. I saw the red diagonal cross on the yellow background flying from the keep. A De Brus was in command. I doubted that it would be Robert. He would be behind the stone walls of Guisborough. We watched for a while. There were sentries watching from the walls and we heard the clash of swords as men practised. Then we saw men leave the castle and head first east and then wend their way south up the snow-covered track which led to the woods we occupied.

Dick said, "Unless I miss my guess these are hunters from the castle."

Aiden had keener eyes than most, "They are soldiers, my lord, they carry swords as well as bows."

I nodded, "Then let us hunt them. Gilles, watch the horses."

There were ten hunters. I surmised they were men at arms. That made sense. When Sir Guiscard and his men had died then those who hunted for him would also have perished. Whoever ruled now in Normanby would only have those men he had brought to hunt and they would be unfamiliar with the woods. It explained the high numbers. Fortune had given me the opportunity of sending an even stronger message to De Brus.

Dick and his archers were not men at arms. They were nimble-footed wraiths who barely left an imprint in the snow. I walked behind, aware that I would be leaving a trail. The men at arms were not the best hunters in the world and we heard them before we saw them. It soon became obvious that they had set traps for game in the woods and were collecting those. Dick halted and looked at me. I stopped and nodded. They disappeared.

I could not see what they were about but it soon became obvious. I heard the sound of arrows being loosed and the soft thud as they struck bodies unprotected by armour. There were shouts as the hunters realised they were being attacked.

There were two cries and then there was silence. Henry Warbow found me, "They are all dead, lord."

I followed him back. Already the bodies were being stripped of anything which might be of use. Aelric held up some rabbits. "They were emptying traps, lord."

Dick held a medallion. He had taken it from around the neck of the leader. "It is the seal of De Brus. This is a sergeant at arms." He gave it to me and I put it in my surcoat.

"Fetch the rabbits and the weapons. Let us return to our horses."

Once mounted we rode to the path they had taken from the castle. As the crow flies the castle was just half a mile from the woods. Leaving Dick and my archers hidden in the woods I rode with Aiden and Gilles down the winding trail. The footprints of the dead hunters marked it.

"Aiden if we are attacked then your task is to take Gilles to Dick and safety."

"Aye lord."

"Why do you bring me, lord? I am no warrior."

"You are learning Gilles. When you became my groom you joined my retinue. All of my men are warriors but there is more to being a warrior than fighting with a sword. You use your head. Aiden here knows that. I would have you watch him and learn." He nodded, "Aiden, have an arrow knocked."

I knew we were seen as we descended the hillside. I had no doubt that the woods were being watched. Whoever commanded would wonder if the three of us were alone and also speculating about the ten men at arms. We did not ride swiftly and the gates opened and five mailed men emerged. I soon saw that they wore the livery of De Brus. I halted and we waited for them. I could see that they were suspicious.

"You are the Earl of Cleveland." I nodded. The young man who spoke said, "Do you come here to surrender to me?"

"And who are you?"

"I am William, younger brother of Robert de Brus. King David has given him this land."

"It was not his to give and far from surrendering I come to tell you that you have until Easter to vacate this castle and go back to Scotland. After that time I will destroy you."

His laugh was not convincing for his eyes flickered around as though seeking out my army. "Bold talk for one knight with two peasants as guards."

It was my turn to laugh, "I have seen little to frighten me here. One callow boy and four men at arms do not constitute a threat."

One of the men at arms suddenly spurred his horse. He managed three strides before an arrow appeared in his throat. I spurred Scout and charged the four. Swinging my shield around I blocked the blow from the man at arms to my left before hacking at the head of the one to my right. He blocked the blow but fell from the saddle. The young knight and the other man at arms wheeled out of sword range. He was not ready to face King Henry's Champion. I swung Scout around and brought my blade into the back of the remaining man at arms who was trying to control his horse. His mail was severed and I heard a crack as bones broke. He too fell from his horse.

Aiden and Gilles were already galloping up the hillside and I followed. The two riderless horses followed me. I smiled. Sometimes fortune favoured the bold. I glanced over my shoulder and saw that Sir William had summoned riders. A dozen men followed him as he pursued us. I shouted, "Aiden, Gilles, collect these two horses."

They reined in and grabbed the reins as the two horses passed them. We continued to twist our way up the slope to the woods and my waiting archers. Two of the pursuing men at arms decided to forego the track and attempt to come directly up the slope. It was an unmitigated disaster and the two horses slithered their way to the bottom of the hill taking their riders with them.

As I neared the top I wheeled Scout around and unsheathed my sword. I smiled as Sir William also reined in to allow his men at arms to close with me. I watched them approach and, when they were just thirty paces from me lowered my sword. Six men were plucked from their saddles and two more were struck by the arrows from Dick and his men. Sir William shouted, "Fall back!"

As they departed I shouted, "Tell your brother this is just the beginning. None of you is safe from my men!"

They ran back so quickly to their castle that we had all the time in the world to collect the swords and mail from the corpses.

Chapter 8

By the time February arrived my gate was finished and my wall almost complete. Those who had come from Cowpen had gone to Norton to begin work on repairing the walls. More easily defended than their own home they were happy to be given the land by me. Their families remained at Stockton while the men cleared all signs of the vicious attack which had made Norton a village filled with ghosts. A rider came south from Sir Hugh Manningham. The New Castle had refused to surrender. His men besieged it but the good news was that the Bishop of Durham had stirred himself and sent some of his own knights north to join Sir Hugh and subjugate the Scots. The men in the New Castle were no longer a threat to us.

As January had progressed we had received a steady influx of volunteers. Men at arms whose lords had died or been killed by the Scots came to my castle. I used Wulfric and Dick to assess them. Not all remained. Some were sent on their way for we doubted their integrity. We were not so desperate that we would take any. We needed men on whom we could rely. Even so, our numbers had swollen and we had erected another warrior hall in the town. The inner and outer baileys were too crowded. We had also had to build another stable. Horses were not the problem.

I summoned all of my valley knights to a council of war. Dick and Wulfric attended too. We had made a good start but there was much yet to be done. None had far to travel and we began early in the afternoon. I told them the news that I had. There was little new. Sir Hugh Manningham kept me informed about Scottish incursions. So far they had not tried to reinforce the New Castle and Norham still blocked the route south.

"We have hurt De Brus. Hartness and Greatham remain empty wastelands. I have Dick and his archers riding there once a week to ensure that the Scots have not tried to retake them. The question remains, 'what do we do about Normanby'?"

No one volunteered to speak. Finally, Dick rose. "My lord I think the castle would not stand long against a determined attack. We halved the garrison."

Sir Richard said, "But what if they have reinforced it?"

"Then they will have weakened Guisborough. Sir Robert has a limited number of men. It is winter and the harsh snows mean that all are suffering. Had Sir John and John my steward not laid in large quantities of supplies then we would be hungry too."

Sir Edward said, "Then let us take from the De Brus family. If we attack their castles then we will lose men and as we all know we can ill afford that. The Earl is right; King David will come in the Spring to punish us and to complete his invasion. We will need all of our strength then."

"You speak wisely, Sir Edward. That is food for thought."

Wulfric smiled, "It would be good for our men at arms to work together. We are all mounted and we could ravage their lands and strip it of all supplies. They rely heavily on the sheep which are on the moors. We could easily capture them. With Dick's archers alongside us, they would need to mount a large force to stop us."

Sir Richard said, "You mean act like brigands and outlaws?"

I shook my head, "You may not have noticed, Sir Richard, but we are outlaws. King David claims this land and we act outside his law. Stephen who claims the throne has yet to stir from his London stronghold. Until we have a legitimate ruler once more then we are outlaws in the truest sense of the word." I could never bring myself to grace Stephen with the title king. He was a usurper. "When William the Bastard took the throne and King Harold was slain my father and Aelfraed were outlaws. They fought from the safety of the woods. It was neither chivalrous nor honourable but it was necessary. Be under no illusions, Sir Richard, we are not fighting for our honour, we are fighting for our existence."

Of all my knights Sir Richard was the one who worried me most. I knew now, beyond all doubt that the rest would follow me over the precipice of rebellion. At some time I would need to address the problem of his divided loyalties.

I was about to send them hence when a shout came from the south tower. "Lord, mounted archers approach!"

We all ran from the hall and up the stairs to the ramparts. Across the river, I saw sixteen archers. Dick grinned and I breathed a sigh of relief. "Tell Ethelred that they are friends. Ask him to bring them over."

The others looked at me and I said, "It is Philip of Selby. He is a relative of the Archbishop of York and a stout fellow. I hope he brings good news."

We descended to the bailey to greet our guests. He had not changed since we had served together but I saw that he and his men now sported leather jerkins and all had helmets and swords. He had seen my archers and emulated them. He dismounted and bowed, "My lord the Archbishop sends you his best wishes. He has offered our services until the threat from Scotland is over."

I felt relief, "I am grateful!"

He lowered his voice, "He also has messages for your ears only."

I nodded. Raising my voice I said to the others, "I pray you to return to my hall. My housekeeper will bring refreshments." I led Philip of Selby to the ramparts and waved my sentries away. "What news then?"

"King Stephen is in London yet and he is securing the support of nobles there. There is trouble in Wales and he has despatched de Clare to subjugate the Welsh."

"And what of Scotland?"

"His grace believes that King Stephen will come north to deal with the problem himself."

That would bring a confrontation to a head sooner rather than later."Thank you and also for coming to our aid."

He laughed, "It is not altruistically motivated my lord. I expect to be much richer as a result."

With the extra men, I was able to send Wulfric and Dick to rampage through the east of Cleveland and they captured huge quantities of animals. Dick and Philip's archers were the difference and each time Sir Robert brought his knights to the field in an attempt to stop the privations the arrows of our archers drove them hence. After two weeks of such raids and, with my men controlling all, he sent an embassy to me suing for peace. It was his nephew who came. We met on the south bank of the Tees beneath the walls of Sir Edward's castle.

He dropped to one knee, "My lord, my brother begs you to stop these raids and to bring peace to our land."

I smiled, "In an instant."

He looked up at me, surprised, "As easily as that? We just ask and you accede."

"Of course not, there are conditions. Firstly you leave Normanby." He nodded, "Secondly your brother and your family take an oath not to attack any of the manors in the valley. If you do this then I will not visit your family with the full force of my men. In addition, I wish restitution in the amount of a hundred gold crowns as indemnity against his future behaviour and to recompense those who lost land to the unwarranted Scottish attack."

"I will need to speak to my brother."

"Then next time tell your brother to send someone who has the power to negotiate or better still come himself. You have three days. We will meet in the church of St. Peter in Thornaby."

I wondered what had prompted such an about face. I doubted that my raids had such an effect. I sent Aiden north to scout the lands to the west of the manor of Hexham. With Sir Hugh still besieging the New Castle, I worried about the dangers from Scotland. The winter snows had gone and while the weather was inclement armies could move more easily.

Sir Robert and his brother arrived at St. Peter's as requested. I had all my knights there as well as my own priest, Father Henry. I wanted a binding oath. Sir Robert's face betrayed him. He did not wish to do this. He had been ordered to do so. The question remained why. The money was handed over. I did not count it. They had lost enough face already. He read the oath and put his hands on the bible. He swore. As he rose to leave he glared at me. Sir Robert and I did not exchange a word. We were enemies despite his oath. I knew then that this was not over.

For my knights, however, it was viewed as a great victory. We now had security in the east as well as the north and west. Their humour and mood improved as it seemed, did the weather. The first shoots of new growth could be seen and we had our first lambs. When Aiden returned, two days after the oaths were taken, everyone was in a state of excitement. Wilfred had had his bandages removed and, although thin and wasted, he managed to speak. Father Henry was delighted and pronounced him healed. I kept my word and told him that I would knight him on the following Sunday. Then Aiden galloped in. His lathered horse told me all that I needed to know. There was trouble.

I hastened to greet him. He threw himself from his horse and pointed north. "My lord an army; it is led by the son of Earl Gospatric and it is heading down the valley towards Auckland. He will be here in two days, three at the most."

He was out of breath and gasping for air. "Someone give him water. Dick! I need an archer!"

"There are forty knights, lord and over three hundred warriors. The baggage train is a mile long."

Rafe ran over leading a horse. Dick had anticipated my orders. "Ride to the New Castle. Tell Sir Hugh Manningham to lift the siege. He must make all speed to reach us. Tell him we march up the Durham road to meet a Scottish army. Ask him to meet us south of Segges' Field."

"Aye lord." He sprang on to the back of his horse and galloped off.

"Send riders to Sir Richard and Sir Edward. I need all of their men. We march at dawn."

"Wilfred, I am afraid you will have to wait a while for your spurs but I leave you in command of my castle. I will need Sir John. I know that I can trust you to protect my home."

Alf's work was evident as we gathered the arrows, swords and spears we would need. Erre and his Varangians stayed at Stockton but all else would come with us. A long baggage train meant they were planning to keep in the field. I had no doubt that Balliol would venture forth from Barnard Castle and swell the numbers Gospatric had. I could expect nearer four hundred and fifty men. Hugh, Tristan, John and Harold were close by. I waved them over.

"How many men can we muster if we strip every castle of archers and men at arms?"

"You would leave them undefended, lord?" Sir Tristan looked shocked.

"They will have to be defended by farmers, boys and old soldiers. If I leave men at arms in the castles then we will be defeated and they will capture the castles whether or no."

Sir Hugh nodded and took a piece of charcoal from the fire. He used my table as a piece of parchment. He made marks as he spoke. "If we assume that Sir Hugh reaches us in time then he will have four knights, forty-odd men at arms and almost forty archers. If we add squires and servants then he will bring almost a hundred men. We can muster seven knights, over eighty men at arms and a hundred and twenty-five archers. The Archbishop's gift was a timely one."

I nodded, "Then we have two hundred and sixty men to face a possible four hundred and fifty or even five hundred."

"Daunting odds, lord."

"Aye but we are all mounted and they will be tired after their travels. If they reach us in two days as Aiden suggested then I will be hopeful. I want to meet them where we can always retreat back to Stockton if things go awry."

Sir Harold said, "And you need a good position."

I nodded, "He will leave Segge's Field and travel down the Durham Road. There are a couple of places between there and Stockton. Layton! It is on a small ridge and it is surrounded by woods. We can use the slope to disguise our numbers and make him think he faces less than he does."

"Aye, and he will have to attack uphill. The woods at the side will allow us to ambush."

Sir Hugh said, "If Barnard de Balliol is with them then he will be suspicious. We have used that tactic before."

"We will ride at dawn and that should give us two or three days to prepare a reception for Gospatric."

Sir Richard and Edward heeded my commands for I did not imply a choice. They arrived at my castle with their men. Sir Edward was happy enough but I sensed that Sir Richard was reluctant. "I brought my wife, Earl. I did not want her alone with Scottish raiders around."

"She will be safe here but had I left you to guard her then the loss of your retinue might have caused us to fail. Our numbers are small enough as it is."

Sir Tristan said, "The Earl knows what he is doing father. We can win!"

I liked his optimism but I had still to convince myself.

There were three farmsteads that lay on the Durham road. They all had the name, Thorpe. We called them collectively, Thorpe, although there was a mile between each of them. Further north on the road lay the farmstead of Layton. It was long abandoned having been ravaged and raided by the Scots many times before. The result was that the farm itself had fallen into disrepair and was now lumps and bumps. There was an untidy tangle of trees and bushes which had grown up around the ruins. It was perfect for my archers. They could hide within the tangle of brambles, elderberry and hawthorn. They would protected from attack.

To the north of the ruined farm were thick forests which came perilously close to the road. As Sir Hugh had said the enemy might be suspicious of an ambush. I intended to use that suspicion. I had my men dig pits and make traps and trips in the forests. When the enemy had lost men navigating them they would see us on the small ridge above the stream which passed behind the farm. The land had been cleared a little in the days when Layton had been farmed and the forests were a hundred paces from the road. We would fill that hundred paces with my men.

We made a camp behind the rise in the road. The Scots would not see beyond our first line of knights and men at arms. We had brought servants to watch the horses. Gilles was with them and I had given him a sword and a buckler. As I had no squire of my own Harold's squire, Ethelred, carried my banner. He would be behind me in the second rank and he would draw the Scots to me.

Until Sir Hugh Manningham and his men arrived we were spread thinly. Ralph of Wales and twenty of my archers were hiding amongst the brambles and wasteland of the farm. They would hide there until the enemy host had passed them. Our front rank consisted of seven knights and thirty men at arms. Our second rank was twenty-five men at arms and six squires and our third rank was twenty-seven mounted men at arms. It was not enough but until our allies came it would have to do. Behind this block of iron were fifty-two archers.

As darkness fell my men returned from their work. The woods and the forests were a death trap. I knew that the Scots would not lose huge numbers. They would soon realise that they did not represent an ambush but by then they would be channelled into one mighty block of men and I hoped to tempt them into charging our small line. All that they would see would be eighty men. Even with wise heads to guide them the wild Scots would charge. It was in their nature. Our horse holders were ready with our horses. Badger stamped impatiently, luckily, he and Gilles had formed a bond. They would both be ready when the time came.

We kept sentries out beyond the farm on the Durham Road. We wanted a clear warning of their approach. I had sent Aiden north to spy out the enemy. I expected him back after dark. We heard the sound of hooves and I heard swords being unsheathed. It was not, however, Aiden, it was Rafe. "My lord, Sir Hugh is camped at Elwick. He will be here soon after dawn. He and his men have marched hard, my lord."

I nodded, Elwick was less than eight miles away. Had we not destroyed the De Brus garrisons at Hartness and Greatham he might have been in danger. "Good, then we can make our plans come to fruition."

Rafe had just begun to eat his meal of cold meat when we heard more hooves. This time it was Aiden, "My lord, the Scots are camped at Bishop Middleham. They will not be here before noon tomorrow."

I was pleased. It meant we had time to refine our defences. The Scots would have more than ten miles to travel. I guessed they expected to camp not far from where we were. From here they could have launched a dawn attack on Stockton. "Dick, I want your archers in the woods to kill any Scottish scouts. I want them to approach this trap blind!"

"I will lead them myself. Philip of Selby can command until I return." There was no greater compliment Dick could give. He trusted the Archbishop's kin.

I went to sleep feeling as happy as I could. We had made our plans and now we would wait for the Scots to come.

Chapter 9

Sir Hugh was as good as his word and the men from the north appeared from the east shortly after dawn. It was a cold, fresh day. We would be aided by a slight breeze from the south and west. It brought scudding clouds overhead. It was a good day to fight.

"Your archer said we had an army to fight?" I told him what had happened. He nodded, "Had I not been besieging the New Castle then I might have been able to bring the news for I would have been watching the wall."

"It matters not," I told him of our dispositions. "I would have you and your knights mounted as the third rank. Your archers can join mine."

He nodded approvingly, "They will not see beyond me and my mounted men." He chuckled, "I like the thought of Balliol searching the woods for archers who are not there. What of your archers in the ruined land near to the farm? They take a great risk."

"Not really. All were outlaws and the woods are just forty paces from their position. Once they are in the woods they would vanish. I do not fear for them."

We had all day to rest, sharpen weapons and prepare the positions to be even more deadly. We had dug pits on either side of the road and covered them with faggots and soil. We would not be outflanked.

It was early afternoon when Dick rode in. "Their scouts are dead and soon you shall see their banners." He led his men behind our lines.

"There, lord!"

Sir Tristan had sharp eyes and he spied the banners above the hedges beyond the bend in the road. As we watched the colourful array came closer. When they neared the woods, which closed along the side of the road, they stopped. If we could see them then they could certainly see us. I watched with amusement as Scottish warriors disappeared into the woods seeking the archers who were not there. They did find the traps. Some would never return from the woods while others would be wounded. It took them almost an hour to discover that there were no men within the woods and then they sounded their trumpets and hurried on to get to us. They passed the deserted and ruined farm without a second glance.

I saw that they had a block of knights at the fore. Each one had a squire and his banner. There were forty of them and behind I saw men at arms. Their numbers were harder to ascertain because of the banners. They filled the road.

We had the time and I turned to my host. "We hold until I give the order. If I fall then Sir Hugh will give the order. Is that clear?"

"Aye!" The answer was roared out and I wondered what the enemy would make of it.

I held my long spear braced on the ground. The long strap on my shield allowed me to hold it in two hands. The men at arms behind us held their spears so that they were resting on our shoulders. To get to us they had to get through over fifty spears. It was a solid wall and we were uphill.

I had Sir Edward on one side of me and Wulfric on the other. None of my knights took offence at the position my Sergeant at Arms took. They knew his worth. Sir Harold shouted, "Now, Dick!" Harold was an archer who was the equal of Dick and he knew the range better than any. The sky darkened as the arrows flew and they kept flying as shower after shower was released. It was the enemy horses that suffered the most. Although some of the knights were struck none was a mortal blow but the horses, without armour, did die. When they died their riders were thrown from their backs. The ranks were so tightly packed that a fallen knight was trampled by those following behind. Some of those who came on were tripped by their own dead and dying horses and still the arrows flew.

The better riders managed to jump the obstacles. It meant that the line of spears that approached us was not knee to knee nor was it dense. It was a few riders who had succeeded in escaping the arrow storm. Their reward was a wall of fifty spears. The horses baulked at the barrier. I jabbed at the nearest knight. He was trying to wrench his horse's head around and my spear sank through his mail, through his gambeson and into his middle. I pulled it out of the side and his entrails were torn out.

Someone was in command of this army and I heard trumpets sound and orders were given. The horsemen withdrew and dismounted. They did this under an aerial onslaught. The arrows fell and so did the men at arms whose armour was not as good as the knights'. Their losses slowed when they locked shields and advanced. Most had lost their spears and they drew swords and axes. They were confident. They outnumbered us. They pressed more men into the solid wall which advanced. Inevitably some of those on the periphery were forced into the ditches. The traps ate them and their screams made those in the middle bunch even more. Soon they were unable to swing their weapons. They advanced with their weapons held before them. I waited until they were ten paces from us and I shouted, "Charge!"

The front two ranks all moved as one. We all stepped off with our right leg and those in the front rank all thrust with their spears at the same time. It worked. The enemy could not move their arms and our spears found faces and found flesh. As they fell the second rank advanced and my rank turned and slipped through gaps to come behind them. The second rank punched their spears and the effect was the same. The enemy line was now reeling. Those in the front had been their best warriors. As the second rank slipped back behind us I drew my sword for my spear had shattered. We had room to move and they did not. The hands which my mentor Athelstan had said were the fastest he had ever seen darted in and out like a serpent's tongue. My enemies could not block my blows and soon my sword was red with Scottish blood.

We worked together. We had fought in such a manner often enough. We had a rhythm to our movements. Our shields seem to be raised as one. The effect mesmerized our opponents. When we struck our well-sharpened steel went through poorly made mail and found flesh. Our feet moved in unison so that we were able to push forward. The spears over our shoulders were used to great effect. Our enemies needed more eyes than they possessed. They had to watch for our swords and for the spears which came over towards them. In contrast to our unified attack they fought as individuals; it mattered not how brave they were. They looked for honour and glory. Fine and skilful knights stepped forward to take on either me or one of my knights and paid the price when they were easily slain. We faced an individual; they faced a band of brothers.

The press of men before us meant that we were tiring. They were wearing us out with their men. I saw two of our men at arms fall and knew that the time had come for the second part of my plan. "Fall back! Now!" The line behind made gaps through which we stepped. We had practised this. I had read of Roman legions doing this and Erre and his Varangians had been taught the manoeuvre. We all stepped and turned as one and the movement was seamless. As the enemy charged they were hacked, stabbed and chopped by my men at arms. They were facing fresh men and they were tired.

"Fall back!" This time we made the gap. Those in the front rank moved back and as the enemy ran to catch them we stepped to meet them. We kept moving back, interchanging warriors, until we were in our original positions. Before us was a wall of bodies. I observed that there was no longer a wall of knights and men at arms. The ranks were intertwined and there were some unarmoured men amongst those before us. It was no longer a wall of mail. It was the time to use Sir Hugh Manningham and his men. They were fresh and they were mounted. They were eager to get amongst men who were tired and had blunted weapons.

"Hexham! Now!" This was our trickiest manoeuvre. There were no traps in the ditches next to us and we all stepped to the side as Sir Hugh Manningham led his fresh knights and his forty men at arms to charge down the road. The charge was also the signal for Ralph of Wales and his archers, hidden in the ruined farmstead, to loose arrows into the unprotected rear of the column. There the men had no armour and few had helmets. I could not see but I knew that it would be carnage.

I could see the enemy as Sir Hugh and his horsemen battered their way through them. They reeled from the ferocious attack of fresh men on huge horses. As soon as the last horseman had passed we climbed on the horses that were brought to us. We followed Sir Hugh and his men so that we were a tidal wave rushing down the hill. Dick and his archers followed us. They would no longer operate as one but as individuals. They would target leaders and knights. I am not certain what broke them the knights or the archers in their rear. Perhaps it was a combination of both. Whatever the reason the enemy host was broken in that last charge. All that was left for us to do was to kill and to chase. To chase and to kill. We pursued as long as it was light. As darkness fell there was nothing left for us to chase. We had won.

We camped where we had fought. Huge piles of arms, armour and helmets were gathered from the dead. We burned their bodies and the heat from the fire kept us warm that chilly night. I sat with my knights. There were wounds: William of Warkworth had a broken arm and Ralph of Morpeth had had his leg mail pierced by a spear but other than that they had survived. Our tactics and discipline had overcome our wild and impetuous enemies.

"Should I return to the siege, lord?"

"No, Sir Hugh. If we close the road to the north at Morpeth then they will be cut off anyway. It will not take them long to realise that they are alone. Now that it is spring our farmers will need to see to their crops and their animals. Our markets will need to be open once more. I hope that with peace restored the merchants will use our roads again. That is what we protect."

Riding back to Stockton the next day, Wulfric said. "You know, lord, we could rid the whole of the north of this Scottish threat. These warriors from the north are not well-led."

"You may be right, Wulfric, but I am loath to lose men I cannot replace to fight another's battle. Until the Empress returns I need to keep as many of our men alive as I can.

That will be a war where we travel further afield. We have gained much in the way of arms. Let us use that to build up our armies and the gold to buy what we cannot produce."

There was both relief and jubilation when we returned to Stockton. I sent one of Philip's archers to the Archbishop with a report of our success. Harold and Sir Tristan went back to their manors. They would make them both good and strong. It was too early for either the now knighted Sir Wilfred or Sir Hugh to return to their homes. Balliol was still ensconced behind the mighty walls of Barnard. There would be time enough to take them but we had much work to do in my town. We went back to the walls and did our further work on the defences. I used some of the gold we had taken to pay William the Mason.

"But lord the work I do is for me and my family."

"I pay my men at arms and I pay Alf the Smith. You are a stonemason and you deserve the financial rewards too."

As my men toiled on the walls I saw Alan of Osmotherley. I waved him to me, "Lord?"

"Are you glad you came north with me or do you wish you had stayed in the vale?"

He smiled, "I was meant to come here. My brother and I always wanted to be men at arms and to serve a great lord but with Sir Ralph in the Holy Land, we did not want to leave our mother and father alone. We feared for their safety." He shook his head, "And yet even being there we could not save them. Had we left then Alfraed might still be alive and they would have suffered the same fate."

"Not quite. Your mother died saving your life. She will be in heaven now, satisfied. No parent wants their child to die before them."

When I was satisfied that the work was coming on apace I spent time with John, my steward. We had the finances of the manor and the valley to reorganise. He was surprisingly philosophical about it all. "If we do not pay taxes either to the King or the Bishop then we can choose what to do with them. You can have your wish to have a larger conroi and retinue while I have other ideas."

"Yes?"

"We need our own vessel. I have spoken with both Ethelred and Alf about this. They have goods they wish to sell. We could send them by road to York but that is the expensive way to do it. A ship can carry more and travel further. You have a manor in Maine my lord and the ship could transport goods from here to there. I daresay the wine you drink would be cheaper from your own estate?"

I smiled, "One would think so."

He nodded, "With your permission, I will have the boat builders begin work on a cog. It need not be overly large. We have sailors already in the borough. All that we need is a captain who knows the seas."

I liked the plan. "Go ahead then John and I will ask the Archbishop if there are any such captains in York."

"I will get it started and then, my lord, there are the sessions. We have many cases waiting to be heard. Some are serious."

"Then arrange them for this peace will be but temporary. Of that I am certain."

March did not come in like a lion and go out like a lamb. It was a wild and windy month. It delayed work on our ship. Its hull, as it was being constructed, looked like a huge fish skeleton. I did not see it being ready for sea before autumn. The messenger to the Archbishop had still to return and I began to worry as did Philip of Selby. "It is not like Jack. He is reliable. I pray naught has happened to him."

"Perhaps, Philip, with the peace you and I may take your archers and ride down to visit with the Archbishop. I feel blind and deaf for I know not what goes on in the outside world. We will give your man one more day and then go."

As I might be leaving for a while I took the opportunity to find out what, if anything, John and Alice needed from York. We produced the majority of what we needed but there were things like cloth which we could not. The two had made a long list and I was debating how many horses I needed to take when there was a shout from the walls.

I left John and Alice and went to the river gate. There I spied, across the river, the Archbishop himself. The reason for the delay in the return of Jack was now explained. I returned to my hall. "Alice move my belongings to the west tower. Prepare my quarters for the Archbishop. We have guests. We will require a feast. John, see if Aiden has been hunting eh?"

"Aye lord."

Alice looked panicked. "My lord, I am not prepared!"

"Fear not Alice, Archbishop Thurstan is a good man and he will understand. Just do your best."

As I went across the bailey I shouted to Sir Hugh and Wulfric. "The Archbishop comes. We may have news."

Sir Hugh followed me to the river. "Is this good or ill, my lord?"

I shrugged, "Speculation will not get us anywhere. We have but moments to wait and then we will find out."

I bowed as Archbishop Thurstan stepped ashore. He made the sign of the cross and then waved a hand at my castle. "I can see why the Scots do not advance south. This is almost the equal of York." I nodded. He saw the men at arms toiling on the new wall. "And I can see you make it stronger." He lowered his voice, "That may be a wise move but I will speak with you in private later."

"I am eager to know of the outside world, your grace."

"And I apologise for the short notice. As you will discover, later on, that decision lay not in my hands. I shall stay but one night and then be gone. However, I have need of an escort from you tomorrow."

"My men and I..."

He stopped and shook his head, "Not you, Earl, not you."

I was a little put out but I saw no animosity in his eyes and I nodded, "Sir Hugh here will escort you. He is a fine knight and his men are the equal of mine." I saw the young knight swell with pride at the praise. "Where do you go? Durham?"

He shook his head and held my gaze, "No Alfraed, Carlisle. I go to meet with King David!"

His words sounded like a platter being dropped in a church; it echoed and reverberated. What did this portend? I had learned patience and I decided that the Archbishop would confide in me when the time was right. Father Henry greeted us at my gate. The Archbishop smiled, "Father Henry, I would give thanks for a safe journey. Shall we go to your church and pray together?"

"I would be honoured for you to grace our humble church." They entered the church and I was left with Sir Hugh.

Sir Hugh was as curious as I was. "Carlisle? The last I heard the Scots were there."

I smiled, "As the Archbishop is to meet with King David then perhaps that explains it."

"But have the sacrifices been in vain, lord? Will the Archbishop give up the land for which we have fought?"

"It is as I said, Hugh, no matter what the high and mighty do I shall not yield an inch of land until Empress Matilda is crowned and orders me to do so. The Archbishop is a friend and good man but he will not order me to do anything I do not wish to do."

He looked relieved and then a frown appeared, "Will we be in danger?"

"From the Scots? No. From Brigands and outlaws? Most certainly. I shall give you a dozen of my archers. They will keep you safe."

Lady Hilda and our other ladies were delighted to have such a dignitary at our table. Alice had excelled herself with the limited fare available and we were all replete. As we finished the last jug of decent wine I reflected that John had been right. I had a good source of wine in my other manor, La Flèche. The sooner my ship was finished the better.

When the meal was over the Archbishop stood, as did everyone else. He waved them to their seats. "Pray to sit and enjoy yourselves. I have matters to discuss with the Earl."

I led him to the west tower. Leopold of Durstein stood on guard. "Let no one close with us. Our words must be private."

"Aye, my lord."

Alice had left a jug and two goblets. A brazier burned and two seats awaited us. As we sat he said, "You have good people around you, Alfraed. I listened while we ate. They follow you as though you were a prince and your men have the look of hardened warriors. I can see why the Scots fear you so much."

"They are the enemies of this land and I bear their enmity as a badge of honour."

"You wonder why I speak with King David?" I nodded. "It is due to you. He sues for peace. Your victories have shown that he cannot hang to the land he has taken. I go to negotiate a peace treaty."

"I was there with the Earl of Gloucester when we signed the last one and that was meaningless."

"You are astute, Alfraed and you are correct. The treaty will last but a short time. It matters not. It gives the King time to build up his forces." The look I threw was a scowl. I swallowed my wine. "I know you like him not but let us be practical. In Anjou and Normandy, there is civil war. Baron fights baron and the land is laid waste. Here there is peace for the country wants a hand at the helm. That hand is King Stephen." I was about to speak and he held his hand up. "Like you, I wish that King Henry's wishes had been observed but they were not. Maud and her husband are destroying the duchy. Would you have them destroy this one too?"

I had no answer to that. "Of course not but I will not accept Stephen as my liege." I poured myself more wine, aware that it was loosening my tongue. "I would rather take my people and go to La Flèche."

The Archbishop leaned forward and put his hand on mine. "I pray you do not do that. You are the last defence in the north. I know that the treaty will not hold and if you are not here..."

I pushed my goblet away. "Perhaps I have drunk too much for I do not understand your words. If I stay then I do not support the King. I will be, to all intents and purposes, a rebel."

"I know and I have wrestled with this. It is why I sent Philip to you. I am on the horns of a dilemma. By my office, I am bound to support the anointed King of England but I am also a man of this land and I know the strength you bring to the border. You are a modern Roman Wall. I need you, England needs you."

"Then I will stay but I will not bow the knee to that man."

"I know. It is the one trait I do not like."

"A man cannot change his nature. Tell me Archbishop is my gold and treasure still safe within your palace?"

"Of course. I gave you my word I would keep it for you. Whenever you have need of it, it is there. In return, I beg you to promise to hear King Stephen before you act hastily."

"Listen to King Stephen?"

The Archbishop finished his wine. "I need to tell you that I do not go alone to Carlisle. I go to meet King Stephen. When the treaty is concluded he comes here to speak with you."

Chapter 10

I did not sleep over much that night and I was up before anyone else. Sir Hugh was also down early to ensure his men were ready to ride. The Archbishop was the most important man they had guarded. I drew him to one side. "A word Sir Hugh." He cocked his head to one side. "You will not be needed to escort the Archbishop back but I would have you wait until he is ready to leave."

"Of course, my lord, but why?"

"Stephen of Blois will be there. I need to know what his plans are so that you can return to me and let me know."

"Does this mean war?"

"I know not but I shall prepare."

He nodded, "Thank you for confiding in me, lord."

When they had departed I summoned Sir John, Sir Tristan and Sir Harold. "Stephen of Blois is in the north. He meets with the Archbishop to discuss peace terms with the Scots. It seems our efforts have saved us from further incursions." They said nothing but I saw questions written all over their faces. "They will return here after they have been to Carlisle. I know not if that means war but we prepare as though it does. I go to speak with Sir Edward and Sir Richard. While I am gone I leave you three to prepare our castle for a siege. You need not tell any what I have said. I will speak with Wulfric, Dick and John myself. The fewer who know this the better."

Sir Harold looked at the other two. They nodded, "Know you, lord, that we have spoken of this. We stand by you even if you are called a traitor. We will be traitors too."

"Thank you but I pray that it will not come to that."

Gilles was hovering close by. "Gilles, get Scout saddled and your own horse. Have Aiden join us. Today we ride abroad."

Wulfric and Dick were both wise old birds. When they saw the activity they were prepared for my words. They nodded when I told them. Wulfric shrugged, "It was ever thus, lord. You are the one who saves the land and yet others reap the benefit. We are better off on our own for some friends you cannot trust."

There was something in his words that had hidden meaning, "Speak plainly, Wulfric."

"I am not certain that all your lords will join this venture. That is all I can say. It is conjecture only for I have no evidence but I have heard rumours from other men at arms. When you speak with your knights, lord, I would look into their eyes for, as they say, the eyes are the windows to the soul. You have the power to see into men's hearts. We need that skill now as much as we need your sword arm."

I began to run through my mind all of my conversations with my lords. I sought clues to their loyalty. Sir Edward was now totally healed. He looked stronger than ever. He knew from my face that I had portentous news. After I had told him he said, "I know you come to see if I stand with you. I understand but you need not fear. Even if I was not oathsworn remember that, like you, I swore an oath to the Empress. I may be a rough warrior but I am a man of my word. I stand with you and we shall make our castle strong."

Sir Richard would be a thornier problem. As I headed along the south bank of the Tees I ran through all of our conversations. He was the one whose loyalty Wulfric doubted. He was Tristan's father and Sir Hugh's father in law. If he did not stand with me then there might be divisions in my own camp.

His wife, Lady Anne, hurried away. That was a sure sign of trouble. After I had told him he said, "Lord, King Stephen has been anointed by the Archbishop. He is supported by God. I cannot, in all conscience, oppose him."

I nodded. We were alone and could speak freely. "Then that means you would be opposing me." He nodded, "And your son, son in law and daughter. Are you prepared for that?"

His face became red. He had not thought this through. "Would they oppose the King?"

"I spoke with them before I spoke with you. They would. They approached me. I did not elicit their support although I am honoured and touched that they offer it."

"I cannot fight my King and I will not fight my son."

"This is a wall upon which you cannot sit. There will come a time when you have to choose upon which side you will stand. I pray you make the right decision. You are an old and valued friend. You have been a rock when we have fought alongside one another and I would not fight you..." I paused, "But do not get in my way, Sir Richard. I stop opposing the usurper when he is dead or Empress Matilda has the throne!"

I did not like the tone I had used but I had to give him honesty. There had been too many twisted words and oaths. From now on I would speak my mind. I was my own man. I was Warlord.

Once back at my castle I took Sir Tristan to one side and told him what his father had said. "I would not, for the world come between a father and son. If you wish to leave then I will understand. And I say the same to you as I said to your father. I would not fight you but the lines are drawn. If you are not with me then do not oppose me."

He shook his head, "Nor do I wish to fight my father but my manor is close to yours. I have fought alongside you for these many years. I will not desert you now but I will not fight my father."

"Nor would I ask you to."

The air was cleared and I joined my men as we toiled from sunrise to sunset. Two days after the Archbishop had left Alf came to speak with me. "Lord, I have heard a rumour that the King comes here."

"It is true." He hesitated. I was lord of the manor and it did not sit well with my blacksmith to question me. "Ask your question, Alf. We have known each other long enough for that I think. I will not be offended."

"Why does he come here?"

"That is an excellent question and to answer truthfully I do not know. I suspect it cannot be good but as he comes with the Archbishop of York who is a friend then I do not fear the worst. Perhaps he comes to know my mind."

There was relief on Alf's face, "I had wondered if we ought to prepare for war as you seem to be."

"I am preparing for the worst but you and those who live under my care have lives you need to lead." I paused, "Do you trust me?"

"Of course, lord."

"Then I tell you that we are in the right, the day when a man's word can be broken as easily as a stick is the day anarchy ensues."

Sir Hugh arrived back four days later. His horse was lathered and he had ridden hard. "My lord the king comes but first he visits with the Bishop of Durham. I am not certain when he will reach us."

"Good. Thank you for your hard ride. Was peace made?"

He nodded, "The Scots keep Carlisle but give up all else."

I shook my head, "What a waste! They held nothing else! We had taken all but the New Castle and that would have fallen."

"Prince Henry is confirmed in his lands in England." He paused, "And Barnard de Balliol begged forgiveness and he keeps his lands."

That made me even angrier but I kept it within. Perhaps I should have let it out for there was a shout from my east tower, "Lord, a ship approaches!"

"To arms!"

I was suspicious of all. We were surrounded by foes now.

The bends in the river meant it took time to reach us and we had time to study her while Gilles and Edgar dressed me. It was a large merchant vessel. It appeared to be harmless but I was taking no chances. "Dick, have your archers watch her carefully. At the first sign of treachery unleash death!"

Armoured and with Wulfric and Sir John at my side I strode down to the jetty. Ethelred and his men were already hunkered behind their new wall with arrows at the ready. A sailor leapt over the side and tied her up.

"What is your business here!"

The captain was disquieted by my tone. "We are here to meet King Stephen."

I pointed to the sailor. "Before you tie up at my port ask permission!"

"I am on the King's business."

"The only King I recognise is now dead and his body lies in Normandy." I turned to Ethelred. "Go aboard and collect the port taxes."

"You cannot do that!"

My anger got the better of me. I drew my sword and sliced through the rope which tied the ship to my jetty. It began to drift away. A second rope was thrown to the stunned sailor who tied that one to the stanchion.

"You were saying?"

"You have ruined a rope!"

"Would you rather I ruined a sailor instead? I can make any demonstration you like and I will do so until my taxes are paid!"

The captain could see that he was defeated. "Send you man aboard but the King shall hear of this!"

I laughed, "I should hope so for you will be taxed each day you are in port and he will be taxed when he leaves!"

"He is the King!"

"Not here, he is not!"

I waited until Ethelred returned with the gold. He was chuckling. "This will make a fine tale, lord! A fine tale!"

Our visitors arrived four days later and they came from the north. I had had scouts out watching for them and I knew when they were imminent. I had my walls lined with my armed men and my new standard flew. My men had all painted the black wolf with red eyes and tongue on their shields. I was impressed by the effect. Sir Hugh had his own livery but Sir John, Sir Tristan and Sir Harold all had variations on my coat of arms. I had sent for Sir Edward as soon as I knew they were at Thorpe so that, he too, joined me on my walls.

It was not a large escort. I recognised the Bishop of Winchester and four Barons. The Archbishop I knew. I also recognised Barnard de Balliol and the Bishop of Durham.

Their escort was less than fifty men. I could, if I had so chosen, have captured the erstwhile King of England. I did not. I had more honour than that and besides the Archbishop was with them and I had promised him that I would listen.

I saw that they slowed as they approached my walls. I might not like him but I respected Stephen of Blois. He was a fine warrior and a passable general. He was assessing my defences. They halted before my barred gates. He lifted his helmet so that I could see his face. "Is this a welcome fit for your king?"

I was not wearing my helmet and I shouted down, "You are not my King. The one I swore an oath to was murdered and his heirs are in France. They are not before me."

He laughed and turned to the Archbishop, "You are right Thurstan!"

The Bishop of Durham called, "Then open it for your Bishop!"

"You were my bishop but you abdicated that title when you fell under the sway of your Scottish spy." William Cumin tried to hide. "Cumin you coward do not hide. If I wished it you would be dead already with an arrow in you. I will come down. I want not enemies within my walls."

"I am not your enemy."

"I was speaking with Barnard de Balliol the foresworn." As I descended I said, "Wulfric come with me and Dick..."

"Do not worry, lord. An arrow will be aimed at each of their hearts!"

My gates opened and I stepped out. Stephen of Blois dismounted as did the Archbishop. Archbishop Thurstan shook his head, "Was this well done, my lord?"

"You know I respect you more than I can say, your grace, but these others come here demanding entry. Not one word of thanks for the fact that it was my men and our force of arms which drove the Scots to the table." I jabbed a finger at Barnard de Balliol. "And I have fought him twice; each time he ran. So pray do not lecture me on manners. The fact that he still lives as does the Comyn spy speaks volumes for my patience." I turned to Stephen of Blois. "Before your captain comes bleating to you I shall tell you that I have charged him taxes for docking here and you will be taxed too. This is not England."

I saw him colour. One of his knights said, "This is one insult too many, my liege."

I turned, "If any feels I have insulted them then let us settle it here under God's eyes. I will fight in single combat any who feels aggrieved. Balliol?" I pointed at the knight who had spoken, "You Highclere?" I turned to Stephen of Blois, "Or perhaps you and I should settle this now. I was King Henry's Champion and I am a Knight of the Empress and one of her champions. Another stands behind me. How about it, Stephen of Blois? You are a fair swordsman. You might win. How about we settle who rules this kingdom here and now. You or the Empress?"

Silence reigned and then he said quietly, "You go too far."

I said, equally quietly, "Not as far, it seems, as you."

I watched as he regained control of himself. "Let us speak quietly as two men who have fought together. We will do so away from the ears of other men. It is your land, which way should we walk?"

I pointed east. "It is quiet down here close to the swans." I turned to Wulfric, whose hand was on his sword. "I will be safe."

"I am not worried, Lord, you and I could handle these apologies for men on our own. None had the spine to fight you!"

As we walked Stephen of Blois shook his head, "Your men are like you, Cleveland, they know their own mind and they are forthright."

"We live on the edge of the world here. Your cousin Gloucester knows the feeling. This is not the civilised world of London or Blois where your enemy is civilised and obeys rules. The Scots and those whose land straddle the border are wild and savage men. There are people from the valley who are slaves in the land of King David!"

He stopped, "Truly?"

"Truly. Thankfully few since I was appointed but enough for me to be angry."

"And I did not thank you for what you did. You were right to chastise me. We owe the peace to you. Can we not be friends?"

I smiled, "Aye, relinquish the crown and support the claim of Maud and Henry as you swore along with me in Westminster Abbey and we shall be the best of friends!"

He shook his head, "I cannot do that. What I do I do for England. I have her best interests at heart."

"I do not doubt that but I took an oath."

"I would not fight you."

"Good for you would lose."

He laughed, "You have a fine castle but you have few men."

"My few men have defeated over a thousand Scotsmen and traitors in the last few weeks and we have suffered a handful of deaths. This is our land and we know it well. And I would not fight Englishmen. I would rather kill the enemies of England but I will not bow the knee to you and that is as honest as I can be."

He nodded, "But you will fight the Scots?"

"Always and it was a mistake to let them keep Carlisle. That is a dagger in our back."

"Of course, if you do not serve me then you cannot break the peace, can you?"

I smiled, "No for I am warlord."

"Warlord; I have not heard that word for some time. It suits you. Then we have a truce."

"We have a truce but as soon as your cousin chooses to come to England then I will support her and fight for her."

"I understand, you are a man of honour. I will speak plainly. I wish you to keep this border safe."

"I promised King Henry I would do that. He may be dead but I obey my king." We headed back to his ship, "As we are being honest with one another I have to tell you that I will kill Balliol the first chance I get. He is evil and he is dangerous."

"I agree. He comes with me."

"A hostage?"

He smiled and I saw his ruthless streak, "A guest."

We reached his ship. Ethelred stood there. Stephen took his purse and threw it at Ethelred, "There are your port fees. "Let us board, gentlemen. The tide awaits us and we have business with the Welsh." He turned to Barnard de Balliol. "Balliol send your men home. You need to come with me!" The gangplank was down and the knights and squires led their horses on board. Barnard de Balliol ran so quickly that he slipped and fell flat on his face. My men laughed loudly.

I moved back towards the two clerics. I said, without turning, "Cumin, you have moments to board this ship and sail away from my land. When I turn I will order my archers to end your miserable life and if I ever see you again then that will be your last on this earth!"

I heard his feet as they scrambled up the gangplank and smiled. Wulfric said, "Not worth spit!" As we watched the gangplank raised and the ship began to turn.

I turned and saw that the Bishop of Durham looked less than happy. "I take exception to your comments, Cleveland. My men did as much as you did."

"And they were led by me while you counted your gold in Durham and shook each time you heard the Scots were about."

"Manningham has sworn an oath to the King."

I smiled, "I am happy that Sir Hugh has made his own decision. At least there is one lord north of here who will fight the Scots." I looked at the sky. It was heading towards the afternoon. "If I were you, Bishop I would hurry home, you don't want to be caught out after dark. Scurry back to your cloisters!"

He wheeled his horse around and men at arms followed him. It left the Archbishop and his half a dozen guards.

"You will stay the night, your grace?"

"That depends... will I be insulted too?"

"I would not invite you if I was to insult you. Do you scorn a man who speaks the truth?"

"There is truth and there is cruelty."

"I was never cruel to any who stood shoulder to shoulder with me against my enemies."

As we went back to my castle Wulfric said, "And that list is growing steadily my lord! We will have a short life, interesting but short!"

Chapter 11

When the gates slammed shut behind us it felt as though it was a final statement. We had nailed our colours to our walls. There would be no turning back now. Sir Richard had not had to choose between Stephen and me but he had made his choice clear. I was slightly disappointed in Sir Hugh Manningham's decision but I understood it. He was no earl. I knew, however, that both he and Sir Richard would continue to fight the Scots. For the time being, they were the enemy. I would have to fight Stephen but not yet. I was grateful that he had decided on a truce. I would have fought him but it would have cost me dear.

No one had mentioned the manors of Hartness or Normanby. I intended to appoint my own lords of the manor. If I had to I would use my own men at arms. Even as I escorted the Archbishop to his quarters I had decided to return with him to York. I trusted him but I needed my treasure in my castle. If he died I would lose it. If he lost power I would lose it. I would hire my own captain and then I would travel back to La Flèche. I had much to do. I needed an army and I need it as soon as possible. Stephen had done me one favour. He had given me implicit permission to raid the Scots. I would do so. Barnard de Balliol would be my first target and then I would range north of Carlisle and make its position that much weaker.

After I had escorted Archbishop Thurstan to his quarters I sought out Alice and John. "Alice, make tonight a feast to remember."

John said, "My lord, the money!"

"And tomorrow, John, you and I will escort the Archbishop back to York where we will access more money than you or your father ever saw!"

He brightened, "Of course, my lord."

Considering the events of the day the meal was lively. Sir Hugh and my other knights seemed to realise that I had burned their boats for them. They had one master now and that was me. I saw the worry on the face of the Archbishop. When the feast had finished I took him to my ramparts. It was a chill night but the stars were bright and my land looked magical.

"Archbishop I know you worry about me and what I will do."

"Your words this afternoon shocked me."

"For that I am sorry but my words were intended for the Scots and Stephen of Blois. The air is clear between us. He has given me permission to pursue my war against the Scots."

"He has?"

"When we were apart we were honest. He may not like my stance but he knows I am the new Roman Wall. I sent a message to King David. Balliol's men will scurry back like rats to their nest and tell the King of the danger I represent. He will wait and he will worry. Soon I will have an army which is large enough to take Carlisle and recover what we have lost." I raised my goblet, "But I do this for the Empress and not Stephen. He knows this. The civil war will begin here when the Empress comes. Does that satisfy you and put your mind to rest?"

"It does but I worry about you. I like you Alfraed but I fear that you are too honourable. You must bend! The times change and you must change with them."

"No, I will not and if you think I will then you know me not."

When we left, the next day, I took Gilles, Wulfric and Dick as well as ten men at arms and archers. We took sumpters to bring back all that we would buy. Our new ship, under construction, would mean we would trade with La Flèche and this would be the last time that I would risk a visit to York.

I had another reason for my journey. I was scouting the land. I might have to fight battles to the south as well as to the north. I wished to be prepared. We travelled at the speed of clerics and we stopped at Northallerton. It had a castle and a lord who was loyal to both Stephen and the Archbishop but I liked the lord and I enjoyed his company. The men at arms and priests who accompanied the Archbishop kept their distance from me. I had challenged a king. It seemed to frighten them. It meant I could ride with the Archbishop and speak with him. We would not be overheard.

"I know that he is a king but King David does not strike me as honest."

"How so your grace?"

"He gave his word to King Stephen that there would be peace but he did not swear on either a relic or the bible. Also his son, Prince Henry, now has a large estate in the heart of England. You are right about Balliol and that cost us. Prince Henry's lands in Huntingdon will pose the same threat. It is a dagger at the breast of England."

"I can do nothing about that and, to be honest, your grace, it is in my interests if Prince Henry causes trouble for Stephen of Blois. I will watch the land to the west. Sir Hugh Manningham might well have gone over to King Stephen but he will watch the border like a hawk. I can now look to the west. Carlisle and Barnard Castle will be kept under closer scrutiny." I had plans for Barnard Castle but the Archbishop was an honest man. I would not compromise him.

When we reached York, the Archbishop gave us beds in his warrior hall. It would not be appropriate for us to stay with him at his palace. It suited us anyway. John had a long list of our requirements and he went with two men at arms to procure them. I went with Wulfric, Gilles and Dick and we collected the treasure I had sent from Normandy when we had fought the French and defeated Guy de Senonche. I had sent half to La Flèche and the other half here to York. Even John would be impressed by it. We took it to the hall where Wulfric assigned two men to guard it. Oswald and Cedric were huge men. Their size alone would have deterred would be thieves.

Thanks to those who had come south with the Archbishop word of my stance had spread so that we were an object of curiosity. I was a rebel who walked free. It helped us in that we did not need to offer explanations for our requests and needs. Wulfric and Dick sat in the inn they called *'The Saddle'*. It had long been frequented by old soldiers and those seeking work. By drinking there Wulfric and Dick would be able to find the men we needed. They would not need to seek them out; they would come to us.

Armed with names supplied by the Archbishop I headed for the river. There were a number of merchant vessels in port. I knew that I would not be able to tempt a captain from his vessel but I hoped there might be a first mate who sought advancement. The equivalent for sailors was the inn they called *'The Blind Beggar'*. I went there with Gilles.

We sat and we waited. "Will we not have to tell them what we seek, my lord?"

"We have time enough and my name is known. We let the curious come to us. The curious are normally the most garrulous and it is their gossip which will draw the right candidate to my table."

Gilles was curious himself and, as we sat and waited he asked me about my stance. "Lord, we have a Duke at home but you argued with a king! Were you not afraid?"

"Of Stephen?" I shook my head, "He is a man. I have fought alongside him and I respect him as a warrior but he is not king. There is not enough oil in the world nor enough priests to make him a king in my eyes for King Henry wished the next king to come from his loins."

"You have strong beliefs, lord."

"And you are wise for one so young Gilles. Aye, I do have strong beliefs. In the end that is all a man has to take with him to the otherworld."

A merchant walked over to us. I could tell his trade for he was well dressed and had soft hands. He bowed, "Lord, you are the Earl of Cleveland?"

"Aye, I am."

"I am Isaac of Lincoln. I understand you are seeking to buy cloth and other items. I can procure them for you at a reasonable price."

"My Steward deals with that see him. I am here seeking seamen."

He looked surprised, "You have a ship?"

I smiled, "Why else would I seek seamen? Are you a seaman?"

He laughed, "No lord. If I were I would sail back to my homeland in the east. I like not the sea." He bowed, "May God be with you."

I smiled, "Now it begins. He will go and sell his information. He will know who is seeking employment."

"But you just said, seamen."

"I know. It means we have a larger group of candidates from which to choose. I will know the man when I see him."

They came in dribs and drabs at first. Their numbers grew as word spread and then they thinned out as I made it clear what I sought. In the end, I chose three. William of Kingston had been the first mate on a ship but had a falling out with the Captain. Others had told me this before I met him. His name had come up as a young sailor but a skilled one. The argument had arisen over the sea captain's daughter. She and William had eyes only for each other but the captain disapproved. When I finally offered him the position he had been honest with me.

"Lord I will take the position but I needs must take Alice with me. Her father may go to the Archbishop."

"You may bring the girl with us but you shall be wed in Stockton. Is that clear?"

He had smiled, "It is our most fervent wish."

"We leave on the morrow. Make your arrangements and meet us at the cathedral."

Henri the Breton was different. He was on a ship where the others did not like his accent or his origins. It happened. He too had been an officer, albeit junior, on a merchantman. His skill lay in the knowledge of the waters around the islands and coast of the land of the Bretons. He was happy to be sailing a ship that would take him close to his home.

Harold Three Fingers was unlike the other two in many ways. He was not an officer. He was far older than the rest. He had lost two fingers as a young man when he had been caught poaching. As a result, he had turned to the sea. He wanted to serve me for he had grown up in Norton before my father had been given the manor. He had something you could not buy. He had experience. Henri and William were young and obviously capable. Harold had seen it all. He would not sail with us for long. He was a greybeard but my promise to him was home after he left the sea.

He had been my last appointment and he had nodded as he shook my hand, "And I take you at your word, lord, for all know that your word is made of steel. It is never broken."

The father of Alice came to see me that night as I made my way back to meet the Archbishop. "My lord, you cannot do this! I do not want my daughter to wed that man."

I nodded, "He is a poor sailor?"

"No, he is the best. I cannot fault his seamanship."

"He is cruel and abuses your daughter?"

"No, lord, he is most gentle with her."

"It is against your daughter's will?"

"No lord, she is besotted by him."

I spread my arms, "Then why in God's name do you oppose this union? You are a fool for you have lost, by your own admission, a good sailor and your daughter. Why?"

"There is a merchant in the town and he will pay a handsome dowry."

I was almost stumped for words, "You would sell your daughter to a man she does not love? What kind of man are you?"

"A man with three daughters and no sons. Alice is the prettiest and will fetch the best dowry."

I was tempted to run the man through there and then. Instead, I reached into my purse and pulled out a gold coin. "Here is your dowry. Take it and be gone." He grasped it eagerly and I saw cunning in his eyes. "And this is the last. Do not think to go to the Archbishop and claim she was taken against her will. Firstly the Archbishop is a friend of mine and secondly, I am Warlord now. The law in my land is my law; I answer to no king. Now go!"

The Archbishop invited me to dine with him. "I know you think less of me, Alfraed, for having sided with King Stephen but I am a man of God. However, I am also a practical man. King Stephen will bring stability to the helm of the ship. England has enemies, not least those close to Normandy. France and the Empire still cast covetous looks at us. England is a prize to be picked. Stephen will stop that.

Even now he is travelling to Wales to drive those enemies back. What do the Empress and her husband do? They raid and plunder Normandy like robber barons. Yet you support her still."

"I know you speak from the heart. However, I cannot be in two places at once. I will sail to Anjou and I will try to steer the Empress in the right direction. I seem to have some influence there but I have to wait until my lands are secure and I can leave them."

"Good. Then I will build up my forces so that, should the Scots attempt to attack again, I will support your forces."

I heard each word, "Support?"

"Even King Stephen acknowledges you the best general we have. My men will fight under your banner... against the Scots. We will not fight our King."

"Then I will lead. And Durham?"

"Geoffrey Rufus knows your worth as do his lords. He will follow your banner against the Scots."

"He still has a Scottish viper close to his breast."

"We are aware of that but he is powerless at the moment."

"Save as a spy where he can pass all of his information back to his master."

"He knows little of what goes on and nothing of my plans. It will have to suffice. So long as he is the papal appointment he is not to be harmed."

I smiled, "I do not need to worry about such things."

The Archbishop shook his head, "You would be excommunicated, Alfraed. And that is a step I believe you will not risk."

He was right. So long as the Pope supported him he would live.

Our convoy left the next morning. My sailors walked for they were not used to horses. Alice rode. She was young and she was pretty. She smiled as I passed, "Lord, thank you for what you have done. I heard you paid my dowry."

I nodded, "It was nothing."

"It was, lord, for it took away any guilt I felt and discharged my obligation to my father. I would be honoured if my lord would give me away when I am wed."

My own daughter was dead. I would never give away another bride. I nodded, "It is I who am honoured."

John, my steward, urged his horse next to mine, "You have a mighty treasure, my lord. Perhaps we could build a second ship!"

"One ship at a time, John. When this one is built I will leave for La Flèche. Before I do you, Ethelred and Alf need to decide what we trade and what we wish in return. This will be my one voyage I may be away until Yule. Until that time it will be my knights who protect my land."

"That is a long time lord."

"Aye, but with the Scots cowed, there is no better time. Besides, the Archbishop will watch our borders and offer aid if the Scots are foolish enough to attack."

We did not stop at Northallerton on the way back. We headed directly north and pushed hard. Our sailors had to sit in the wagons for they were holding us up. Once we passed Alan's former home at Osmotherley we made good time. I waved Dick and Wulfric forward and we rode ahead of the convoy.

"I leave for Anjou as soon as my ship is built," I told them of the words I had spoken with the Archbishop.

"He is a good man, my lord, I trust him."

"Good, Dick. And I believe that Sir Hugh Manningham will do his duty. Before I go I intend to ride to Barnard Castle. I want Sir Hugh to command there."

"We cannot besiege it, lord. We would lose too many men."

"We will not do so, Wulfric. You know the garrison. Do they like the Scots?"

"Most do not, lord."

"Then we use that. We trick our way in to the castle and we use our new men at arms and archers to do so." We had taken on five new archers and five men at arms. "Alan of Osmotherley has proved himself a doughty warrior. We send him and the new men to Barnard. They offer to fight for

Barnard de Balliol. They open the sally port and we enter. We give those within a choice, serve Sir Hugh of Gainford or leave."

"And if they fight, lord?"

I smiled, "Wulfric you and I will be there and Dick will have his archers on the walls. Do you honestly believe that having faced us three times and been thrashed three times they will try to fight when the outcome will be their death?"

He laughed, "You are right and with Barnard Castle in our hands, we need not worry about an attack from the west."

"Aye, for the alternative is to build a new castle at Gainford. This is the better way. Then, while I am away we can patrol the Tees as far as Barnard Castle. Your job while I am away is to make my castle impregnable and to make my conroi invincible. We are buying time. Let us use it wisely."

Our return threw the castle into a frenzy of activity. Our new sailors needed homes built. The cloth was made into new surcoats for my men at arms. Any labourers not toiling in the fields were thrown into the maelstrom of shipbuilding. I rode with Sir Hugh and Sir Tristan to Yarm. Before I left I needed words with Sir Richard.

I took only my knight's squires and Gilles. I was not going in force. Sir Richard was in his bailey practising. He stopped when we entered. He gave a bow. "Sir Richard we need to talk. I wish the air between us to be clear. You are my neighbour and we cannot have bad blood between us. These are your children and I would not drive a wedge between you."

"Aye, lord, come into my hall." I noticed his wife throw her arms around Sir Tristan. Tears coursed down her cheeks.

Once at the table I spoke. "You know that I have made my position to the... to Stephen, clear?"

"Aye lord."

"What you may not know is that there is a truce between us. I have been charged by the Archbishop to defend the land against the Scots. I will do so. I would have done so without the request but the support of the Archbishop is important. It allows you to fight under my banner and yet not compromise your loyalty to the man you call king."

He looked relieved, "Lord, that will aid my sleep."

His wife nodded, "It is true, lord. My husband paces the room at night. He does not like being torn."

"I am afraid the day will dawn when your husband will have to decide whom he follows: Stephen of Blois or Empress Matilda. When the rightful heir comes to England to claim the throne I will support them."

Sir Richard nodded, "I understand lord but that day is some way off."

"It is. I will leave you now so that you may speak with Sir Hugh and your son. There will be things you need to say."

Lady Anne followed me out. "Lord!" She bowed her head, "You are an honourable man. Try to understand my husband. He knows that without you he would have nothing and yet now that he has such a fine manor he is afraid to lose it by being a traitor."

I lifted her head, "I know he is a good man but someone who breaks an oath loses their soul. This world is fleeting but heaven lasts forever. Hopefully, it will all turn out for the best."

As I rode back to Stockton I said, "Gilles you have proved your skill with my horses. They are all happy."

"Thank you, lord."

"Would you like to learn skills with weapons too?"

"Aye lord."

"Good for you and I will go alone to Anjou and you may need your sword there. I will have you a surcoat made and we will see if Alf has some mail which will fit."

Father Henry was happy to marry the young couple and, indeed, it proved a great celebration for the whole town. It was a day away from the hard work which we had engaged in for, what seemed, a lifetime. I was surprised at my emotion when I gave away young Alice. Perhaps it was the proximity in the church of my dead wife and child. Adela would have approved and that made me fear that I might break down. The fact that it was such a happy day for all gave me the strength I needed.

My ship, to be called *'Adela'*, was almost complete and so we headed for Barnard Castle. We had heard that many men had defected from Barnard de Balliol. Some had joined us and so we had a better idea of the garrison. Our new warriors, led by Alan, were quite happy to take the risk. They would present themselves as a band of mercenaries. None were known to the men in the castle and the only one who had fought against them was Alan. I doubted that he would be remembered. We waited in the forests where we had ambushed the Scottish army. Our eleven men marched off to the castle. They looked the part.

Once it became dark we approached the walls. We already knew where the sally port was and my forty men waited there. The door creaked open and Simon the Jew stood there. He waved a hand and bowed. We entered. Dick and his archers scurried up to the walls where the sentries had been trussed and bound. Sir Hugh and I went with Wulfric and my men at arms to the warrior hall. All lay asleep within. There were just thirty men. We each went to a bed and held our weapons to the men's chests. I nodded and said, "Awake, the castle is taken!"

The man beneath my sword opened his eyes and they widened in terror when he recognised me. "Lord I pray you do not kill me!"

I spoke loud enough for them to hear but not loud enough to wake the rest of the castle. "None of you will be harmed if you remain silent. Rise and come over here. Wulfric, watch them."

"Aye lord."

Sir Hugh and his six men at arms followed me and we went to the quarters occupied by Sir Barnard. We opened the door and entered. There were two women in the bed but the man was not Sir Barnard, it was his castellan, Robert of Bowes. Stephen must have retained Balliol as a 'guest'. Sir Hugh held his sword at the man's throat and one of his men brought in a brand. One of the women woke and gave a scream. The other two woke immediately.

"Get dressed and come down to the Great Hall. Sir Hugh escort these to the hall and then find any other servants, slaves and warriors."

There were a few scuffles and shouts. One or two of those in the castle had to be cuffed by my men but, by and large, it was painless. The men at arms and sentries were brought to the hall. They were cowed by my men who surrounded them. I stood on the table so that all could see me.

"You all know me, I am the Earl of Cleveland and now Warlord of the north. My avowed aim is to make this land free from the raids and privations imposed by the Scots. Your lord, Barnard de Balliol, is a traitor and a coward. I challenged him to combat and he refused. He now hides with Stephen of Blois in London. This castle now belongs to me. I give it to Sir Hugh of Gainford who is now lord of the manor. He is under my protection." I glared around the room but none dared gainsay me. "I intend no harm to any. Even Robert of Bowes is free to leave. When dawn breaks all those who do not wish to serve Sir Hugh and myself will leave. You will leave with only that which you can carry. All horses, sumpters and palfreys will remain within these walls. If you stay then you swear an oath to myself and Sir Hugh, on a bible. I hope I have made myself clear. The sun will rise soon. You have until its first rays peer through the wind holes to decide."

When the gates were opened and those who had chosen to leave left it was a surprisingly small number. The priest and Robert of Bowes were among them. It mattered not; Sir Hugh had his own priest who had fled Gainford with him. After they had been sworn in the new retinue of Sir Hugh of Gainford went about their business. Sir Hugh said, "I will send my men back for my wife and my things. We will be out of your hair, lord."

I smiled, "I mind not the company. Are you certain? You are now the western border."

"This is a strong castle and I have learned much from you, lord. My wife is keen to be the lady of the manor again. She will enjoy furnishing this castle."

I nodded, "As would the Lady Adela. You know that while I am away Wulfric and Sir John are just a day's ride away?"

"I do. I cannot thank you enough for this honour."

"Aye well, when Sir Wilfred has rebuilt Piercebridge then you will be more secure here. In days gone by, he would have acknowledged you as overlord and when the Empress is returned to power that may be true again. For now, I wish my knights all to be equal."

"And we are happy to be so. A round table has no head save you, Warlord."

His words reassured me and I headed back to my ship which was almost complete and ready for sea.

Anjou

Chapter 12

We sailed a week as soon as my ship was ready. The Archbishop wrote to tell me that Stephen had held a grand court in London where he had made edicts. He had reversed Henry's policy on the forests. I smiled at the news. I had done so already. He had also confirmed all titles and earldoms. He did not say that mine was to be removed. I found that interesting. He also spent lavishly. He was trying to buy the barons. It would work. Those around London were the ones who rarely had to fight for anything and they took whatever was on offer. Ominously I heard that the Welsh had begun to eat into the lands of the Welsh marches. His knights had been defeated. The Earl of Gloucester's lands were diminishing. Robert de Brus had already ingratiated himself with Stephen and sworn fealty. In return, his titles had been confirmed. He now held both Hartness and Guisborough. Although disturbing I still had his sacred oath. The problem would come when I fought Stephen.

The *'Adela'* was a fine ship. Ethelred and John had used their own money to commission a second, smaller version. It was their coin; I did not mind. It would be built while we were in Normandy. We took neither horses nor banner. My standard would flutter from my battlements and I would buy a new horse, if I needed it, in La Flèche. Sir John and Wulfric knew my orders and we had three castles under construction. William the mason was helping Sir Harold, Sir Tristan and Sir Wilfred to build strongholds against the Scots and any other enemies.

As we headed down the Tees, and thence out to sea I stood at the stern with Gilles and Captain William. This was a new crew. The sailors came from my town while the three officers had never worked together before. I was happy to watch them grow together. Gilles was excited to be travelling back to his homeland. He had grown in the time he had been with me. The helmet and hauberk fitted him, albeit loosely, and, with his new surcoat, he looked like a squire now rather than a stable boy.

Once William realised I was not watching him critically he relaxed and we talked of my hopes for his ship.

"I have two manors, William, and you are the bridge between them. Your men will need to become warriors for these seas are dangerous and I have many enemies." I laughed, "You can count my friends on Harold's fingers!"

"Your men of Stockton are all skilled with weapons and have brought their bows. We will get better."

"Good. And I am happy for you and your crew to benefit financially from these voyages. John and Ethelred have both become rich through trade."

"Thank you, lord, it is rare to find a master who is sympathetic to such needs."

"I think you will find, William, that I am unlike other lords in many ways."

We docked at Angers rather than St. Nazaire. I did not wish to have to hire a berth on a salt barge. I needed speed. William knew what we had to buy and he would have enough time to negotiate a good price. I wanted to speak with Philippe, Leofric's steward before William sailed home.

The Empress was at home with her two sons. The sentries told me that Geoffrey of Anjou was busy raiding castles in Normandy and that my son rode at his side. When I spied Maud I saw that she was with child again. She and the Emperor had been unable to have children. She had proved now that it was not her fault. She bloomed and I felt my heart race again at the sight of her. At her side were her two boys. I could not help noticing how much young Henry had grown. As I recalled he was now three. I was delighted when he saw me and shouted, "Mother! It is the wolf! He has returned! Now we shall have victory!"

I smiled and the Empress blushed a little, "You must forgive him, Earl Alfraed. He loves the tales your son tells of you and he remembered the wolf on your livery." She pointed to it. "I see it has sported a red tongue and eyes."

I nodded, "I have much to tell you."

She turned, "Margaret, take the boys to the bailey where they can play. Judith, take the Earl's squire and his belongings to his quarters."

They both curtsied and gave me a knowing look. They were the ones who knew our secret. They were the guardians of the tryst and the secret of the child.

"Come, my lord, we will walk by the river, it is pleasant at this time of year and it is quiet. We may talk there."

I told her, as we walked, of all that had happened in England. I was careful not to criticise the strategy which had allowed Stephen to steal a throne. I needed to speak with William and Rolf first. We stopped by the bank. She seemed distracted. "You are ever the Knight of the Empress. I cannot thank you enough for your efforts on my behalf."

I looked at her. This sounded very formal. "I swore an oath to your father. I do not break oaths."

She took my right hand in hers, "Alfraed there should only be truth between us. We have shared a bed, our hearts and a son. You and I have something between us that was ordained by higher powers than we. I know from your face and your words that you are disappointed in me."

I shook my head, "Never. Stephen took advantage of a situation and, perhaps, you were slow to react but I am convinced, in my heart, that your son will become King of England."

"Our son."

"Yes, my love, our son."

"But I shall not be Queen?"

I shook my head, "I shall be honest with you. It is the only strategy that will work. There is too much bad feeling about what the Angevin have done in Normandy. You are seen as the wife of Count Geoffrey. Those with estates here and in England are bitter for they fought Count Fulk for years. It has increased support for Stephen. He will lose that support when he has to tax them for he is spending your father's treasury far quicker than he ought."

"What else could we have done, Alfraed?"

"Had I been here I would have pursued the war ruthlessly and conquered the dukedom quickly. From what I heard the Count has conquered, pillaged and withdrawn. The best way is to keep an army in the field until you have defeated all. There are too many enemies out there for hit and run."

I was aware that she still held my hand. It was hard not to envelop her in my embrace.

"Will you stay? I know the Count will heed your advice. Teach him how to conquer Normandy. If we control that then we can look to England."

"I will stay until summer is gone but then I must return home. The Scots fear me but if I am not there..."

"I know. We need you in your valley."

"What of your brother?"

"Robert was distraught at our father's death. He blamed himself."

"He could have done naught about it. Where is he now?"

"He is in Caen. He holds it for me."

"He is a mighty leader who should be drawing men to your banner."

"You are here now. Things will improve." She let go of my hand and we looked into each other's eyes. "Life is not fair, my love. We can look, we can remember and we can dream but we cannot be as we would be."

"I know. We had best go within before tongues wag." As we made our way in I said, "And what of Rolf? Is he well?"

"He is healed now, my lord, and he acts as a mentor to your son William. Young Cleveland has proved himself to be a fearless lord. My husband thinks highly of him. He now has men at arms of his own."

"And where is he now?"

"He is with my husband on the Norman border."

"I shall join them after I have visited La Flèche."

"Your castellan has made a difference there. The people think well of him. His marriage was a fruitful one. His wife is with child and the act has made the castle and the town much closer. You have made a wise choice, my lord."

I gave a rueful smile, "Sometimes I do."

We were still outside the castle, "We could never have been as one. I was the daughter of a King. I was used as a pawn in a game of chess. I was married to an Emperor and then a Count. My father saw me not as a daughter but as a prize heifer."

"You sound bitter."

"I am. All I wished was to run away with you as you asked and to begin a new life somewhere but we were both too honourable for that. Duty came first. On my grave, it should say, *'she did her duty'*."

We heard a squeal from the bailey and then Henry hurtled out brandishing a wooden sword. Gilles followed him waving another one. "Protect me Uncle Alfraed, the Scots are after me!"

"Always remember young knight, that you never run from the Scots; you face them and roar even louder. They will run." I winked at Gilles. Henry turned and roared. Gilles obliged by running away. Judith, Margaret and the Empress all laughed.

Maud said quietly, "You do not just bring hope, you bring joy and, to me, peace." We went indoors. The moment had gone. We would now be Empress and loyal knight once more. As I bowed to go to my quarters she added, "Go to my husband. Advise him. Make him fight the way you and my father fight. He has changed and that is thanks to you. I wish it."

"I will do as you command."

Later, as I changed for the feast I said, "Thank you, Gilles, that was well done."

"I had a little brother just like the young lord. I used to play like that with him."

"Where is he now?"

"He died of the plague along with my sister and mother when my father served on campaign with you. He was but four when he died."

There was little else to say. Everyone had their secrets and some were sadder than others. The meal was pleasant for it was us, the Empress, her ladies and her boys. I forgot, albeit briefly, that I was Warlord. I smiled and joked with

Henry and Geoffrey and we regaled them with tales of knightly deeds.

We borrowed two horses from the Empress and rode the next day to my manor on the Loir. The castle still looked small but it was solid. My standard still flew from the gate. We had brought a new one as well as new surcoats for my men at arms. It was Brian who was at the gate and his beaming smile told me that he was pleased to see me.

"My lord! An unexpected pleasure!"

I dismounted, "And how is your new home? All that you hoped?"

"Aye lord. We had some trouble when the King was killed but we drove the raiders hence and we have had peace since then."

"And Leofric is to be a father I hear?"

"Aye, lord, at harvest time." He looked at Gilles, "And who is this, my lord?"

"This is Gilles son of Guy of Tours. He was my groom but I am training him to be a squire. In the absence of Wulfric perhaps you can give him some lessons."

"Aye, I will. And you will be here for a while, lord?"

"I will go back after summer. The Scots need keeping in check."

Leofric came from the keep, "My lord! You should have warned me!"

"I have much to tell you and I know that you have much to relate to me!"

It was good to have an unending supply of wine and I relaxed as I had not done for many months. Here I was safe. There were no intrigues and no enemies trying to harm me. This was a sanctuary. I wondered if King Henry had second sight when he gave it to me. I idly wondered if I should stay here and leave Stockton to Stephen. The thought flitted from my head almost as soon as it had entered. Like the Empress, I knew my duty.

When I finished relating events to Leofric he asked, "Do you want our men to return to England?"

"No, for if things go ill this will be our home. I will, however, be using our new ship to trade twixt my manors. It will be mutually beneficial. I have some spare weapons Alf made. The bulk of his output we used but English arrowheads and English fletched arrows are the best. We also have new surcoats for you and your men as well as a new standard."

"I have hired more men at arms. The civil war has left many without their lords. Brian here chooses the best."

"I will need four to escort us to the Count. I have offered my services as an adviser to him. The Empress thinks it will help."

"Of course."

"My ship will be ready to sail at the end of the week. I would have her filled with some of the produce from this manor: wine, cheeses, oil and spices. Have it sent down with the Empress' horses and bring back the timber, iron and arrows from the ship. Make a list of all that you need from England. I intend to have Captain William make this a monthly voyage; at least until the weather worsens."

Three days later I headed north with Padraig and three of the new men at arms. "How do you find it here on the Loir, Padraig?"

"I am happy. My life has changed. I have a woman now, lord. I only understand half of what she says but that may be an advantage eh? I miss English ale and I miss the lads. I even miss Wulfric although that is to be expected, I am happy here. I am grateful for the opportunities you have given to me." We rode in silence for a while then he said, "What will happen in England, lord? Will the Empress become queen? She should. She is a good woman."

"I am afraid that many in England and Normandy feel differently. Know this, Padraig, I will never cease to fight for that which King Henry wished. The King of France may have had our King poisoned but it is Englishmen who will decide who rules us."

"Amen to that, Earl."

We headed to the border where fighting was going on. Count Geoffrey was laying siege to the castle of Falaise. Even before I reached there I knew that it was a mistake. The castle was well made and would easily withstand a siege. It was better to strike where damage could be done rather than lose men in fruitless attacks on thick stone walls.

We reached the siege works by nightfall. I saw the wounded being brought back from the walls. I headed towards the tents of the Angevin. I gave my reins to Gilles, "Padraig find us a tent."

I heard raised voices inside the tent. One of them was Count Geoffrey's, "I do not want cowards. I want men who will assault the walls. I want men like William's father who leapt up a burning tower to save the Earl of Gloucester. I saw none of that today."

There was a clamour of voices that suggested that the speakers had been drinking. I strode in. It was a large tent and those who were on the periphery bridled as I pushed past them. Then they saw who I was and the complaints became cheers. I saw William, looking slightly flushed, and he was seated next to the Count of Anjou. He raced to me.

"Now we shall have victory for my father, the champion of King Henry, is arrived!"

He rushed to me and embraced me. He smelled of wine. Count Geoffrey stood, somewhat unsteadily and came towards me. "You are here! We prayed that you would come! God has sent you."

I saw that not all of the knights were as drunk. "I have come from England where Stephen has declared himself King. He claims Normandy for his son Eustace. The Empress and young Henry need us to regain the land of King Henry for them. Arguing among ourselves will not achieve that. Tomorrow we hold a council of war. Until then I bid you all depart so that I may speak with the Count and my son."

The drunks were not happy but those who had been drinking less heavily nodded and nudged the drunks out of the way. Soon we had the huge tent to ourselves.

"Earl, had we known you were coming we could have celebrated."

I spoke quietly. William was less drunk and he heard the censure in my voice. "Have you won a victory? Has Falaise fallen?"

The Count said, "No but now you are here. We will win."

"How many men did you lose today, lord?"

He waved a hand as though the number was immaterial, "Ten, twenty..."

"If you gain the castle what will you achieve?"

I saw William shake his head as though to clear it. He had a mind which Wulfric and I had trained. He began to use it. "We will have a castle, father."

"The Earl of Gloucester controls Caen and that is close to the coast. The garrison cannot move far for you would be able to capture them."

"Then what should we do?"

"Hit them where it will hurt. Rouen is their capital. It is the centre of their power."

"And it has the greatest citadel in Normandy, saving Caen."

"I did not say attack it. I said hurt it. Stop the ships travelling up the river and starve them to death. Stop them gathering their crops. Close the roads from the rest of Normandy."

"Some will get through."

"Aye but some is not enough. Eventually, they will have to meet you on the field and that is where you win."

Count Geoffrey said, "I feel unwell."

He raced from the tent and I heard him vomiting.

"Is he often thus?"

"When we fail then aye. It is good to see you, father."

"And I. you. I hear you now have your own conroi."

"I do. Men speak of me as the wolf cub." He sounded as though he resented the word '*cub*'.

"Do not worry about what men say. Idle words mean nothing. It is yourself who will be your sternest critic." He nodded. "The Empress has asked me to advise her husband. If you have any influence then I beg you to use it. Until we conquer Normandy England will suffer under Stephen's misrule."

My words sank in, "I am sorry. I can see it now. We have been playing at war. We should have been making war."

"Aye, my son. It is not glorious and there is little honour but if we wish to win then we make war and squeeze the enemy until they have no other recourse than to accept young Henry as their Duke."

"Not the Count?"

"Normandy fought his father for too long to accept the Count of Anjou as their new Duke. That is why you have been opposed. From tomorrow we change the strategy."

"But the Count..."

"The Count will listen or he will lose all!"

Chapter 13

I was up early and I walked the camp. I wanted to get the mood and feel of the men whom I would be asking to fight. It was ill-organized. Those within the castle must have been lax for a sortie could have ended the siege in one fell swoop. I recognised some of those on duty and I spoke with them. There was an air of despondency about the men. They had had success in the early days but, speaking with them, that had been the wooden castles that had fallen. I saw that they had tried a mangonel but it lay wrecked and broken. They had no siege engineers. As I headed back to the tent of the Count I saw that they had, at least, plenty of horses. That was where their strength lay. I learned from some of the Normans a little of the geography of the region and an idea began to form in my mind.

William was awake when I reached the Count's tent. Gilles had already cooked some eggs which we had bought on the road and he was cutting up yesterday's bread.

"Come, William, join us for some bread and eggs."

"I am not certain that my stomach could take it."

"Then all the more reason to eat. Sit. I command you!"

I said it with a smile and William gave a mock bow, "Then I shall do so!"

I made sure that Gilles divided the food equally into three and we sat around the fire, eating. "I did not see Rolf last night. I heard he was ever at your side."

He nodded, "I think that, like you, he did not approve of the way the war was being fought. He made an excuse and he headed back to Angers."

"I must have missed him on the road. Perhaps when I visited Leofric." I was disappointed. Rolf was someone on whom I could rely. I trusted his judgement. He would have made an ally for my arguments with the Count. The fact that he concurred with my views was reassuring. I would have to use my influence to persuade the Count to a different strategy. "Do you like it in Anjou, William?"

"Aye father, I do. It is neither as cold nor as bleak as Stockton and the Tees in winter and in summer there is a bounty." He held up the bread, "Here we eat fine bread every day."

I knew that many Normans objected to eating barley or wheat bread. They felt it inferior. I had grown used to it. "You would stay here?"

"Aye, father. The Count has given me a manor not far from La Flèche, Sablé-sur-Sarthe. We captured it just before Easter. The wooden hall burned down and we will have to build a better castle there but it has a fine position and brings in a good income."

"Good. I am pleased but there is always a manor for you in the valley." I told him of the raids and the deaths. "Norton has no lord of the manor. Should you return to England, it is yours."

"Thank you, father, but here I am not the son of the King's Champion. I am William the Bold who stormed the castle at Sablé-sur-Sarthe and fought the lord of the manor before killing him. Here I am my own man."

It hurt but I understood. He did not have to live up to my name. He had his own. "Well, William the Bold, you can help me persuade the Count to a more productive strategy," I explained to him how we could defeat the Normans more effectively. William had always had a clever mind and he understood quickly.

"It is not as glorious but it would be effective. I will aid you. The Count likes me, I think."

"If you are close then tell me who was the knight who was poisoning the Count's ear?"

"I am making informed guesses but I think it was Sir Hugh of Langeais. When I first joined the Count he would often be closeted with Sir Hugh and after those meetings, he would speak harshly of the King."

"And now; with the King dead?"

"Sir Hugh died too. He led the attack on Sablé-sur-Sarthe. I was with him. One reason I was given the manor was that I not only killed the lord of the manor, but I also stopped them despoiling Sir Hugh's body." He shrugged, "They made much of it but I have seen you do such things often enough."

We heard a groan as the Count staggered from his tent. His face broke into a weak smile when he saw me. "Earl! Then it was not a dream."

"No, my lord. You and I need to talk."

"First I need a drink. My mouth feels like the inside of my mail."

"Gilles find some small beer for the Count."

"Aye lord."

"Small beer? I need wine!"

"No Count, you need a clear head." I waved an arm around the camp. "With respect, Count, this is not working. You are losing men and the castle is no closer to falling. We need a different strategy."

He slumped on a log and held his head in his hands. "Different strategy?"

I sat next to him, "What is the purpose of this raid into Normandy?"

He looked at me as though I had taken leave of my senses, "Why, to conquer the lands that were left to my wife and son."

"And how does taking Falaise achieve that end?"

"Well... I ..er. It is a castle in Norman hands."

"And to the north is Caen which is held by the Earl of Gloucester. Falaise is nothing. Rouen is where the power lies. That is the heart of the Dukedom."

"But we have not enough men to take it."

"Is that why you chose Falaise, Count? You thought you had enough men for the task?"

He had the grace to smile, "Perhaps. But I wanted to be seen to be doing something. We captured so many castles on our way north that I felt sure Falaise would fall."

"The men of Anjou are fine horsemen. You have many horses and they give you speed. Leave your foot soldiers surrounding this castle. It will fall when they have to eat their horses. We take your men and we cut the Seine. We can strike along the river. Those who rule in Rouen bring in their iron and their weapons along the river. They send their goods to be sold along the river. Honfleur is a small castle. We could take that one by stealth rather than by siege. With that one in our hands, we would control the mouth of the Seine. We could raid from there and make the land between the Seine and the Orne yours. Falaise would have to fall and then we would have the west of Normandy."

"That leaves the east."

"And we can take that too. When we have Honfleur I will speak with Robert of Gloucester. This piecemeal attack does not help us. We need to combine all that we have and force the rebels to acknowledge the Empress as ruler."

He drank the beer which Gilles had brought. He pulled a face but he drank it. "My wife sent you here?"

"She welcomed my advice, yes, Count."

"And I am glad. I will summon my men and we will do as you say. I would rather be on a horse than watching my men die on the walls."

The mere fact that we were moving away from the walls of Falaise seemed to motivate the men more than even I would have believed. A hundred men were left under the command of Sir Stephen of Azay to keep the defenders bottled up while the rest of the Count's men, all mounted, left with us for the forty-mile ride to Honfleur.

William had not been idle since he had been in Anjou. He knew the worth of good scouts and archers. He had hired six such archers. They were all English but had lived in Normandy for ten years. We sent them to scout Honfleur.

"How do we take it by stealth, Earl?"

"I am hoping that they feel secure there. They will close the gates at dusk but I daresay they will allow travellers to enter during the day. Eight of us arrive in ones and twos or perhaps we say we are a caravan. We hide our surcoats beneath cloaks. I am certain that there will be horses which are not fit to be ridden amongst those your men have. We use those to gain access to the castle. We say we need to have our horses looked at. Once inside we overpower the guards at the gate and we take the castle."

"You make it sound easy. If it was this easy then every castle would be taken this way."

"We may not be granted entry and then we would have to think of another way but this is worth a try rather than appearing with a host which tells them that there is danger. They will know you besiege Falaise and they know that the Earl of Gloucester has not stirred from Caen. Whom should they fear? Merchants like their trade and they want visitors to their towns. We will take off our surcoats and hide our mail beneath our cloaks. William and I will say that we are on our way to take a ship to the Holy Land for a crusade. We say that we are Englishmen who are unhappy with Stephen of Blois. That should put their minds at rest for Stephen has claimed Normandy too."

"Who would go?"

"My son, his squire, four of his archers and Gilles here. You have your men watch the gate and we will signal when we have taken the gate."

The archers returned. "They have a close watch on the gate, lord, but it is open. There are ships in the harbour."

William asked, "Did they see you, Harold?"

He shook his head, "I am insulted, lord!"

There were woods four miles from the gates of the small port. We took the poorest eight horses from the horse train and we trudged the last four miles, leading the horses. The dust from the road soon covered our mail and our cloaks. We looked like road-weary travellers. The walk meant we reached the gates an hour or so before dusk. There were eight men at arms at the gate.

"Halt, what is your business?"

I patted the rump of the tired-looking palfrey I led. "We need lodgings for the night and we need a smith to look at our horses."

The sergeant at arms laughed, "Better find the butcher. That is all that they are good for. Who are you?"

"We are knights who have fled England and the tyranny of King Stephen. We like not his ways and we seek our fortune in the Holy Land."

"You are many miles from the Holy Land and you are far from England. Whence came you?"

"We took ship but a storm took its rigging. The captain put us ashore at Trouville-sur-Mer while he made repairs. He told us that there are ships here in Honfleur."

"Aye, there are. Have you enough coin?"

I patted my purse, "We have a little."

"Then if you lighten it here we shall grant you entry."

"But we are pilgrims."

He smiled, "And the Lord will smile upon you when you reach his land a little poorer." He held out his hand.

I played the impoverished and outraged knight. I took out two coins and put them in his palm. He kept it there. Three coins later he nodded. "For another coin, I will tell you of an inn where you will not have your purses cut." I handed it over. "The inn is the '*Wheatsheaf*'. It is just inside the gate. They have a stable. Tell the owner that Henri sent you. I may join you when my duty is over for a glass of wine. The landlord is my brother!"

Scowling as though we had been robbed, I led us into the town. The inn was where he said and we played the game. Henri's brother was as much a thief as Henri and we paid too much for poor rooms and even worse food. I consoled myself with the thought that we would get all of this back.

We spoke English in the inn. It fitted our story and meant we could talk a little freer. Raymond, the owner, came to chat with us. We were the only visitors in the inn. It was no wonder his brother had sent us there.

"Is there a war in England as there is here?"

"No, but King Stephen is ridding himself of those he does not like." I waved a hand around the empty room. "Has the war affected your business then?"

"A little. There are fewer travellers but we get the trade when ships enter. All the goods which go to Rouen come either here or at Harfleur to the north. It is either a feast or a famine. There are more ships expected tomorrow." He smiled, "Your rates will go up when they do for rooms will be at a premium."

"But we agreed on a price!"

"The fortunes of war my friend." He glanced outside and said, "The gates will be closing soon and my brother and his men will come for their food." He went over to the four men who had been seated in the corner drinking since we arrived. "You four had better get on duty. You know my brother has a temper on him. He will not like it if you relieve him late."

They rose reluctantly and dropped coins on the table. Four guards were manageable. As Raymond cleared the table, ready for his brother no doubt, I sent all but William to our small room, ostensibly to rest but in reality to prepare for the night's work. Henri came in and his brother brought him food. He waved over affably. I knew that my purse was attracting him like a moth to a flame. I intended to use that to ensure that there was no suspicion attached to our presence.

After he had eaten he wandered over. "You have poor horses there, lord. Perhaps I can be of some assistance."

"How so?"

"We have horses here in the garrison. Baron Thierry rarely ventures forth and they just grow fat. If you were to make it worth my while I could exchange your horses for his. The Holy Land is hard on animals, I hear."

"You are right but would you not get in trouble for this?"

He laughed and tapped his nose, "What the Baron does not know will not hurt me. Besides, he rarely leaves his keep. So, do we have an arrangement?" He rubbed his finger and thumb together.

I handed over a silver coin. "We have an understanding but I withhold the rest until I see the horses."

"Of course. I will bring them to the stable tomorrow when I come on duty. You have made a wise choice, lord."

We retired as soon as Henry had left the inn. A short while later I heard the door as it was barred. I had worked out that apart from Raymond there was just his wife and son in the inn. That was all. I detailed two of the archers and Gilles to take care of them. If anyone came I had no doubt that Raymond would wake when he heard the bolt slide back. Our shields were with the Count and his men. We just had swords and daggers. I hoped it would be enough. There were five of us and only four guards. From what I had seen they had consumed a large amount of wine. I did not think they would be as alert as my guards. I had also noted that none wore a helmet and they had no mail. Their short swords and spears told me all I needed to know about them. They were the town watch and they were not men at arms.

Leaving Gilles and the two archers to wait for the innkeeper to come we went to the door and unbarred it. As I expected it creaked and I heard the floorboards groan above as Raymond stood. We slipped out of the door. William had handpicked his archers. They would deal with the innkeeper. There was a brazier burning next to the gate. I saw a sentry silhouetted on the wall. He was staring to the south. A solitary guard sat by the brazier staring into its glow as though he was determining the future. The other two lay huddled beneath their cloaks. I took out my dagger and held it by the blade. I pointed to the sentry and the archers. They nodded and slipped towards the stair. In two strikes I was behind the guard at the brazier. I brought my dagger pommel down on the back of his head. William's squire, Henry, grabbed him before he fell.

I sheathed my dagger and drew my sword. William did the same. As Henry trussed up the unconscious guard with the rope we had brought I kicked one of the sleeping guards. As I did I heard a slight noise above me as the archers incapacitated the sentry. My kick and the noise made the sleeping guard open his eyes. The tip of my sword was but an inch from his eye. William kicked the other guard. They both had terror on their faces.

The archers descended, one of them carrying the unconscious sentry. "Truss them up. William, take a torch and make the signal." I pointed to one of the archers, "Come we will open the gate."

We lifted the bar and carefully laid it on the ground. Then we swung the two gates open. Outside it was silent. Where were they? I peered into the darkness. There was a limit to how long we could guard the gate. I knew that the town watch would be walking the streets looking for fires if nothing else. They would come to the main gate; perhaps to get a warm from the fire.

I thought I saw a movement in the dark. Suddenly Rolf appeared on foot leading his men at arms. He grinned when he saw me, "Trust you to make this war more interesting."

"And it is good to see you too. Come we must get to the keep as soon as we can."

I wondered how he had transported himself from Angers to Honfleur but that was not important. I stood aside so that he and his men could enter. The Count had wisely decided to leave the horses outside and his army flooded into the town. I joined Rolf and William and we headed through the streets to the keep. We needed to get there as quickly as possible.

The streets were thankfully empty and we moved without anyone noticing us. This was not a town on a war footing. When we reached the keep I saw that the door was closed. I guessed that it was barred. I waited until some of the Count's men joined us. "Keep watch here and let no one in. If the door opens then you know what to do."

We ran towards the river. It was not the Seine it was a tributary, La Morelle. There were two small towers guarding this side of the harbour and I saw, from within, the glow of a brazier. The town watch were here too. Behind me, in the distance, I heard an altercation. I guessed the town watch had seen our men. As the doors on the two towers opened I ran towards one of them with sword drawn. The guard tried to close it but my blade darted in and found soft flesh. I pulled his body from the door and ran inside. A dagger was thrust at me and I could not avoid it. It caught on my mail and I used the hilt of my sword to punch the man in the face. I did it three times before he fell backwards. I skewered him as he lay at my feet. William and Henry raced up the stairs to the top of the tower.

I went back outside. The alarm had been given. I heard a bell from the keep. Rolf emerged from the next tower. I pointed to the ships which were tied up to the harbour wall. "Quick. We must stop them from leaving! We need them."

I was alone when I jumped aboard the first one; it was a small merchant vessel and the nearest to the harbour entrance. I had my sword out as the three crew rose sleepily from their blankets. "Do not be heroes. I have a sword."

One, I took him to be the captain or owner, ignored my warning and ran towards me. He held a wooden spike in his hand. I feinted with my sword and, as he raised, his wooden spike, I punched him hard with my mailed left hand. He crumpled to the ground. I shook my head, "I warned him. On your knees!"

The town was now in an uproar. In contrast, the river seemed almost peaceful. Our prompt action had secured all of the ships, all four of them, and we had the port. More of the Count's men arrived led by one of the knights I had trained, Baron John of Nantes. "Make sure the ships do not leave. I would secure the crews and put your men in the tower."

"Aye lord, you bring us luck and success again!"

As I led William, Rolf and our men back to the keep I wondered how long I could rely on such luck. The sun had risen in the east and the town was no longer in shadows. The area around the keep was deserted. I saw two of the Count's men sprawled untidily in the square with crossbow bolts sticking from them. We used the narrow streets around the square to make our way to where the Count and his men hid behind their shields.

"Almost a perfect attack, Earl. It is a pity about the keep."

"Have you spoken to him yet? The Baron?"

"Not yet. Will it do any good? He is ensconced in his tower. How will we winkle him out?"

"Let me try." I turned to one of the men at arms who was sheltering in the doorway. "Give me your shield."

I raised the shield above my head and stepped out. As I had anticipated three bolts thudded into it. I held the shield high above my head to afford the maximum protection.

I shouted, "Baron Thierry. I would speak. Cease!"

"Who is that, the Count of Anjou?"

"No, it is Alfraed, Earl of Cleveland." There was silence. "We have you surrounded. There is no help coming your way."

"You cannot take this keep. It is made of stone."

"And how much food and water do you have Baron? How many bolts can you afford to waste striking shields?"

"We will not surrender."

"I have warned you. Whatever happens from now on is your doing Baron. I gave you the opportunity to end this peacefully."

"Do your worst, Englishman! This is a Norman keep and it will keep you at bay until help arrives!"

I returned to the Count.

"See it is hopeless."

"No, my lord, it is not. Have as much firewood gathered as you can."

"Firewood? Why?"

I pointed to the keep. "This is a well-designed keep save in one respect. There is but one way in and one way out. We set fire to the door. The flames will be sucked inside and race through the whole building."

He smiled, "See to it!"

With shields protecting them the Count's men piled huge amounts of wood next to the only door. Our archers kept down the heads of any on the battlements. I sent three men to fetch the brazier from the front gate. They hurled it onto the firewood. Those inside the keep knew we were up to something but they had no idea what. The brazier soon set light to the bone-dry kindling and firewood. Suddenly the flames took hold and whooshed up the door. I heard cries of alarm from the keep. They tried to pour water from the top of the keep. When two men fell pierced by arrows that stopped. The water had little effect for the walls of the keep actually protected the door.

As the smoke began to pour from the top we heard, "We surrender! Douse the flames! The town is yours!"

The Count nodded and men ran to pour buckets of water onto the door. When it was out there was still smoke coming from the keep. The door was suddenly flung open. It was a mistake for the draught fanned the flames from within the tower. They raced up the wooden stairs within. Men ran out covered in flames. Our men used blankets and cloaks to put them out but some were dead even as the flames were extinguished. I heard screams from within. There were women inside.

"William, Rolf, wet your cloaks. We cannot allow women to suffer because of a foolish knight."

I immersed my cloak in a bucket of water and then put it over my head. I ran into the keep. One of the staircases was still standing. The one by the door was burning and out of control. I ran to the other stairs and raced up them. The Baron's quarters would be on the first floor. The door was close to the other set of stairs and was burning. I shouted, "Stand clear of the door!"

I ran at it and hit it with my shoulder. It crashed open and a wall of heat through which I ran flared towards me. Inside, cowering on the bed was a woman and three children. William ran through the door behind me closely followed by Rolf. "Grab the children and put them under your cloaks."

Even as I gave the order the flames from the door, now fanned by our entrance leapt across the ceiling and the room was in danger of becoming an inferno. I grabbed the woman who stood petrified and pulled her under my cloak. Rolf and William had already raced out of the door. The woman shook her head, "My husband..."

"Forget your husband and think of your children." She nodded and I pushed her towards the door. I had just stepped out when huge burning timbers fell onto the bed where we had just stood. The second set of stairs was now on fire. Even through my mail leggings, I could feel the heat. The woman stumbled as we reached a turn. I picked her up and threw her over my shoulder. I ran down the stairs two at a time. I could feel a wall of heat behind me. I remembered the sensation from the time I had been in a burning siege tower. I saw, through the smoke and flames, daylight. It was the door. I burst through and, as I did so we were doused in water. Gilles shouted, "My lord, you are afire!"

I realised that the cloak was burning and I threw it away. The three children ran to their mother who lay on the ground. "She lives, I think children."

The boy, who looked to be about seven, looked at me and said, "Father?"

I turned and looked at the tower. Flames wreathed it and black smoke billowed from it. From inside came the sounds of screams. I had barely made it out alive. No one else would. I shook my head, "You are now the man. Care for your mother eh?"

The Count came to me, "That was bravely done but was it necessary?"

"The day we make war on women and children is the day I leave my sword sheathed and become a priest."

Chapter 14

The deaths and the destruction of the keep had been unnecessary. Baron Thierry had been foolish. The Baroness and her children were taken to the church where the priests could care for them. The Count gathered together all the men we had captured. I saw Henri. He saw me approach and feared the worst. I smiled and, rubbing my finger and thumb together, said, "You have some coin of mine I believe."

He nodded and handed over his purse, "Will you kill me, lord?"

"No for this town now belongs, as it should, to Empress Matilda. I hope you will serve her better than you served your former lord."

I walked over to where the Count was speaking with the burghers. "I have just had them swear allegiance to my wife, Earl. We have had great success and our men are all richer! What now?"

"We close the river. Have your men sail the boats in a line across the Seine. Link them with ropes and chains so that they form a barrier. You will need to secure them to the northern bank and guard that end. Then we need to find a bridge and cross to the north shore. We have taken Honfleur. We now take Harfleur."

"The ruse will not work twice."

"I know but they will have seen the smoke. We take the Baroness and her children and ask for Harfleur to give them sanctuary."

"Let them go? Why?"

"They will be more persuasive than we could ever be. They will tell of the horror we inflicted and our requests will seem reasonable. We use the name of the Empress. This is hers by right. Her father gave it to her. If you take it then you are doing what your father, Count Fulk tried to do."

"But we are married. The result is the same."

"It is not, my lord. Trust me. Now we need our horses for we must move quickly. Time is of the essence."

After three days Harfleur agreed to surrender. The Baroness had, indeed, been persuasive and my name still had an effect, even across the Channel. The huge Angevin army and the horror of the fire-related by the Baroness had the desired effect. We now had a gate at the mouth of the Seine. We had a double row of ships which stopped any we did not want from progressing up or down the river.

The Count, of course, was delighted. "Earl this is better than I could have hoped. We now control the west of this land and it is not even summer. Why we could conquer it all by harvest."

"Do not get ahead of yourself, Count. Tomorrow I ride to meet with the Earl of Gloucester. If I were you I would send a messenger to Falaise to tell them that we now control the Seine. Ask them to surrender again."

"Will you go alone?"

"You will need William and Rolf. I shall take Gilles. I should be safe enough."

We took advantage of the newly captured horses and we rode two of the Baron's best. I had not worn my surcoat but my cloak was ruined and we had to take one from one of the Baron's men at arms. As we rode the twenty odd miles to Caen, Gilles asked. "Lord, will my father be safe?"

"Safe?"

"If Rouen is in the hands of the rebels what of my father's farm?"

"I think he will be safe but when we have visited with the Earl there may be an opportunity to ride towards Rouen."

He nodded, "He is a proud man, lord. He would not suffer orders from others."

"I know, Gilles, he served me well. It was only one campaign but you know a man when you have fought alongside him."

The Earl was out hunting when we arrived at Caen. That disturbed me. I had thought that, perhaps, the Earl was building up his forces and was preparing to join his sister. There appeared to be little evidence of a war footing in the castle. I was known and I was given quarters. Gilles took the opportunity to groom our two new horses. The one we had given him was the first that belonged to him. He would be like a child with a new puppy. We would have to drag him away from the stables.

I was looking out of the south window when the Earl returned, "Alfraed! You are a sight for sore eyes! I wondered when you would return."

"As I wondered, my lord, when you would stir yourself and ensure that your dead father's wishes were carried out."

"You go too far."

"Do I lord? We are both Earls. You are no longer the son of a King and until Maud is made Queen we are equals. Why should I not express my opinion? Even now your cousin is emptying the English treasury of all that your father built and buying favour. Your lands are being eaten into by the voracious Welsh and yet you hunt. I think I am entitled to be, shall we say, a little peeved."

His servants had deemed it a judicious time to leave and we were alone. Robert clenched and unclenched his fists. Then he threw his head back and laughed, "God but I had forgotten just how outspoken you are. Perhaps I am used to toadies and lickspittles who yes sir me to death!" He came closer to me. "You have seen Geoffrey of Anjou. All he wants to do is to storm castles regardless of the result. There is no strategic plan!"

"Then perhaps you should have given him one."

"He would not listen to anyone."

"We took Honfleur and Harfleur. The Seine is under our control."

I could see by his face that I had stunned him. "How many men did you lose?"

"None," I told how we had achieved it.

"Incredible. Then we have more than half of Normandy under our control."

"But I fear we do not have enough men yet to finish it. Rouen and the land to the east have many large manors and, as you know, Earl, the French and the Flemish are very close. I believe it would be a mistake to push the Norman barons there into the enemy camp."

"What do you suggest? You seem to have thought all of this through."

"We raid until the barons beg for peace and a truce. We extract a fine and use that to build up the Empress' army. We both know that this will not be ended here in Normandy. It is England where we will decide the outcome. At some point, the Empress will have to invade England and when she does she will need a mighty army. That needs money. We tax ships using the Seine and use the Angevin horses to control the lands between the castles. The Count has found, to his cost, how hard it is to take stone castles."

"Then I prepare my men and give support to my sister."

"Your name alone, my lord, will bring vacillating barons to our side. All know what a mighty leader you are."

He laughed, "Do not make the mistake of underestimating yourself, Alfraed. I am sure that your name will draw men to our banner."

"I will ride back, on the morrow and tell the Count of our plans."

I was not used to this role as a mediator. I was brokering alliances but it appeared to work. When I told the Count he was delighted. "And Falaise has surrendered. I will send for the Empress and my sons. She can stay in Argentan. It is a good castle and she will not be in danger there. The babe is not due for three months."

"Is the move wise, my lord?"

"She will be delighted. She will be close to her husband, her brother and her favourite knight, her Knight of the Empress and King Henry's Champion. When I send word I dare say she will leave immediately"

In the event, he was right and knew his wife better than I did. It made sense for Angers was remote; it was in Anjou. Argentan was in Normandy. It showed her intent; she would be Duchess of Normandy. Robert of Gloucester also concurred. We spent a week planning our strategy during which time the Empress reached Argentan and set up her court there. For the first time, the balance of power was shifting away from Stephen and towards Maud, in Normandy at least.

It was early summer when our three columns of knights and men at arms moved out. I was with the smallest. With my son, William, and Rolf the Swabian we had but three knights and twenty men at arms. I was more than happy with the quality of the ones with whom I rode. We were the central column and we headed directly for Rouen. Our aim was to make the land south of the Seine untenable for the rebels. Guy of Tours lived in Tostes which was just four miles or so from the Seine. I had made the decision to start there and work my way back towards Falaise and Argentan. I reasoned that if we did it the other way then they would be expecting us. I had also promised Gilles that he could see his father.

Gilles came into his own for he knew all the greenways and backways in the area. We moved like ghosts through forests and woods. The handful of men we saw was there illegally. They were poachers. We passed each other with a tacit acknowledgement that what we both did was less than legal.

The carrion above Tostes should have warned us what we would see but we were not prepared. The hamlet had been devastated. Birds picked at bodies that had been roughly covered in branches and leaves. I could not stop Gilles who galloped up to the largest hut in the village. It was his father's. "Rolf, William, see if any live yet."

I was not hopeful. Gilles was bent over disturbed leaves. He reverently pulled them from the face of the corpse. Even though the birds and rats had feasted I still recognised my old man at arms. I moved the leaves and branches a little more. There was a wound in his chest which suggested he had been lanced. His armour and sword were gone.

"None live, lord."

I stood. Gilles grieved by his dead father. "Someone made a half-hearted attempt to bury these bodies. Find whoever it was. I would know what went on." I went to Gilles. "We should bury your father." It was not what was on my mind but I knew the young man needed to do something for his dead father.

"Aye lord. There should be a shovel out of the back of the hut." He sounded numb as though he could not comprehend what we saw.

The simple act of finding something with which to bury his father gave him focus and he forgot, albeit briefly, the horror of what he had seen. I helped him dig the grave as William and Rolf organised my men to find whoever had tried to give the dead some dignity.

We had scraped out a depression in the earth when I heard William say, "Here! I have him!"

They pulled an old man with one arm from the bushes some fifty paces from the village. Gilles said, "It is old Henry! He was the swineherd."

"Be gentle with him. He looks frightened!"

By the time they reached us the old man looked a little less terrified than he had when William had dragged him out.

"Tell me, my friend, what happened."

"It was a week ago, lord. Men came from Rouen. It was Sir Hugh d'Elbeuf. It is a manor north-west of here. They came through and just killed everyone."

Gilles said, "But why? This village is small and there is no lord of the manor here."

The old man shook his head, "I know not, Gilles. They were drunk. They rode down the animals and your father remonstrated with them. They slew him and then slaughtered the rest. I would have died too but I was with one of my pigs who was giving birth. I hid. I am sorry Gilles! I have one arm! What could I have done?"

I put my hand on his shoulder, "Nothing my friend. And you buried them as best you could with one arm."

"Aye lord. I would have done more but..."

"William, have one of your men take him to the Empress. She will care for him. Make sure she knows what went on here."

"Aye father." He went to speak with his man and we buried the dead.

When we had finished William said, "I have heard of this Hugo d'Elbeuf." I nodded. "He was the cousin of Sir Guy de

Senonche. He has a reputation for evil which is the equal of Sir Guy."

"Then we begin our war at the manor of Elbeuf. Your father shall be avenged, Gilles."

As we rode through towards the Seine Rolf said, "It will be a well-made castle, lord. I thought we were raiding."

"And we are Rolf. I will not throw away lives recklessly. I go to spy out the castle and see the roads the garrison use."

It was just three miles or so through the forest to the river. The river was wide. We sent scouts east and west and one returned within a short time.

"Lord, there is another village down the river. It too is burned out and filled with the dead."

"It looks like this Hugo d'Elbeuf is ridding himself of all he thinks will oppose him."

The other scout took longer. "I have seen the castle, lord, and it is strong. It is on the bend of the river. There are no bridges across the river."

I nodded, "It protects the road to Rouen from the east. We go to these forests to the east of the town. I would observe the castle myself."

It was a short ride but the forests were dense and they teemed with game. We moved down the hunter's trails. It was a risk, especially if the knights were out hunting but I relied on the fact that we were looking for danger and they were looking for game. I saw the castle in the distance. There was no natural hill and they had used the river to afford some protection and built up the bailey so that it stood up from the land. The road which led from the castle went to Lisieux. That was also held by rebels.

"We will go through the forest and head west. Let us see if we can cut this road and tempt Sir Hugo from behind his walls."

The breeze was in our faces as we headed west. It brought smells and it brought noise. The scout who led us, Edward, held up his hand and we halted. Suddenly a stag came hurtling down the trail. It veered to one side as soon as it saw the line of men. We drew our swords. The stag was being hunted. There were six hunters and they were as surprised as the deer when they burst into our midst. William, Rolf and I spurred our horses forward to engage them. If they were hunters then they came with Baron Hugo's permission and they would be knights.

The leading hunter thrust his spear at me. I deflected it and used my powerful mount to force his small horse to the side. He fought to control his animal and I stabbed at him with my sword. He was agile, despite the fact that he looked to be a little older than me. Even so, he could not avoid the edge of my sword and, as he was not wearing mail, it sliced deeply across his right arm. He tumbled from his horse.

A second man, I took him to be the knight's squire, came bravely at me. He jabbed his spear at my face. It was an easy blow to avoid and I ducked. Holding my sword out the squire impaled himself upon my blade.

And then it was over. Two men had died and four were captured. I returned to the knight whose arm I had slashed. He was making his own tourniquet. I dismounted and said, "Yield!"

He laughed, "There is little else I can do although I fear I shall bleed to death before you receive ransom! I yield."

I sheathed my sword and tore a piece of cloth from the dead squire's garment. I tied it tightly around the knight's arm.

"Thank you, Earl."

"You recognise me?"

"I fought alongside you when we fought the rebels. I saw the wolf and knew that we were in danger. I am Baron Charles de Touville." He shook his head. "We thought you in Honfleur. Sir Hugo will be annoyed that you are loose in his lands."

"He will be more than annoyed when we are finished here. Did you know what he has done with the villages along the river?"

"They are his lands. Each of us rules in a different way."

"And yet you accept his hospitality."

"The winds have changed, Earl. King Henry is dead and Stephen has claimed the English throne. There are many who vie for the Dukedom. Baron Hugo would make a strong Duke."

"There is Empress Matilda and her son."

He shook his head, "She is a fine lady but she is just that, a lady and her son is a child. As for her husband... I fought Count Fulk too many times to accept his son as even the consort of a Duchess."

"William, have these men sent to Honfleur and we will ask for ransom. They have all yielded?"

"Aye father."

I helped the wounded knight to his horse, "Think what King Henry would have wanted Sir Charles. Would he be happy with Sir Hugo as Duke? King Henry was a hard man but he was just and he was fair."

"I will think on your words for I know you to be an honourable man. But your lands are in England and you will leave." He leaned forward and spoke quietly, "The French are already eyeing this land. King Louis has sent emissaries already to discuss alliances. I look to my own land, Earl."

They put their two dead on the back of their horses and William's six men at arms headed back to Honfleur.

After they had gone I reflected on the words of the knight. He seemed a reasonable man and what he said was probably the view of many. I knew that Count Geoffrey was not the same man as his father but his actions until I had arrived must have seemed like a child trying to achieve what his parent could not.

"We continue west." We had smaller numbers now. There were just thirteen men at arms until William's men returned.

We followed the road but saw no one using it. The land appeared devoid of people. Perhaps that was understandable. This was forest and if Sir Hugo wanted that for the game and the timber then there was little point in living close by. As evening approached we went into the forest and found a clearing close to water where we made camp. Rolf and William were both much like me. We could sleep under the greenwood. Three of Rolf's men went to hunt our supper while we got a fire going. I doubted that there would be any danger during the night but, in the morning, Sir Hugo would seek out the missing three knights and their squires who had not returned from the hunt.

We still had sentries set but we were relaxed as we sat around the fire. Rolf was silent and I saw his face was troubled. "What ails you, brother?"

He shook his head and forced a smile, "I am sorry, Alfraed, but when I see you and your son together it reminds me of what I do not have. So long as Karl and Godfrey rode by my side then I had a family with me constantly. Since they were killed I have been alone. I have no family and I am no longer needed as Knight of The Empress. What is my purpose in life? Why do I fight? The ransom we collect I will spend on ale and horses."

I understood his thoughts. They were the dark ones I had experienced after the death of my wife. He was right, William was my future, as well as my dark secret, Henry. My son, however, was young and he did not see the problem.

"Sir Rolf you are not too old to take a wife. Count Geoffrey would grant you a manor as he did me."

"I know, young William, but I am a grizzled old warhorse. Any woman who took me on would need the patience of a saint. I would not inflict that on any."

"You are the last of the Empress' Swabians. Karl, Godfrey, the others, they would have wanted families had they lived would they not?"

"Karl, certainly."

"Then you owe it to them to do what they cannot."

He nodded, "You always were the wise one amongst us. I will give it some thought." He lay back and laughed, "Just so long as some rebel sword does not end my thoughts and my plans eh?"

He was soon asleep and William and I talked a little longer. "You should think as Rolf, William. I married your mother when I was but a little older than you. Think about how quickly your mother was taken from me and now I have but one son. The King and the Queen had but two children.

One died at sea and look at the problems the Empress has. Find a wife and father children!"

He nodded, "You wish to be a grandfather! I will do my best!"

"I did not say that. I said, marry. The rest will follow naturally."

We were up before dawn for we were in the land of our enemies. We headed back to the road. William pointed west. "If the river is closed then they will have to send goods along the roads. Lisieux is their front line."

Rolf had awoken more energised than the night before. "Then they will have to come from Rouen. We could find somewhere to ambush on this road."

"A good plan Sir Rolf. The men I sent to Honfleur will join us here and then we will have sufficient numbers again."

"Good. We ride east until we find a good site to ambush."

We had travelled further through the forest the night before than I had realised. The road was some way from the eaves of the forest and we found no suitable ambush site in the next mile. Half a mile later however we did find danger. We came upon a conroi. There was a bend in the road and as we came around we suddenly saw, a hundred paces from us, five knights with their squires and ten men at arms. At such times a knight has to make decisions quickly. We could run or we could charge. Perhaps I was arrogant or I thought we were better knights. Whatever the reason I shouted, "Charge!"

William and Rolf naturally rode on my flanks and we drew our swords as one. My quick decision meant that we were moving more swiftly than they. I heard the leading knight shout, "Charge!" They spurred their horses on but we were already closing. We had reacted quicker. We had swung our shields around from our backs and our swords were in our hands. They were still trying to get their weapons out.

There was enough space for them to form a line. They would slightly outnumber us and there was a chance that they would outflank us but our speedy charge allowed us to close with them quicker. The knight who led had a yellow surcoat with a black boar. I went for him. The horse I had taken from Baron Thierry was a powerful horse. He was closer to a destrier than a palfrey and this was the first time I had had occasion to use him in a real battle. He did not let me down. As we closed I veered towards the leading knight and brought my shield to protect my front. The knight in the yellow surcoat was still trying to bring his mount up to speed. He was distracted.

As we closed I pulled my arm back and swung hard at the black boar on my enemy's shield. My horse leaned to the right as I did so. He had been trained well. My sword smashed into the shield with all the force I could muster. The knight lost his balance and he tumbled to the ground. My sword was still before me when the man at arms jabbed his spear at me. He should have aimed at my face but he did not; he went for my shield. His own shield was on the left and he had no protection. My sword struck him in the throat. The blade ripped through his ventail and he fell backwards over the cantle.

I wheeled my horse around and came upon a surprised man at arms who was racing to aid the four knights who remained. I jerked back on the reins and my new horse lifted his mighty hooves and struck the horse and the man at arms. Both beast and man crashed into the forest. I pulled the reins around and rode after the knights. I saw one knight, in addition to the leader, was down. William was fighting two. I spurred my mount and yelled, "Stockton!"

One of the knights turned to face me. Our swords clashed and sparks flew. I had power in my arm I knew not that I possessed. I was fighting for my son's life. It was an unequal battle. I used my knees and my left hand to pull around my horse's head. It snapped and bit at the knight's mount. His mount tried to pull away and as it did so exposed the knight's left side. I lunged at a gap I saw between the shield and the sword. It sliced through the leather strap holding the shield and the reins. As the shield fell, the reinless horse pulled its head around. I swung backhanded and hit the already unbalanced knight in the chest. He fell from the horse and cracked his head against a tree. He lay still.

I turned. I saw that the leader had managed to mount a horse brought by his squire but he had but one knight remaining. then, looking west, I saw the seven men at arms from William's conroi returning. Our enemy fled.

We had not escaped unscathed. William's squire lay dead and three men at arms would never follow our banner again. Two knights, including one I had knocked into the forest, lay dead. The last knight began to stir. We had a prisoner.

I dismounted and went to him. I saw that he too had a yellow surcoat but his boar was a much smaller one. I held my sword to his throat as he opened his eyes. "Yield!"

He nodded and said, "I yield."

I sheathed my sword, "What is your name?"

"I am Geoffrey d'Elbeuf and you have made a grave mistake for I am the younger brother of the next Duke of Normandy, Sir Hugo d'Elbeuf!"

Chapter 15

My men at arms ensured that knights and the survivors of our attack had headed back to their castle. We had two knights, a squire and four men at arms as prisoners. As well as our dead four of the men at arms were wounded. Rolf said, "As much as I would wish to press on, Alfraed, I feel that we should return to Honfleur."

He was right, of course. We had succeeded beyond our wildest dreams. We had cut the road for Sir Hugo would not dare risk supplies being sent along the road while we prowled. Our reinforcements would have made him think we were a larger conroi. "I agree. We will resupply and return in a day or two."

Geoffrey d'Elbeuf laughed, "The next you come, knight of the wolf, my brother will have assembled all of the knights who are allied to him and you will be swept aside."

William smiled, "Strong words for a man who will have to wait to be ransomed. Curb your tongue."

William was changing. He was becoming a man. He had flown the nest and was now a hunting bird himself. I felt satisfied. I could return to England confident that my son needed me no longer.

We reached Honfleur in the early afternoon. We had had to skirt the castles still held by those loyal to D'Elbeuf. My original plan had long since disappeared. We had had just two encounters but they had yielded more than we could have hoped. The other two conroi were still raiding. The keep at Honfleur still reeked of smoke and the upper floors were uninhabitable but the ground floor had been cleared a new door replaced the burned one. We secured our prisoners there and sent a man at arms back to Elbeuf and Touville with demands for ransoms. We sought more than we would have in England for we needed to break this rebellion and if we hurt their finances it would end it more quickly.

Gilles had been quiet on the way back and I took him to one side. "Your father?"

He nodded, "He was a good man and deserved to end his days in peace."

I shook my head, remembering my father and his oathsworn. "He died with a sword in his hand, Gilles. Your father was a warrior. He went too early but the alternative would have been like old Henry the swineherd. He would have lived alone. The coughing sickness or some other plague would visit him and he would have died with none and no purpose to his life. His death had some value for you now know what you wish, do you not?"

"Aye lord, but how did you know?"

"I saw it on the road there where you were eager to close with our enemies and you fought with a wild look in your eyes. You wish to be a knight."

"I do."

"Then we must train you. My son has lost his squire. You can tend to us both until he finds a new one and he can teach you how to fight better."

"Why not you, lord?"

"He was recently my squire and learned the lessons from me. Besides I have much to do here to further the cause of the Empress."

Over the next four days, while we waited for the return of the Count and the Earl, Gilles trained hard each day with William. There were no suitable candidates for squires in Honfleur and William was happy to develop the skills inherent in Gilles. I wrote letters. With Honfleur and Harfleur in our hands we could send ships anywhere we chose. I wrote to the Archbishop. I could not risk sending a ship to my river but I trusted the Archbishop. I used our code and told him of the French conspiracy. I knew that the message would get to Stephen. He had diplomatic routes not available to me. He could appeal to the Pope and to other allies.

The Earl and the Count were able to use their own castles at Argentan and Caen as well as the recently liberated Falaise to raid into rebel territory. On the fifth day after our return, they arrived in Honfleur.

We had all been successful to varying degrees but Sir Charles' news about the French was disquieting. I think the old man regretted what he had said but in his heart, he was still King Henry's man and sometimes the truth will out even if you do not wish it so.

The ransom arrived the same day and that surprised me. Perhaps we had not asked for enough or perhaps Sir Geoffrey was important to his brother. I knew that the ransom would have impoverished Sir Charles' family but if it had not affected Sir Hugo then how much did he have?

After our hostages had left and while Rolf and William divided the ransom equitably the Earl of Gloucester and the Count of Anjou held a council of war to which I was invited. We had a crude map on the table. I jabbed my finger at Lisieux. "See we have the rebels pinned back all the way along this line save for Lisieux. It holds out still. Sir Hugo was on his way thither when we met him. If we can isolate it then we have a chance to gain all the land to the Seine."

"We cannot assault it. The castle is well made."

"I know, Count. We cut the road to the east. Argentan and your wife hold the road to the south and Honfleur guards the road to the north. They will have to relieve it."

The Earl nodded, "And when they do we meet them in the field." He looked at the map. "Here at Thiberville, the ground begins to rise after the road passes the town. We could spy our foes from some way away and meet them there."

The Count was dubious, "If they come that way."

"It is the main road. It is D'Elbeuf land and he will feel confident about the roads close to his manor. It is a pity we do not have more archers. If we had then we could end this rebellion there in one fell swoop."

"We have doughty knights and men at arms, Earl. That will have to suffice. This is not England."

"Archers, as the Earl and I know, give us an advantage. This is not a game to see who can win the tourney, Count. We fight for your son's birthright. For that reason we make sure that we are as strong as we can be and when we fight we do so to win and not just to gain glory."

"Alfraed is right, brother. We need to prosecute this war ruthlessly."

Whilst the Earl of Gloucester did not possess as many archers in Normandy as we would have liked he did have excellent scouts. Twenty of them ranged far to the east and the Seine. They reported back regularly. Our preparations were also sound. The Count and I went to Thiberville where we had cut the road and established a camp. We had enough men to stop a sortie from Lisieux but not enough to fight Sir Hugo if he stirred. We relied upon our scouts for advance warning. The Earl of Gloucester meanwhile, was raising an army to join us. We hoped that by midsummer's day we would be in a position to fight Sir Hugo on the ground which we had chosen. A week before midsummer we heard news from our scouts. Sir Hugh, too, had mustered an army and they were preparing to move to relieve Lisieux. We had to change our own plans. Riders were sent to Caen to summon the Earl. We would have to fight with the army which was available to us and not the one we might have chosen.

We waited on the high ground to the west of Thiberville. We had been there long enough to prepare the ground. The fields to the left and right of the road had been prepared with pits and spikes. The limited number of archers and crossbows we had were behind sharpened, fire-hardened stakes. We had brought lances and spears from Caen for we intended to use our knights to destroy this enemy host. This would be one battle to decide how Normandy would look over the winter. If we won then we would retain control of the Seine and with it the lifeblood of Rouen. If we lost then we would have to retreat to our line of castles and plan for a spring offensive.

Our scouts brought regular reports so that we knew when the Norman army left Elbeuf. The Earl of Gloucester brought his forces in the day before we expected our enemy. The scouts we had sent kept us well informed as to the enemy's movements. Our numbers were not as great as they might have been but we had enough. There were sixty knights with their squires and three hundred men at arms. The archers and crossbows were an insignificant number; just a hundred of them. They would guard our flanks. The men of the levy were left, all two hundred of them, as a reserve and to guard the horses.

Rolf came to the Earl and the Count, "My lords I know that you plan to use dismounted men at arms to tempt the enemy on. I beg you to let me lead them. They need a knight and we Swabians fight as well on foot as we do on a horse. With my men at arms in the centre, we will be a rock on which the enemy will shatter their spears."

"An excellent idea, Rolf!"

I shook my head, "Let me do it, lord. Rolf has still not fully recovered from the poison which killed your father."

Rolf laughed, "Alfraed, old friend, I will not let that witch who now rots in hell have the satisfaction of knowing that she kept me from a battle." He lowered his voice. "This is meant to be and this day will be long remembered. This Sir Hugo will remember the courage of Rolf and his Swabians." Raising his voice he said, "And I will claim a boon when we are victorious!"

"You shall have anything you desire Rolf! I shall give you a manor!"

"Thank you Count. I shall fight even harder with that reward in mind." He turned and clasped my arm, "Do not be too reckless eh, old friend."

"And you take care too."

"I am with my Swabians! We will be a solid wall!"

From our scouts, we knew that we faced eighty knights and squires as well as over three hundred and fifty men at arms. They had brought far more of their levy. The scouts estimated four hundred of them. It was a daunting number but we relied upon the quality of our men. When the scouts told us, towards evening, that the enemy was on the other side of Thiberville we sent our men to sleep where they would fight. Fifty of our best men at arms, commanded by Rolf, would fight on foot in two ranks between our pits and traps. Behind them would be our forty archers. I rued not bringing Dick and his men. They would have slowed down the enemy attack. We would have to use what we had. Our knights would be mounted and would be led by the Earl. The men at arms would absorb the enemy attack and brunt it. Our job would then be to become the hammer that would smash them apart.

It was Gilles first real battle and I took him to one side. "You need not carry my banner tomorrow. I would have you keep three spears with you and a spare horse. When my spear is shattered find your way to me and give me a fresh one. If my horse falls then bring my spare. When we break the enemy then follow close to me and watch my back."

"You are confident that we will break them, lord?"

"Not confident but hopeful. We plan for success, Gilles, not failure. If we do not break them then we try something else. Now sharpen our swords and daggers. By mid-morning, they will be as blunt as an iron bar!"

We rose before dawn. It was so dark that Gilles thought it was the middle of the night. We had heard our enemy arriving during the previous evening. I thought that the Normans would scout our lines out but would not attack. I was proven correct. Our own sentries caught and killed four such scouts. There would have been others of that I was in no doubt. The priests we had brought with us as healers now blessed us we prayed in the dark for success. I knew that our enemy would do the same. We each believed that God was on our side. We ate cold meat and cheese washed down with the beer we had brought with us. And we waited for dawn to break. We had the advantage that we were in the darkness of the west. Although the sun would illuminate us it would highlight and silhouette the Normans as they advanced from Thiberville.

Gilles was nervous and did as many men did on such occasions, he talked. "Lord, why have we made them a present of Thiberville? They will have food and they will have shelter."

"Aye they will but we have height and a good soldier never gives away height, but more importantly it blocks their escape. I told you last night that we plan for success. When we force them from their positions they cannot run freely. They either use the road which will be congested or they use the fields and we hunt them down. In a month or so we shall go home and by then I want Normandy to be more settled than when we first arrived."

He nodded. He was of low birth but he was bright and he learned quickly. He would remember the lesson of the battle of Thiberville and it would help him in battles yet unfought.

Dawn broke and still Sir Hugo kept his army behind Thiberville. The Count of Anjou became worried. "Perhaps he will not take the bait and attack us!"

"In which case, he loses Lisieux. They must be short of food. His people cannot even begin to harvest for our men are guarding all the roads. If he is willing to lose the castle then he does not attack."

"Suppose he tries to outflank us?"

The Earl smiled, "We chose this place because to go around would mean an extra twenty or thirty miles and our scouts watch those routes. He has not made that move yet. You can see his banners beyond the town. He will be working out a strategy to defeat us. He sees our dismounted man at arms and debates how best to counter that."

"Suppose he chooses not to use his knights. He could use his men at arms dismounted as are ours."

It was my turn to smile, "Then we will win."

"You are so sure?"

Robert of Gloucester said, "The Earl is correct. We can hope that he is foolish enough to try that. Dismounted men at arms charging uphill against Rolf and his Swabians would give us an advantage."

In the event, as the sun rose and our armour began to weigh down upon us, Sir Hugo chose to charge with a mixed force of mounted men at arms and knights. He was not going to oblige us by making the attack we wished. There were fifty men in the three ranks which came up the road towards us. He had a further fifty lightly armed Breton horsemen on each flank. They were armed with javelins. They were unexpected but not a difficult problem. They walked their horses until they were a hundred paces from us and then began to trot. At a hundred and twenty paces our archers began to loose arrows. The knights and men at arms held up their shields. Once again it was horses that were felled and not their riders. On the flanks, the Breton horsemen discovered our pits, traps and stakes. The crossbows we had brought felled many.

At forty paces the lines of knights and men at arms charged. Rolf and his men suddenly presented a wall of shields three shields high and with fifty bristling lances protruding. Had they had archers making life difficult for Rolf and his men then the Norman charge might have had more success but, as it was, their horses could not breach the wall of steel. Our archers rained death on the horses at the rear of the line but the battle line itself was a stalemate. Swords were raised and crashed down on shields that did not break. Eventually, a horn sounded the retreat. Our men were well trained and they did not fall into the trap of pursuing the enemy. I saw that there were gaps in our lines. Men had fallen. Rolf reorganised them and fresh lances to replace the broken ones were passed forward. The Bretons fell back too. In all their attack had cost them over twenty men. In addition, I saw at least ten horses that were dead and many others who wandered around with arrows showing their wounds.

"Send water to the men at arms!"

Squires raced to the men who had fought and passed water skins amongst them. Sir Hugo was not a leader to try and then retreat. As our men were watered I saw him organising a wedge of men at arms. It was every man at arms he had available. He had damaged our men at arms and now he gambled with his own. I had not seen one of those for a while and never one as big. It was a bold stroke. One man stood at the front and the rest formed up behind. I was grateful that it was Rolf who held the centre of our line. With his Swabians around him, they would break against him. The Norman who led the wedge was a giant of a man. That was not always an advantage. Rolf had fought enough big men in the past for me to be confident about the outcome.

I nudged my horse closer to the archers. "Lay your arrows in the centre of the wedge! Force them to the side!"

The disadvantage of a wedge was that it was wide at the rear. So far only the Breton horses had fallen into the traps and they had been further away from the road. The wedge used the road. I wanted it to spill over into the fields. I hoped to cause more casualties with the wedge.

When I rejoined the Earl and the Count I said, "This may be our time, Earl. We caused casualties amongst their knights and see how they rest by their horses. They think we stay on the defensive."

"We will see. I am loath to lose the high ground."

The fact that they walked without horses and held shields above them meant that the men at arms suffered fewer casualties than the mounted men. However, it also meant that they were struck by far more arrows. Inevitably some arrows found a gap and men fell. When men fell holes in their lines appeared and more men died. It was not sudden but slow; it was like a man bleeding to death, slowly. Men at arms rushed to fill the gaps and to gain the protection of their fellows. As they did so the rear of the wedge widened and some of those fell into the traps. And then the two sets of warriors met. There was a clash and a crash as men and metal met men and shields.

The archers continued their work. Those in the centre of the wedge were the ones who fell. The heart of the wedge, the part where they should have had all their strength was hollow. Rolf and his Swabians at the centre were being forced back. It was inevitable. Our line bowed and surged around the giant. I saw Rolf's sword rise and fall. The giant was no more. The front lines ebbed and flowed. Had this been my men at home we would have interchanged the ranks but these did not know each other and I knew that Rolf and his men would be tiring.

Suddenly I could not see Rolf and his men rushed forward. Their line became a circle. Rolf had fallen. His men at arms were oathsworn. They were a throwback to the days of my father and they fought to the end to protect the body of their fallen leader. They all died but the enemy paid such a heavy price that I saw our line, reinforced from the rear, pushing forward.

I turned to the Earl of Gloucester, "Now lord. They are pushing back the men at arms. Their line is thin."

"I am not certain."

"Commit only the Count's men with me and my son at the head. Let us use my name to sow fear into their hearts. You still have your knights and men at arms if we fail."

He smiled, "But you do not believe you will! Aye, do so." He nodded, "Avenge your friend!"

I took my lance. The Count was keen for this was what he craved, a glorious charge. For me this was not about glory it was about hitting them when they least expected it. Sir Hugo and his knights were not ready for a fight. They were resting and watching their men at arms bleed. We formed up behind the men at arms. I saw, in the distance some of the Norman knights as they viewed our arrival. The Earl's herald sounded the trumpet three times and our men at arms suddenly broke and fled back up the slope. I spurred my horse and we moved down the road even as our men at arms passed between us to form a line behind us. The Norman men at arms had their heads down and when our men at arms fled they surged after them. All order was lost. Our archers released another shower of arrows and then we charged.

There were only thirty-two of us. A paltry number in the scheme of things but as we thundered down the road the men at arms found themselves without their fellows' protection. It was like sticking static pigs. I pulled my arm back and punched my lance into the face of a sergeant at arms. He fell backwards and I allowed his body weight to pull it from my lance. I pulled it back as another man at arms braced himself with his sword and his shield. I feinted to his head and as he raised his shield changed my aim and gutted him. This time he broke my lance.

I raised my hand and shouted, "Lance!"

Gilles must have been close by my horse's rump for he was there in an instant. I took the lance and saw that we had broken their line. They were streaming towards their knights who were hurriedly trying to mount. It was too late for the men at arms impeded any chance they had of charging us and the men at arms were broken. I was not the only one to have bloodied his lance. I spurred my horse and he leapt at the knight who was struggling to turn and face me. He failed and I punched with my lance and struck him in the right shoulder. My horse was both heavy and powerful. My blow was delivered with all of my strength and it penetrated deep into his body. The blow knocked him and his horse to the ground. His fall took the lance from my hand and I released it.

As I reached for my sword I glanced to my right and saw a spear coming at my own unprotected right side. I was a dead man. Then Gilles thrust my last lance into the helmet of the knight. It was a good blow and it pierced his coif and his neck. The lance fell from his dead fingers. I nodded my thanks and kicked on. This was not the time to pay compliments. I swung my sword at a knight who was trying to control his rearing horse. I thrust my blade into his side. It had been freshly sharpened and had not been used. It came out to the other side. I ripped it out and he fell from his horse.

William appeared at my left. His sword was bloody. "We have outrun the Count's men. We must hold!"

Shaking my head I said, "Look, Sir Hugo's standard. If that fails then we win!"

There was still confusion in the enemy ranks. I heard the trumpet as it kept making the new call. It was the signal for the whole army to attack. I need not turn around. The Earl was bringing all of our mounted men against the Norman knights! I rode at the standard-bearer and the squire of Sir Hugo. He was busy trying to control his horse. William leaned forward and brought his blade against the squire's shield. It was a powerful blow and he reeled. Gilles still had his lance and he punched it at the standard-bearer who tried to use the banner as a spear. It was brave but doomed to failure. The head of the lance glanced off the standard and struck the standard-bearer in the eye. He could not help himself and he dropped the standard as he put his hand to his face. I had chosen Gilles for his skills on a horse and he showed them by leaning down and catching the standard before it reached the ground.

Sir Hugo roared in rage and spurred his horse towards Gilles. My horse was tired but he had enough energy to leap when I spurred him. Our beasts met in a tangle of mane and teeth. I swung my sword at Sir Hugo. It was not blind but I knew I would not cause a wound. He had to use his sword to deflect it and that gave Gilles time to turn and take the standard back towards our lines.

Sir Hugo tried to hit me with his shield but I pulled my horse's head around so that Sir Hugo hit fresh air. I lunged at him for the punch with the shield had opened up his side. He barely had time to use his own sword to block the blow. Behind me, I heard the wail as the Earl's men struck the disorganised men at arms and knights. I heard cries of "Mercy!" Sir Hugo whipped the head of his horse around and joined those of his men who had been able to extricate themselves. He fled and the field was ours. We had won. There were no faces before me only the fleeing backs of men who had broken.

The men of arms of the Earl pursued the survivors while we tended to our own. I rode back, with William, to the last stand of the Swabians. He had been my friend but he had also been William's guide. The bodies had been hacked and slashed so that they were barely recognisable. They had been faithful until death. Gilles, with Sir Hugo's standard, made his way to us as did William's men at arms.

I dismounted and looked at Rolf's body. He was beneath his men. I saw that it had been a slash to the neck which had felled him. The huge bloodstain on his surcoat told me that he could have lived only for moments after the blow.

"We bury Rolf and his oathsworn here at the side of the road. Gilles, take the standard you captured from the pole. We wrap him in the banner. It was his victory."

William dismounted and sent men back to get us tools. The rest of the army was busily looting the dead and dispatching the wounded men at arms. In the middle, there was peace and calm as we honoured our dead. All ten of us set to work with silent fortitude. Some of William's men had fallen also and they, too, would be placed in this one grave. The soil was both soft and sandy and we made good progress. We were just laying the first body in the grave when Geoffrey of Anjou and Robert of Gloucester rode up.

Geoffrey was ebullient. "Come Alfraed! It is time to celebrate our great victory. We defeated them easily!"

I looked up at him. Each time I thought he had changed and become the man the Empress and I hoped he would be he said something like that. "First we bury our dead and do them honour."

He looked perplexed, "But your men can do that!"

I pointed at Rolf's body, now wrapped in a shroud made of the Elbeuf banner, "This is the last of the warriors who protected Empress Matilda. They never faltered in their duty and all have now died in the service of Anjou. I know my duty, Count. He was my friend and I shall see him to the Otherworld and then I will mourn for him. When that is done I will celebrate this victory but if you thought it was easy then look at these men who paid for that victory with their lives."

There was an edge to my voice and Robert of Gloucester said, "Come brother, Alfraed is right. There will be time to celebrate but it is not yet."

By the time we had finished and the dead had been laid in the grave, we covered them in soil and finally lined their grave with turf. We were the last ones on the battlefield. It was silent. The wounded had gone and the enemy dead still lay where they had fallen. We stood with heads bowed and I spoke, "Rolf and his brothers, Sir William's men at arms, we salute you. You were warriors to the end. Now you will be with those who have gone before and you will have great tales to tell. The last stand of the Swabians will be told and retold for it was a deed of great courage. Farewell, my friend."

There was a silence that was only broken by a flap of wings from the nearby wood. I saw a hawk rising slowly to climb the thermals. It seemed to circle overhead. I unsheathed my sword and, pointing it to the skies said, "Rolf, Knight of the Empress!"

All those around the grave did the same and said, "Rolf, Knight of the Empress!"

The hawk took flight and headed heavenward to hunt. In my heart, I knew that was the spirit of Rolf.

Chapter 16

We prepared to ride to Lisieux but some survivors must have fled the battle and reached it already for they capitulated before we reached there. They pleaded for peace. Their only chance had gone when Sir Hugo had been defeated. The baron there accepted the authority of the Empress. We set off north-eastwards towards Elbeuf. We were met by a delegation of Norman knights. "Sir Hugo would like to discuss a truce."

The Count and the Earl were delighted. The year had begun with the loss of Normandy now more than half had been recovered in a couple of months. The Earl made arrangements to meet at Elbeuf. After the Normans had departed the two of them began to talk animatedly about the reparations which the defeated knights would have to pay. I knew it was necessary but Rolf's loss was still too raw.

"My lords I will return to Argentan. I must speak with the Empress about Sir Rolf and then I will take ship for England. It is now July and I said I would be home as soon as I could. You no longer need me here and England calls for me."

The Count looked crestfallen, "But Alfraed this is as much your victory as ours! Surely you wish to be there when we humiliate our foes."

I saw that the Earl did not like the words either but this was not the time for a disagreement, "You do not need me there, lord. My son can stay if he wishes."

"No father for I would return to my own manor too. This is not over. Next year we will begin to fight once more and I need to train more men."

The Earl nodded and clasped my arm, "Once again, Alfraed, Earl of Cleveland, I am in your debt. You were ever my father's man. We will send your share of the reparations to your castles. You shall have your share."

"Thank you."

As we headed towards Argentan William was reflective, "Sometimes I think that the Count is just like you, and then at other times, I wonder if he is two people. How can that be?"

"Men are complicated, William. We are made by our fathers and by our experiences. The Count was made vindictive by his father. The Empress has made him a man but sometimes the old Count, the son of Fulk, rises to the surface. One day the demons within him will finish fighting and we shall see the real Count of Anjou."

Word of our victory had reached Argentan and we were greeted like heroes. The details were unknown but they had heard that we had sent the rebels packing and all were in the mood for celebration. The castle was also in high excitement for the Empress was about to give birth to her third child. Despite her confinement, she sent for William and me as soon as we arrived.

"My two heroes!" Henry and Geoffrey were with her in the solar and their faces were filled with joy too. "Tell us all."

"Rolf is dead," I said it flatly and it seemed to puncture the very air of the room. As soon as the words were out I regretted saying them.

The Empress judged my mood and said, "Judith would you take the boys to the hall perhaps young William will tell them of the battle?"

William looked at me and I nodded. He grinned and held his hands out for the boys. "Come and I will regale you with the tale of how your father fought alongside mine to defeat the rebels at Thiberville! How we charged our enemies and drove them from the field!"

There was just Margaret left in the room. The Empress gestured for me to sit next to her. Margaret closed the door so that we would not be disturbed. Maud took my hand, "Tell me all and do not spare my feelings. He was the last of the men the Emperor hired to protect me. I would know how he fell."

By the time I had finished tears coursed down her cheeks. I took the handkerchief and dabbed them away. "Do not grieve for him. He told me, not long before he was killed, that he did not want to waste away. He died the way he wished. He would not have been a burden on any. He is at peace now. It was a good death for he was ready."

"His last visit to Angers now makes sense. He arrived not long after you had left. When I told him you were back he determined to follow you but before he did he asked to be freed from the obligation of being my bodyguard. He said that there were other younger men who could do that." She sighed and squeezed my hand a little tighter. "He left me his treasure. It is in two chests in his quarters. He was ever frugal and over the years he had collected coin and treasure as well as the payments we made. They are for you and for William. He said that William was as close to his own son as he would ever get and that you were like Karl, Godfrey and the others, you were his brothers. The two of you are his heirs."

I nodded, stunned by the gesture, "Then his death was planned. I guessed as much from his words before the battle. It puts my mind at ease."

The Empress nodded. I wondered if I should have been so honest in my account. She shut her eyes. I knew what she thought. Had she known it was the last time she would see him she would have spoken from the heart. Then I saw her wince as a sharp pain seemed to grip her.

"When is the baby due?"

She smiled, "I think you should call my women, Alfraed. You have many skills but delivering a child is not one of them!"

I leapt to my feet and ran to the door, "Margaret! The child! It comes!"

She nodded as she entered, "Be calm my lord. She has had two before. This one will be easier. Find Judith and send her to me. You can care for the boys until we have done." She smiled, It will be good for you to get to know Henry."

Judith smiled when I told her, "You stay with the Earl, boys, while I see to your mother."

Geoffrey was seated upon William's knee and Henry climbed on to mine. His hands played with the blue pommel stone on my sword. "Mother says that you will win back my kingdom for me, lord. Will you?"

"I swore an oath to your grandfather that I would make sure that his wishes were observed so aye I will."

"It will take time will it not, lord?"

"It will." I pointed to a dove that was gathering twigs to build a nest high beneath the castle walls. "Watch that dove, see how he builds a nest." As we watched the dove tried to put three twigs into place. Two fell but one held. It flew away to gather more. "It will take time for that bird to build a nest for its young but it will persevere. When the nest is strong enough only then will the bird trust it to its young. That is what we will do. When your nest is strong enough then you and your mother can come and claim the throne that is rightly yours."

"That may be many years hence."

"Aye, it may."

"Then I shall fight alongside you and William and I will help to regain my birthright!"

"And we will be proud to fight alongside you too. We will help you become a great warrior!" There was a cry from inside and I said, "I am guessing that you have a new brother or sister."

We rose and Judith came running out, "Come boys, you have a new brother. Come and meet William!"

I think my son was more delighted than any. I knew that the baby had been named for his great grandfather but my son took it to be for him. It made him closer to the youngest of the Empress' children.

I had planned on a brief stay but it was not to be. The Empress and her ladies wished me to stay and I could not, in all conscience, say no. I sent Gilles to La Flèche to bring back some men at arms to escort the treasure back to my manor. The inheritance from Rolf was not the only chests we had to escort. Over the next few days, our share from the victory was brought from Caen.

William left before I did. He had enough men to escort his share. "You will return to Stockton father?"

"Aye, I will."

"Would you have me return thither with you?"

I smiled, "Do you wish to do so?"

"Truthfully? No. This is my home and I will be needed to regain the Dukedom for the Empress."

"I think it is for the best. Until we have Normandy I do not think that either the Earl nor the Count will contemplate invading England to reclaim the throne."

William said, "I am not certain that the Count will wish to leave Normandy."

My son had become wiser. "I believe you are right. When Normandy belongs to the Empress again then join me in England."

"What of your manor? Leofric's"

"That will become a place where my men are trained. I will need more men in England and now I have the coin to pay for them. La Flèche is a rich manor and I will use it to keep the north safe. I believe it is what King Henry would have wished."

The Count arrived a day after William left. He was delighted with his son. He saw it propitious that his new son had been born within days of his great victory. My departure for La Flèche was delayed by a further week as we celebrated the birth of his child. The result was that I did not leave for La Flèche until August. I felt I had done more than enough for both the Count and the Earl. I needed to be in England. When Gilles had returned with the men at arms he told me that my ship, *'Adela'*, was in Angers. That solved one problem at least. I would not have to wait for him.

We had captured horses, mail, weapons as well as four chests of coins. I was happy to have my men at arms guard it. The convoy would be a tempting target for any brigand or bandit.

The Empress and the Count came to see me off. The Empress said, "The Count and I are grateful beyond words, Alfraed. When other former allies defected, you remained loyal and we will never forget it. As much as I want the throne of England do not be reckless. You may have to bend. We will understand."

I smiled, "Then you do not know me, lady. I will hold on to the island that is Cleveland and, when the time is right for you to bring forth your forces to England I shall join you."

She nodded and kissed me on the cheek.

The Count clasped my hand, "You stand alone against a sea of enemies. I admire you and your courage. I would that my son learned some of those qualities for he will need them when he attains the throne."

I caught the Empress' eye and she nodded. I reached down to ruffle Henry's hair, "And know this, Henry of Anjou, that I will be at your side when you come to England to claim your birthright. I will be your champion as I was for your mother and your grandfather."

He impulsively threw his arms around my neck and hugged me. It was a struggle to maintain my dignity. I saw the Empress and her ladies well up too. I mounted my horse and left Argentan. I had the seventy-odd miles to La Flèche to reflect on my situation. Gilles was coming to know me and he remained silent as we headed south. We could have stopped along the way; the castellan at Le Mans was keen to speak with one of the heroes of Thiberville but I was anxious to get to my castle. The result was that it was dark when we crossed the bridge to my Angevin manor. Leofric was pleased to see me and his new and heavily pregnant wife also made a great deal of fuss over me.

"My sympathies, my lord, for the death of Rolf. I only served with him briefly but he was a mighty warrior."

"And his death was equally mighty. It was he who won the battle and made the truce. The harvest can be gathered without fear of raids and invasions. Our people will prosper." I waved a hand at the horses which were being unloaded. "I leave some here to pay for the wine and other supplies which I will now need. I rely upon you and your steward to fulfil all of my orders."

"You return to England then lord?"

"You think I should stay here?"

"King Stephen will soon tire of your rebellion, lord and bring his army to crush you."

I shook my head, "Do you have so little faith in me, Leofric? Have you grown so comfortable here? Do you not know how we have fought against great odds many times before?"

He looked distraught, "I am sorry, lord! I meant no offence. I just thought that it was time for you to enjoy some of the riches you have acquired."

I was thinking of Henry of Anjou as I said, "I do this for my son and for the Empress. I gave my word to Henry's grandfather. I will keep my word."

"I understand."

As we made our way in to the hall I said, "You have another task for me while you are castellan. I do not expect you to come to England and fight as much as I would value your skills." I saw his wife breathe a sigh of relief, "However I expect you to train and supply me with a steady source of men at arms. Now that the truce is in place there will be men at arms who seek employers. Spread the word that you are interested. Have Brian and Padraig select the best and they will be sent to England. You can keep any of the rest."

"I will, lord, but we have enough men here now."

"We have bought peace but war will return, Leofric, and you must be ready. This castle was in disrepair when I came here. I would have it better than it was."

"Aye, lord."

I spent a few days at La Flèche and made sure that Leofric had his fair share of the weapons, coins and armour. The remaining horses, however, would be needed in England. Leofric could buy more and I could not. I sent the goods to be transported down to *'Adela'*. William would need time to load the valuable horses.

As I was leaving I said, "What we lacked at Thiberville, Leofric, was archers. I know the skill does not come naturally to the Angevin but have Griff of Gwent seek out those local youths with potential. Pay them well and have Griff train them. You and I will need them before too long."

The next time that my captain, William, sailed for Anjou I would have him bring the ship to La Flèche. The journey to Angers was too long. I was impatient to get home and as I headed down the road I wondered what problems lay in my land and what mischief the Scots had in mind. The *'Adela'* was heavily laden. When I reached Angers I could see that William was eager to leave.

"The horses have been a little restless lord. They like not the ship."

"Fear not William, Gilles can speak to horses and as these are Norman he knows their own particular language."

I allowed him to concentrate as we negotiated our way through the busy river and headed downstream to the sea. Once we left the crowded river and struck the sea he was able to hand over the helm to Henri the Breton. He knew the waters as well as any and I could hear, from their banter, that they worked well together.

"How is the ship, William of Kingston? Does it match your expectations?"

"She sails well enough but when time allows I will balance her ballast a little better. I can sail her closer to the wind."

I did not understand what he meant but it sounded good. "And the crew?"

"Ah, they are a different matter. I cannot fault them. They work well together and are good seamen. We have begun to train with war bows as you suggested."

"Good. And the Tees is it still in our hands?"

"Aye, lord. It is quiet enough. There appears to be peace and your castle prospers. The wine you sent last time was much appreciated and the spices sold for a high price. I bought some more on my own account." He gave me an apprehensive look, "You said that I might."

"Of course. And I shall want you to return immediately we dock. Leofric will have more goods and, perhaps, men when next you dock. I would have you try to sail up the Loir to La Flèche. The salt barges manage it and it will save you having to negotiate the Loire."

He tapped Henri on the shoulder, "Henri, the Loir, can the *'Adela'* navigate it?"

"Oh, aye captain. There is a good channel. You mean La Flèche?" I nodded, "We can reach there. I used to work the barges. It is easier to dock there too."

"Then I can do as you wish, Lord."

We were lucky with the weather. August could sometimes bring brutal squalls from the southwest. The winds still blew from that direction but they were gentle. We beat through the Channel and towards our home. It was not a swift voyage. We were heavily laden and the winds were not strong enough but it was a safe journey. I put my mail on when we passed the mouth of the Humber. King Stephen might have declared a truce but I had made enough enemies over the years for one of his knights to, perhaps, decide to make a name for himself and capture the Earl of Stockton.

I viewed my river differently from my other journeys home. Now I was sailing through land controlled by those who sought to defeat me. There were no castles and defences until you reached Stockton and I wondered how long it would be before someone decided to try to build on the salt marshes and sandy shores. Even As soon as the thought came into my head I dismissed it. Stockton was the only place upon which one could build a castle. So long as I held the castle then the river was mine. Had King Henry deduced that too? Was that why he had made me Earl of such a strategic valley?

The fluttering wolf on my keep was a welcoming sight. I had fought for others and now I would fight for myself. I now knew that it would be years before Normandy was conquered and the Empress was able to think about England. Until then I was the only hope. I knew what I had to do.

The smiles and cheers when I stepped ashore were heart-warming. This was not Normandy, this was England and I could never be attached to Normandy. England was in my blood. And so long as that blood coursed through my veins then I would fight for her.

Warlord

Chapter 17

I almost felt suffocated when I landed. I was pressed on all sides. John my steward had a smile as wide as the River Tees and a bundle of documents in his hand. Alice curtsied and smiled and asked how long I would be at home. John, my castellan, was keen to know how Leofric was and Wulfric and Dick had the looks of men with much to say. I held up my hands, "Thank you for your welcome. John and Alice, there are spices and other goods on my ship which require carriage to my castle. There are horses whose unloading Gilles will supervise. They need stables. When that is done then I pray you to come to my hall so that I may speak with you." They bowed, curtsied and hurried off. "You three come with me I know you have much to say."

"Aye lord, " John sounded almost worried.

Wulfric nudged Dick, "And that is why the Earl is such a good general, he knows how to avoid an ambush and beat a hasty retreat without losing face."

"You have never been married, Wulfric, it is a skill every married man learns!"

Once in the hall, I sat on my chair. My legs were still a little unsteady after so many days at sea. John poured me some wine. I drank deeply. My Angevin manor produced good wine. "Now, pour yourselves some wine and then speak. Tell me the news which is bursting from within you."

They both deferred to John. "My lord, the usurper has lost more of Wales. One or two castles hold out but it is largely lost." I nodded, I had heard that. "Balliol and De Brus are now in London. They are reconciled with Stephen the Usurper and he gives them honours and titles. It is said he is angry that you gave Barnard Castle to Sir Hugh."

"I shall not lose much sleep worrying about upsetting a usurper. However, I do not like the fact that those two have benefitted from Stephen's favour. The next time they are in my sword length they shall die. And the Scots themselves?"

Dick shook his head, "I have had my men spying upon them. They see an opportunity to defeat you whilst not upsetting Stephen or breaking the peace."

That was more serious and a threat I would have to deal with. "Have they made any moves yet?"

"No, Earl. I have had patrols watching for the places they might cross into the valley. Sir Hugh has done the same. Sir Hugh Manningham also sent a man, Oswald, to tell you that he has heard of plans being made north of the border. They are rumours which are like a will o' the-wisp. They are hard to put flesh upon."

Wulfric downed the last of his wine, "My fear, lord, is Durham. The Bishop is a weak man. I would not like them to come through our back door. We have made the west a solid wall but the north..."

"Then we plan for an attack from there. Any more news?"

Wulfric stroked his beard, "I think there are spies operating close to the castle or the town. If I am honest I think the town."

"What makes you say that?"

"We have found camps which we did not expect. There are fires that our people did not make. If we have spies close to Scotland then it stands to reason they have the same. We just cannot find them."

Dick nodded, "It was my hunters who spied them. The problem is that there are many people who come to Stockton to trade and for work. Some of the camps may well be honest travellers but..."

"But you do not think so?"

"No lord. Travellers leave more signs and clues as to who they are. All that we find are the burnt-out remains of fires and footprints which are hard to read. These are people who know how to hide their tracks. That sounds like spies to Wulfric and me."

"And what have you done to find them?"

"It is difficult, lord, for we know not if we seek a man, a woman, a youth, a couple... it is not like Lavinia who sought work in the castle. None have done that. We can spot spies who are soldiers but...these may well be ordinary folk. I am sorry lord, we should have done better."

I waved a hand, "I should have been here and now I will put my mind to that. Do you think that they have much to report?"

"Numbers of men, defences, that sort of thing. Where our archers patrol. They will be looking for a pattern and, perhaps, weakness."

"Then, Wulfric, let us change the numbers and the routes our men patrol. We are now on a war footing." They nodded. "On a more optimistic note, I have brought treasure, horses and weapons from Normandy." I smiled, "We were successful."

"And how is William?"

"He has his own manor now and a conroi of his own. He fought well. He is a man now and reflects well the training he received from you Wulfric and you John."

"He was easy to train, lord. He had a natural ability like his father." I nodded my thanks. From many men, it would be empty flattery but Wulfric was always honest. "And Rolf?"

"He is with his brothers in the otherworld."

"He died well, lord?"

"He won the battle for us and his oathsworn died protecting his body."

Wulfric nodded his approval, "As they should. I hope that I shall go the same way."

"Do not rush, will you, Wulfric? I fear I shall need you by my side for many years."

"Aye, I will, lord."

"And I have asked Leofric to find more men at arms for us. With the cessation of hostilities in Normandy, there should be men looking for a banner to follow. Perhaps they will choose mine. Brian will ensure that they are of the right standard." John refilled the goblets, "How goes the training of the archers?"

Dick shook his head, "Slowly, lord. It is the strength we need to build up. Until they have muscle and can pull back the war bow it matters not how accurate they are. It is a matter of strength but we progress, we have another ten archers. Perhaps by Spring, we may have another ten."

"I pray we have until Spring."

"Amen to that Lord."

"And my other knights how do they fare?"

"Sir Tristan and Sir Harold have improved their castles immeasurably."

I laughed, "In Harold's case that would not be hard! He only had a hall!"

"He now has a stone tower and a ditch. He has diverted the two streams to form a moat. I think his new wife has made him worry a little more."

"Norton?"

"The people there are happy enough, lord and we visit each day. I have two riders go out each day to visit Norton, Hartburn and Elton. It is good training for them and they combine the ride with hunting. We eat well."

"Let us not hunt too many of our own animals. Next week let us hunt in the woods close by Guisborough. If De Brus is with Stephen of Blois then he will not need his own animals."

They left when Alice and John my steward arrived. Both were more than happy with the coin and the supplies I had brought. "And your ship, John, the one you and Ethelred are building; how goes it?"

"Not as fast as we had hoped lord but it will be ready by Spring."

"Until then I intend to send *'Adela'* to La Flèche every month. William of Kingston is happy about that. He will bring back wine, spices and men. There will be plenty of room for your goods on board."

"Thank you, my lord,!"

I smiled, "And of course, William will not charge you excessively!"

He shook his head ruefully, "You are learning from me, my lord."

"Alice, I need women of the town to make surcoats for the men I have yet to hire. I will pay them. Could you organise that for me?"

"Of course, my lord."

"And now that Gilles is my squire he will need to have chambers in the hall. John you must teach him to read and to write."

John did not look happy and Alice said, "Lord, I can read and write. I would enjoy the task."

I think John was surprised by her offer. I was not. She had not been able to have children and the opportunity to be as a mother to Gilles was appealing. "Thank you, Alice, I would appreciate it."

I rode, the next day, to tell my knights of the news from Normandy. I knew that it would bring them hope. It brought the day that the Empress would come to England that much closer. I also told them of Rolf. They all knew him and it saddened each of them. Edward was affected the most. We had fought together and now there were just three knights of the Empress left. Edward was feeling his mortality.

When I went to visit I took Gilles and Aiden with me. I had plans for Aiden. As we returned from visiting Norton I said, "Aiden I wish you to travel to Sir Hugh Manningham. But you must use the back roads and the secret roads. I want none to know that you go on an errand for me."

"I will do that lord. Is that why you brought me here with just you and Gilles?"

"It is. There are spies operating in my valley. Dick has found their camps. You must have seen them too." He nodded. "Sir Hugh is still a friend and he may now know who conspires against me. Is it Gospatric or is there another? If I know the name of my enemy then I can do something about it."

Aiden nodded, "There is another way, lord. Let me hunt them."

"When you return from your mission we will do that but it is the head which must be removed. While you are away I intend to sweep and scour my lands."

Gilled asked, "Why Sir Hugh in Hexham, lord? Surely the west of your land is where the Scots are the most dangerous."

"They are but both Wulfric and Dick fear danger from the north and I am inclined to agree with them. The Roman Wall is the easiest place for an enemy to slip through. Sir Hugh Manningham has fewer men now for he must watch the Tweed too. If Baron Hexham has heard nothing I will send to Sir Hugh of Gainford."

"I will leave before dawn, lord. It will take me some days to take the greenways and the backways."

"Just be safe."

I organised the hunt for the spies as soon as I got back. While Aiden was heading north I had every archer and every man at arms not on sentry duty riding through my woods and forests seeking out those who might be spies. When we returned at the end of the day I discovered that there was no sign of recent camps. John had fretted about the camps for he felt that he should have done something about them in my absence.

"If I had been more vigilant in your absence, lord, this would not have happened."

"When we look back, John, our eyes can see much further! It is in the past and it is gone. Let it go."

"But what do we do now, lord?"

"It has made our task easier."

All three looked at me in surprise. "Easier, lord?"

"Yes, John. If the spies are not in the woods then there is but one place left for them. Stockton. The camps were needed while they established themselves."

"Spies? More than one?"

"The camps we found were occupied by more than one person. They will be in Stockton."

"But we have had many new incomers of late."

"These spies have to get their information back to their lord and master. We look for someone who comes and goes. They will be one of the spies. A spy who stays in Stockton is useless to his master."

It was a place to start but, before I ate I visited Alf. Taking him to one side I explained the news we had discovered. "Are you certain, lord? All of those who have joined us seem to be the kind of people we would welcome."

"If you were a spy in a Scottish camp you would say good things about King David and you would insult me would you not? That is what makes them a spy. These people will appear to think as we do. Remember Lavinia."

"Aye lord." He rubbed his chin. "If you are right then there are but four people whom it could be. Ethelred has a new man who travels to Barnard Castle for him. Ethelred has a number of women in Barnard town who spin wool for him. The wool of the upland sheep is good. This is but a recent turn of events. It has only begun since Sir Hugh of Gainford became lord of Barnard. Stephen of Coxhoe is his name. He appears to be a diligent worker and Ethelred is pleased with his honesty."

"He sounds likely. He could easily pass a message to another spy in Barnard. We may not be the only place they have spawned. And the others?"

"Father Henry has a new servant. He travels once a week to York. The priests of Durham still send messages to York. Since we hold the ferry they only come south as far as Stockton."

"And his name?"

"Alan Squint Eye."

"He too is likely. This may prove harder than I thought. The third?"

"Edgar son of Tom. He gathers wood for Harold the Fletcher. He travels far afield to seek the best shafts. Sometimes he is away for two or three days at a time. He always brings back good wood but he could meet someone on our borders. You could travel many miles in two or three days."

"And the fourth?"

"Robert of Whitby. He is a fisherman. He plies his trade at the mouth of the river and beyond. He is a popular man for he always catches bigger fish than the river fishermen."

"Surely he comes back with his catch each day?"

"Normally he does but sometimes he has to travel further out to where the fish congregate. He says the mouth of the Tees, whilst dangerous, is rich with fish. I have known him to be away for two or three days at a time but he always returns with a good catch."

"This will take some careful planning but I will catch these spies. Tomorrow I will return, Alf and you shall take me around my town so that I may see these four. We will say that I am keen to see how my people fare. I want to know who these four see regularly. It will be those who are incomers anyway."

"I am sorry for this, lord, but I find it hard to believe that there could be a spy. These four are hard workers. Robert of Whitby and Alan Squint Eye are religious. They are often found in the Church."

"The Pope himself uses spies, Alf. If it were not for the well-disguised tracks in the woods I would agree that these four may be innocent but I have seen the evidence with my own eyes. There are spies in our town. The alternative is even more worrying that someone we know well spies. We are now outlaws, Alf and must rely upon our own resources to survive."

When I told Wulfric he was a little more direct. "Lord this is easy. Have the four arrested and let me question them. I will discover the truth."

I shook my head, "That may well be a solution but we will try other ways first. If we are wrong then arresting these four alerts the real spies. These are the ones we investigate first. I have ideas about how to trap them but let us just watch them first."

Over the next four days, I saw all of the suspects. None, at first sight, appeared disloyal. As I had learned to my cost first appearances could be deceptive. When Aiden returned he brought equally disturbing news, "Lord Sir Hugh knew nothing of spies but he has heard from his own spies that Barnard Balliol's cousin, Baron Skipton, is raising an army north of the border."

Baron Skipton's land was to the south of the Tees. It was almost in the centre of the country and if the Scots held that then we had a dagger held at the heart of the north. With Balliol and Stephen reconciled it could well be that they thought it a good time to retake their lands. As I ran Aiden's words through my head I remembered that Balliol had also claimed the manor of Piercebridge. King Henry had given it, instead, to Wilfred's father.

"Did Sir Hugh know where this army would march?"

"He said to tell you that it would not be on his side of the country but when the poor weather closes in then his control of the Roman Wall is tenuous at best. He said that men could slip over. He is right, lord. I have done it many times myself. There are few roads north of the wall but many well-used trails. The gates through the wall are now open. Once through there is naught to stop an army."

"Except for Barnard Castle which blocks that route and the other is through Auckland and towards our back door. You have done well Aiden."

"And tomorrow I will take my falconers Edward and Edgar. We will seek out these camps."

"We have looked and they are all cold."

"Nonetheless I will be happier lord when I have cast my eye over them."

My three lieutenants were as disappointed as I was with the news. The watch over the four would be spies had yielded nothing. I began to wonder if Wulfric's draconian solution was the only one.

"At last, lord, we can prepare for their attack in winter. We know from whence they will come and we can be ready."

Wulfric growled, "You may be right, Sir John but remember how we took Barnard Castle. Unless we have rid ourselves of all spies then they may well be within our walls and that could spell disaster. They could open the gates for the barbarians."

"Then we must smoke them out."

"How lord?"

"We use William the Mason. I will prepare him. The great danger to our enemies is that we make it harder for them to gain entry from the north. We have just improved the western gate to the town but the north gate is still largely wood with a stone foundation. If we were to say that we were building a better gate there then the spy would have news to take north. We have each one watched by a pair of Dick's archers and when they leave, we follow them. If they go about their lawful business and do not leave a message or meet anyone then they are innocent."

Dick nodded his approval but Wulfric said, reasonably, "Why not actually improve the gate? It makes sense."

"William and his masons are still helping Sir Harold and Sir Tristan. I would not leave those two exposed. We shall improve the north gate but that will be in spring."

Dick said, "I will have my archers watch them anyway."

"Will that not make our suspects suspicious, Dick?"

"No Sir John, my archers are busy at this time of year making arrows. We do not do it in one place. It will help make our suspects less alert. They will become used to their presence. It is like a hunter in the forest. He hides until the animal no longer sees him."

William was happy to be part of the deception. He and I went to the north gate and we took measurements and discussed, loudly, what stone we might need and when the work might begin. I hated to deceive both Alf and Ethelred but when we came into the main square we discussed the improvements with the two of them. It meant that, by nightfall, the whole town was talking about the new gate and how it would make us safer.

The only one who left was Robert of Whitby. He left on the evening tide. He was the only one we could not follow. Dick berated himself, "I should have thought of this problem."

"Dick, ask the archers who watched him to come here." When they were brought to us I asked, "Who are the ones Robert of Whitby speaks with?"

Long Tom said, "He is a queer stick, my lord. He keeps to himself but he is a religious fellow. He visits the church each day and prays for half an hour or so."

I felt the hairs on the back of my neck begin to prickle. "When he is in there is there anyone else inside the church?"

"Sometimes Father Henry although he was not there the last time he visited."

"No one else?"

Rafe who had been watching with Long Tom said, "There is only that servant, Alan Squint Eye. He cleans the church."

I turned to Dick. "I think we have our two spies. Unless I miss my guess when Robert returns, Alan Squint Eye will visit York. It is clear now. The two spies allow our enemies to have two avenues of communication. I have no doubt now that Robert makes contact with Guisborough. We know the de Brus are traitors. There will also be a spy in York. I will send Philip of Selby to speak privately with the Archbishop."

Wulfric, who was now with us said, "And then do we question this fisherman?"

"When Alan Squint Eye has left for York, aye we will."

The fisherman returned two days later. Now that we were watching for him his movements became clear. He unloaded and sold his fish remarkably quickly. I could tell that he had not charged enough for his customers were delighted at the prices they had paid. He then went immediately to the church. Alan Squint Eye must have been watching for he followed him into the church. Now that we knew the conspirators their collusion was obvious. After the fisherman and Alan Squint Eye left the church Alan hurried in to speak with the priest.

"Wulfric, take three men at arms and get on the York road. When he gets to York then see whom he meets. Apprehend him on the way back. We know he will be going there and if you are before him then he will not be suspicious. Shadow him in York."

"And if he sees us, lord?"

"Offer to escort him and tell him you have a letter for the Archbishop from me. He will be slower than you. I would wait at the inn in Easingwold until he has passed."

Wulfric quickly left and I saw him and his two men at arms on the ferry. They crossed, thereby giving them a lead over the spy. That would ensure a healthy gap between them and Alan Squint Eye. The spy emerged and led the poor sumpter he used to the ferry to wait. I found Father Henry tending his small herb garden. "Your servant is going somewhere, Father Henry?"

He nodded, "I have to keep in touch with the Archbishop. He needs a record of the births, deaths and marriages." He shrugged, "And he likes to keep in touch with the church here. We are part of the Diocese of Durham, lord."

"I know and I was not criticising. I merely wondered why he was going today."

"Ah, he reminded me that I needed some more candles for the church. We used our last one three days since."

"You should have said, I would have brought some back with me from Normandy. They make fine ones there."

"And I will do so for it is annoying when we run out. He is a good and hardworking servant but sometimes he forgets to remind me of such needs. Still, he is always happy to travel the long road to York for me."

After I had left him I felt guilty for deceiving him however if I was wrong I would have upset him for nothing. Meanwhile, John, along with Erre and Sven the Rus had gone down to the river to fetch Robert of Whitby.

I waited for them in my hall. When he arrived he looked confused, "Have I done wrong, lord? Why have I been dragged from my boat by these two Vikings? I am an innocent man."

I smiled, "Then you are truly blessed. Erre are you an innocent man?"

He laughed, "Why no lord, I have done many things which I should not."

"And I know that I have committed crimes and sins but perhaps your frequent visits to the church means that you have absolution and that you are, truly, an innocent man. Is that it, Robert of Whitby?"

For the first time, a look of doubt flickered across his face, "I do visit the church regularly, lord. Is that a crime?"

"Of course not." I smiled, "You came to my town when I was in Normandy and I know you not. My men tell me you are a good fisherman but somewhat lonely."

"I am happy with my own company it is true."
"You seem to have a good friend in Alan Squint Eye."
"I know him but..."
"Did you know him before you came to my town?"

This time his eyes flickered. Whatever he said would be a lie. "No, lord."

"I am not satisfied, Robert of Whitby. I need to investigate more. Until then you shall be my guest."

He tried to rise but Sven the Rus' hand clamped on his shoulder. "My lord, I protest."

"Protest all you like until I am happy then you stay here. Sven, take him to my dungeon. Have him watched." When they had gone I turned to John and Erre. "Well?"

Erre said, "He lies."

"I am not certain."

Erre shook his head, "The trouble is, Sir John, that you have not met many liars yet. I lived in Miklagård. I can smell a liar."

"Thank you both and now we wait for Wulfric."

I know that I was jumping at shadows but I liked not this conspiracy. I wondered if I should visit my wrath upon Guisborough. If there were enemies there I should rid myself of them. Why did Alan go there first and then speak with the church spy? It made no sense. Either way, a message could not reach north of the border for many days. Dick and his archers had reported that the other suspects never left the town except on legitimate business. They would still be watched but as they had not risen to the bait then they were no longer such good candidates.

Wulfric and my men returned three days later with a very unhappy spy. He looked to have been knocked about. Father Henry happened to be in his garden when Alan Squint Eye was brought to my gate. "Wulfric, what are you doing with my servant?"

I stepped forward, "He is obeying my orders, Father. I pray you to join us and listen to what Wulfric says before you judge us."

He knew me well enough to agree and he followed his servant.

Once in my hall, Father Henry and I sat. I said, "Wulfric tell me what you saw."

"We followed this man when he went to York. He did not go to the Archbishop's palace. He went directly to the *'Blind Beggar'*, the inn by the river and sat there for an hour until the captain of a small merchant ship docked and came to speak with him. They spoke for an hour. This man gave the sailor a document and then he left and went to the Archbishop. The merchant ship left straightaway. They unloaded nothing else. The ship arrived just to meet with this man."

Father Henry frowned. Until that moment I believe he thought we had lost our minds.

Alan Squint Eye said, none too convincingly, "It is a lie."

"Why did you not go directly to the Archbishop as I asked?" Father Henry spoke calmly. I knew he was looking for a reasonable explanation.

He said nothing and Wulfric put the final nail in his coffin, "When I delivered the letter to the Archbishop I asked his clerk about Alan Squint Eye here. He said he never stayed long and often left before the Archbishop could see if a return message was needed."

Silence hung in my hall like some heavy weight. I spoke quietly. "The fact that you had no reason to speak with this captain who came just to speak with you strikes me as damning evidence. Your defence is to call Wulfric a liar. Even I would not do that. He speaks the truth. We know about the messages passed to you by Robert of Whitby. I need to know who is your master and why you use such a complicated method." The spy remained obstinately silent. I let the silence hang in my hall and then delivered the killer blow. "Robert of Whitby lies in my dungeon."

There was fear in the spy's eyes. What did we know?

He appealed to Father Henry. "I had to do it, Father."

"Speak the truth, my son and I shall absolve you of your sins. There is little point in deception any longer. The Earl knows your perfidy and treachery."

"And if I tell you the truth, what then?"

"You will be sentenced to labour in the borough for ten years."

"Ten years! That is a lifetime!"

"No, the punishment, if you do not tell the truth, is death, that is a lifetime."

He suddenly became defiant. "Your town will not last for ten years! Baron Skipton will have taken your town before the year is out."

"Why did your fellow spy have to sail to the mouth of the river and back?"

Father Henry said, "Speak. Hard labour is better than death."

"There is a lookout on Eston Nab. The men of Guisborough keep a watch there. They look for the arrival and departures of your ship. When Robert sails and he wants to tell them we have news then he hangs two lights from his stern. A message is sent to Whitby and then a ship sails to York. I meet the Captain and tell him what we know." He shrugged, "We thought it foolproof for you cannot land a ship in the swamp between the river and the hills. I had plenty of excuses to go to York and to give the message. They were spoken so that none could trace them or intercept them."

I nodded, "And the Baron will attack soon."

He looked afraid, "I am not certain, lord. I believe so. Your new gate means they will find it harder to attack."

"You seem knowledgeable."

"We were both men at arms who served the Baron. When my eye was injured I could not fight as well as once I had and Robert had the coughing sickness. He is my brother."

I nodded, "Take him and put the brothers together." Once they had gone I said, "I am sorry Father but I could not tell you until I had proof."

"I understand. And now we will be attacked again?"

"I fear so. We could not stop the message being sent and when they hear that we are making our gate stronger they will attack sooner rather than later."

Wulfric said, "Aye lord and now we know that they are watching for our ship they will find out that we are being reinforced."

"Then tomorrow we ride and destroy this tower. Have the men prepare to ride before dawn."

I prayed that they would wait until we had the harvest in before they attacked. If not, it would be a long and hungry winter.

Chapter 18

It was an hour after dawn as we made our way up the southern side of Eston Nab. There looked to have been an ancient fort here. It had long gone but the lords of Guisborough had built a tower of stone in the centre of the mound of lumps and bumps. We spied the castle from some way away. It looked, even from a distance, to have been crudely built. We dismounted and made our way towards it. I guessed that they would keep watch on the river rather than the land to the south. We used the natural cover which was to the landward side, De Brus land. I saw hoof prints as we moved across the scrubland which was covered with stunted trees and hardy bushes. I saw a horse tethered to a post at the bottom of the tower.

The stone tower was thirty feet high and newly built. The mortar was bright and lichen had yet to colonise it. The tower itself reminded me of the tower at Otterburn. As we drew closer I saw more of its features. There was a door that was ten feet or so from the ground. Obviously, they had a ladder which they lowered. I had brought twenty men at arms and eight archers along with Sir John and Gilles. I had deemed that to be more than enough. I planned on destroying it the way I had the keep in Normandy. I would burn it to the ground. Hopefully, the sentries would give in first but one way or another I would destroy it.

The door opened and a ladder dropped to the ground. As the sentry began to descend he saw us. He raced back up the ladder. There was little point in hiding. "Run!"

We ran towards the tower. The ladder was pulled up and the door slammed before we could reach it. The problem would be setting fire to the door. It was too high for us to build a fire next to it. Crossbow bolts flew from the top of the tower. They were ineffective against our shields. Dick's archers let loose with the bows. Hiding behind a wall of shields held by our men at arms they were able to rain arrows at the top of the tower. A warrior, still clutching his crossbow, fell to earth. His neck was transfixed by a goose feathered shaft.

We ran to take shelter next to the walls of the tower. They could do us no harm there. With my archers watching for movement on the top there was a stalemate. I went to the door and shouted, "This is the Earl of Cleveland! Surrender and you shall live. Fight and you will die."

A voice from inside said, "Do your worst. When our relief comes they will bring help from the castle."

I turned to Sir John, "Take four men at arms and ride towards the castle, ambush the relief."

Wulfric and Leopold of Durstein were with me. I said quietly, "He is right. We cannot winkle them out."

Wulfric knelt down and rubbed his axe along the lime mortar about three stones up from the ground. The mortar came away. He went to the dead crossbowman and took the man's short sword and dagger. He handed the dagger to Leopold. "Scrape away the mortar. They have done a poor job of building. This was not done by a mason." As the two of them began to scrape I saw what he meant. They had not used finished stone. They had taken whatever lay about. The result was that the courses were uneven. A mason would have ensured that the foundation levels were solid and well laid.

I went to the crossbowman and took some of his bolts. I waved over Alan of Osmotherley and Gurth. "Here do as Wulfric is doing to the next stone along." I did the same on the other side.

Soon we were loosening three stones in a row. Wulfric and Leopold finished first and they used the short sword and dagger to lever out the stone. They began work on the one above. Having levered one out Alan and Gurth made short work of the second stone. Mine took longer by which time Wulfric was ready to take out the next one. A small crack appeared above the large gap we had made.

"Now the level below. We make it unstable, my lord."

The men inside raced to the top of the tower when they heard us working and peered down but were driven back by my archers. They could hear us but I doubted they knew what we were doing. The more stones we took the easier it became. The gaps meant we only had three sides of each stone to chip away. When the next three stones came out the crack lengthened.

"Fetch kindling. Wulfric, try the inside stone." The tower had been built with a double course of stones. There was a slight gap between. It was hard work once more as Wulfric and Leopold attacked a secure stone on the inside of the tower but they persevered. By the time they had levered it out kindling had been brought. I saw a wooden frame on the other side of the hole. "Pack it with kindling. Wulfric, loosen another few stones while we may."

Dick came over with a flint. He had gathered some wool from the gorse which lined the hill. Soon his spark set light to the wool and then the kindling. The gap in the walls drew the flames up. They also sucked the fire inside the tower through the small gap which Wulfric had made. Within a short time, it was too hot for us to work. Wulfric and Leopold levered their last stone and then ran with us to a safe distance. The door opened and the ladder, now on fire, was lowered to the ground. The small garrison who remained, all five of them, descended. I saw that the last one had his clothes burning.

"Dick secure the prisoners and make sure they do not burn to death. One must have still been inside for a fireball emerged and tried to climb down the flaming ladder. It broke and he fell. I hoped he had broken his neck for he continued to burn at the foot of the ladder. The prisoners were brought over and we all watched as the flames consumed the tower as the crack which Wulfric had started raced to the top. It was a race between the flames and the damage to the tower. Without warning, there was a sound like a crack of thunder and then the whole tower tumbled down the hill. The hillside was set alight.

I went to the prisoners. "I should kill you for I gave you fair warning."

"We throw ourselves upon your mercy."

"Bind their hands behind their backs and put a halter around their necks. We will take them to Stockton for judgement."

We had just mounted and were setting off down the hill when Gilles rode up, "Lord, there are horsemen from the castle. They are heading here. Sir John and the men at arms are lower down the hill. He said he would hold them until you came."

"Dick, leave two men with Gilles to guard the prisoners. The rest of you, follow me!"

I drew my sword as I led my men at arms towards the distant sound of metal on metal. I had been the first to mount and Scout was eager to run. We hurtled recklessly down the trail. I spied Sir John and the men at arms ahead. They were fighting against overwhelming odds. Mounted men at arms had ridden from Guisborough; obviously, the smoke had alerted them. The only thing which was saving my men was their armour. That would not save them for long.

Common sense said to slow down but I did not employ common sense. I saw Theobald son of Henry struck simultaneously by two blows and he fell to the ground. I watched as a man at arms raised his spear to skewer the fallen man at arms. Sir John bravely urged his horse forward so that he took the blow on his helmet. I saw that he was stunned. I crashed through the enemy. Riding with just my knees I punched with my shield as I slashed with my sword. When a maniac attacks you then you turn. The enemy pulled their horses' heads away from my headlong flight. I saw one Scot trying to pull away but his horse had panicked As I grabbed my reins and jerked Scout to the left I swung my sword to slice through his arm and to bite into his chest. I did not wait to see the result. I headed back up the hill. Wulfric and my other men at arms had reached our fallen man and Dick and his archers loosed arrows with unerring accuracy. Even as I swung my sword at a man of arms who was trying to flee, it was over. My sword took the Scot's head which flew into the air and then rolled to a halt by John's horse, staring at the sky through dead eyes.

Edgar leapt from his horse and knelt by Theobald. The ones who had not been slain surrendered. "How is he?"

"They are bad wounds, my lord. Leopold, fetch a burning brand from the tower. I have to stop the bleeding."

"Wulfric, bind our prisoners and collect their horses."

I rode up to John. He had taken off his helmet and I saw blood dripping down his face. "That was brave, John. You do not need to prove yourself whether to me or to my men at arms."

"I could not let him be speared like a wild pig."

"Aye well, next time try a fighting withdrawal rather than taking on such superior numbers. I cannot afford to lose such a good knight as you!"

"They came at us really quickly, Earl. We only saw them late."

Leopold brought the brands and the archers brought the other prisoners. I heard the hiss as the wounds were cauterized. "Sir John, you and Wulfric, escort the prisoners back to my castle. Dick bring your archers. We will ride to Guisborough and let them know I am displeased. Come, Gilles!"

As we joined the road which led to Guisborough, Gilles asked, "Why do we not bring men at arms, Earl?"

I laughed, "I do not need them. With Dick and his archers, I am as safe as I would be behind a wall of armour. Any who try treachery will not make two steps before they are slain."

When we reached the castle, I saw that the gates were barred and the walls lined with warriors.

I lifted my helmet and lowered my coif so that they could see who I was and I shouted. "I have either slain or captured the men you sent. Your tower is destroyed and you have broken the peace. Robert de Brus promised me that he would not fight me. I come to tell you that I intend to make you and your people pay for the attack. If you wish your men at arms to be returned to you then the price is ten gold pieces for each one. If you do not, then no matter, we need slaves to make our castle even stronger. You have seven days to bring the coin to my castle after that do not bother."

I did not wait for a reply. I pulled Scout around and we headed towards Sneaton and home. I had achieved what I intended and more. While we waited for the attack from the north, which I knew would not be long in coming, I would punish the De Brus clan. Harvest time was coming and I would tax them by taking what they had grown. I would seize their animals and I would burn their farms. Their treachery would be punished.

Theobald recovered from his wounds but he would not be riding to war when war came. He would take time to heal. And there was no doubt that war was close by. We were now on a war footing. I warned Alf and Ethelred that I expected a warband from the north. My archers rode around the outlying farmsteads to warn them of the danger and to look for enemies. Aiden and his falconers scoured the woods looking for signs of spies. When my ship arrived with eight new men at arms I felt a little relieved. I could afford to leave more men at arms to guard my castle. There would be little point in destroying an enemy warband if I left my castle open for attack.

The shipwrights had finished Ethelred and John's ship. We crewed her from the town for William of Kingston would command the tiny flotilla. With his own trained archers on board, the *'Adela'* would give any attacker a shock; she had teeth.

The captives were not ransomed. Perhaps the de Brus feared treachery or did not have the money. It may have been that they were waiting for word from Robert de Brus, now campaigning with Stephen of Blois against the Welsh. Whatever the reason the men at arms now wore yokes around their necks and were tethered at night. They would be more mouths to feed but their former masters would be paying.

At the end of the seven days, I had allowed, I led half of my men at arms and archers and we began to raid the farms which supplied Guisborough. We took only the lord of the manor's share. We harmed no farmer but we took half of their crops and half of their animals. If they were sensible they would tell the reeve that we had taken it all. On the second day, the other half of my men, led by John continued my raids. The newly acquired labourers toiled to build new granaries and storehouses. Now that the men of Cowpen had moved to Norton we used the outer bailey we had built for them. The animals were penned by the river. With a solid wall and a tower there they could be better protected.

By the time the second week of October came there were neither crops nor animals left to be gathered from the lands to the east of us. A letter came from the Archbishop in the first week complaining of my privations. I got the impression that it had been written to fulfil an order from London. It felt like a slap on the hand, and a gentle one at that.

We had still no word from Hexham of any danger. My archers rode, each day, to the borders of my land and beyond. I went with my new men at arms to visit Sir Hugh of Gainford. He also had spies out. I hoped that he had heard something. He had not been idle at Barnard Castle. There were new defences. The ramparts had small roofs over them so that there would be protection from arrows. When he greeted me I no longer saw the boy who had survived the massacre of his family all those years ago; I saw the man. I realised the difference when his wife showed me their new child, a son.

"My lord this is Richard our son. He is a healthy boy."

"Aye," Sir Hugh stroked his son's head, "I now understand much more about being a knight lord. Young Richard is a reason to fight to protect his birthright from all enemies."

I led him away from his wife. I did not wish to upset her. "And have you heard anything about an attack?"

"There have been scouts and spies but my archers have sent them packing. The bodies of ten lie unburied in the woods to the west."

"And from the north?"

"Nothing! Why, Earl?"

"I have it on good authority that the Baron of Skipton intends to come south and attack my lands. It may be that he comes this way too but he hates me and he might see us as being weak now."

"Do you need my help, lord?"

"I need you to hold the west. Unless I hear from you I will put all my defences to the north." I took a deep breath. "And now I must ask a delicate question. What do you think Sir Richard of Yarm will do? He has not spoken to Sir Tristan for some time. I wondered as he has a new grandson who has his name if he had visited or spoken to either of you."

"We wrote and told him and we had a letter from Richard's grandmother congratulating us but that was all. You cannot think that he would betray you, lord?"

"I hope not but he guards the south of my land. If you hear aught from him or of any Scots, however few, in the north of your land then let me know."

"And Normandy, how goes the war there?"

I told him all including the death of Rolf. Like my other young knights, it was a blow for they had liked him. "Then there is just you and Sir Edward left from the knights who fought together all those years ago."

"Aye and the only other knights who yet live from those times are Sir Hugh Manningham and Sir Richard of Yarm. They are no longer true allies. I am now in the hands of the young knights I trained."

"And we will not let you down."

As we rode back to Stockton I looked more closely at Gilles. He had grown considerably since he had joined me. Much of that had been Alice's doing. She was fond of him. She fed him well. Wulfric had done his best to train him but that had not been a priority. The youth was brave but did he have the skills to survive in battle? Those skills would be tested soon. I looked up and I tasted, in the air, a change in the weather. In England the seasons were unpredictable; winter could be early or late. One year winter had lasted but a day. The rest had been wet and damp but we had had no snow. I could smell and feel the cold in the air. The wind was from the north. Perhaps the weather was an ally of the Scots. I spurred Scout on, the Scots were coming.

Perhaps it was the hard ride I gave him but whatever the reason Scout was limping when we reached Stockton. Gilles' real skill lay with horses and when he saw his limp he examined him for me. His face was sad when he turned to me. "Lord your horse is old."

"Aye, Gilles, I had him when I first came to England all those years ago."

"He cannot ride to war again. The lameness is a sign of age. It will heal but when you need him to run hard he will not be able to. Perhaps we should...." he left unsaid the words neither of us wished to be uttered.

"No, Gilles, Scout is as much a part of me as my armour. I will not have his life ended to save some winter feed. He stays with me in the castle. I will ride him when there is no war but he shall be looked after with Hunter, Badger and my newly acquired horse, Rolf. I will use Rolf from now on. He is younger than the others and has a little destrier in him." I went to Scout and rubbed his nose. "I shall miss this nose, Scout, for it sniffed out enemies who would have slain me. Perhaps you can teach others how to do it." He always seemed to understand me and he raised his head and whinnied.

The first news came to us just before All Hallows Eve. The weather had been growing colder since my return from Barnard Castle. There was no snow and no frost but the viciously cold north wind scoured the land. Oswald of Hexham, one of Sir Hugh Manningham's scouts arrived at my gate after sunset. Ralph of Wales was the captain of the guard that night and he knew him. He was admitted.

"My lord I have a message from my master. The Scots are coming."

"Come to my hall and eat. You can tell me all as you do so."

I had seen how he was almost blue with the cold. The freezing ride south had been hard. Alice laid bowls of stew and bread before him. He wolfed them down, telling me between mouthfuls his news. "We saw signs of men gathering north of the Tweed. There were camps towards

Jedburgh. Sir Roger of Norham reported many men moving west along the Tweed towards the border."

"When did this begin?"

"At the end of September, the start of October, lord."

I nodded. That was about the time we had apprehended our spies. "Go on."

"Sir Hugh sent a messenger to you with the news down the Durham Road. He did not return. Sir Hugh knew that I would get through," he smiled, "I know the backways and greenways like your scout Aiden."

"How many men were there?"

"It was hard to estimate but Sir Hugh said to expect at least forty knights."

Forty knights meant at least three hundred in the army, perhaps more. "I will send an escort back with you."

"You need not, lord."

"I do for Sir Hugh must know that I have received his news. Besides, I have a message for him. When you have told me yours I will give it to you. It will be spoken. We want nothing to fall into enemy hands."

"Enemies, lord?"

"The land between Hexham and Stockton is England and not Scotland. If the other messenger died..."

Oswald nodded, "Aye lord. Then it means that we cannot trust those who live in Durham. I will give you the rest of my news. Sir Hugh sent men to identify those who were camped. They are led by Earl Gospatric. It is largely those who rebelled against King Henry."

Even as he said it I wondered why they had not thrown their lot in with Stephen. It seemed obvious to me that he would have given them back their lands if only to keep me in check. If they did not want to serve Stephen then that meant they were working for King David. He would not be breaking the peace but, if he could capture Stockton then Cleveland would be his and he would have a toehold in England. The Baron of Skipton could retake his castle and the land between Stockton and Skipton would be a dagger held at the heart of the north. Even York would be threatened.

"Here is my message for your master, Oswald: the Empress now controls more than half of Normandy. There will come a day when he can choose once more to either serve the usurper or the rightful ruler of England. Tell him I understand his decision but I know his heart."

"Aye lord and I would rather serve you than the Bishop of Durham."

When Oswald was led to his quarters I summoned Aiden. "I wish you to escort Oswald back to Hexham. How many archers will you need with you?"

"None, I take Edgar the falconer and Edward. It will help their skills and they are silent in the forest."

"Are you certain for when you have done that I would have you find the army which is camped close to Jedburgh? They are coming here."

"Then I will definitely take my two falconers. We will be invisible."

They left before dawn. The four of them, by riding hard, could reach Hexham by nightfall. We would then seek out our enemies. Even as they were galloping from my gate I was speaking with Dick, Wulfric and John.

"War has come. It is days and not weeks away. Dick, have riders go to my knights. Sir Hugh should be warned. The others should prepare to bring half of their retinue to serve with me. I want them here in three days."

"Aye lord."

"Wulfric, we need a garrison leaving here but I want our best men ready to ride. I want to meet this army far from our borders. I fear this is just the start. We will have a winter war."

"Do not fear, lord, we are prepared."

Chapter 19

I visited Alf and warned him of the dangers. "We have improved our walls, lord, and built, as you have, both granaries and pens. We keep what we have."

"I will leave a small garrison but I am happy now that we have enough men in the town to defend the walls."

Alf nodded, proudly, "Thanks to Dick and his archers every man in the town can now use a war bow. We have made plenty of arrows. We are not as skilled or as quick as your archers but we can give a good account of ourselves. All of our boys have slings. If the Scots come they will find us a hard morsel to digest."

We had a healthy population in Stockton. There were a hundred and eight men who could use bows and fifty boys who could use slings. If you kept an enemy from your walls then you had almost won the battle. I was satisfied.

We had a flurry of snow on All Hallows Day. It was followed by an icy blast which made the snow a deadly place upon which to step. When my men began to arrive they led their horses rather than risk them slipping on the slippery stones. When all were gathered I spoke with the knights and the sergeant at arms.

"We ride tomorrow for the north road. I have information that a band of Scots intend to use the chaos that is England to capture Stockton and begin to reclaim the land south of the Tees. We will stop them. Remember, when we fight, that we are the last true Englishmen. It may seem daunting that we, alone, must fight for King Henry's heirs but we are just the first stones that are rolling down the hill. They will gather pace and then we will become the avalanche which sweeps away the usurper and restores England's crown to its rightful place!"

I had deliberately chosen my words and they had the desired effect. There were just twelve of us in the hall and we had had greater gatherings but the crescendo of noise which arose had never been equalled. We might be alone but we had the heart to take on anybody. When we passed through our northern gate the next day we received an even greater cheer from my townspeople. The men lined the walls, showing the world that they were armed and ready to defend their homes.

Once we reached the Norton Road, Dick sent out his scouts. I hoped they would meet Aiden and give us a better idea of the whereabouts of our enemies. If we heard nothing else from our three advance scouts we would head up to Jedburgh. We had passed Segges' Field when Mark rode in with Edgar. "My lord, Aiden sent me. The Scots are moving south. He and Edward will keep watch on them. If Edward does not come south it means they have kept to the old Roman Road." I nodded. That meant they were skirting the Palatinate and coming through the emptier lands to the west between us and Barnard Castle. "They have taken Otterburn and put the garrison to the sword. It held them for a day."

Phillip of Elsdon had fallen. The Bishop of Durham had neither stirred nor raised his voice in their defence. They were his people and yet they had died. William Cumin had much to answer for. "How many did you count?"

"Aiden said he counted forty-two banners and half of the army were horsed. He estimated four hundred men in total but some were just farmers. They wore no mail and they had crude weapons."

"What of Sir Hugh Manningham?"

"We did not see his patrols once we had left Oswald with him but there was a message from Sir Roger of Norham that Scots were massing on the Tweed."

I turned to Sir Edward, "They have drawn Sir Hugh away to the north. It is understandable for he is the defender of the north now that I am restrained to our valley. It means they will put as much distance between themselves and Hexham as possible."

We turned to the west. I would head for Wolsingham. If we could reach it before they did then we would use the two rivers, the Wear and the Waskerley Beck to stop them. Dick said, "Lord if we head north by west along the old greenway we can reach the confluence of the rivers in four hours."

We headed through Auckland and we passed the old Roman fort at Binchester. Knowing that they were within two days' march of us gave added urgency to our journey. I rode Rolf, the mount I had taken from Baron Thierry. He seemed to enjoy leading the cavalcade of knights. He almost pranced. He was a different beast to Scout. We would have to get used to each other. Badger and Gilles were with the baggage train. We had spears, lances and arrows in great supply. We would use the wagons, when we emptied them, as barricades. I had no doubt we would be outnumbered.

It was late afternoon when we reached the village of Wolsingham. St Godric had long departed and the famous Erik the Hermit had either died or simply disappeared. The village served one purpose only, to feed the Bishop of Durham. I had been hunting there before with Bishop Flambard in the forests close by the village. It was not a large place and had no defences. Dick had established sentries north of the bridge across the Wear. He had left a couple of men close to the ford which was half a mile east of the bridge.

"Sir Edward. Have your sergeant at arms take your archers and ten of your men at arms. Stop the enemy from crossing the ford to the east."

"That will leave us thirty men short, lord. Can we afford it?"

"Can we afford being outflanked? We will have to use the cloth we have been given."

We made camp south of the river. Dick had some of our archers in the forests to hunt game. We were defending the Bishop's land. The least he could do was to feed us. I sent Edgar the falconer back north to find Aiden. I needed to know exactly where our enemies were.

The few houses in the village were to the north of the river. The beck joined the river just after the ford. Its course meant that we had the right flank of any line we chose well protected. The Roman Road was well maintained. This was the Bishop's land and, as such, cared for. An ambush from the forest would be difficult. The only place I could see which suited an ambush was just where the road crossed the ford on the Waskerley Beck. The two fords would prove crucial. Edward still worried about our division of men. "Earl what if they do not come through Wolsingham? If they head further east then we will miss them."

I spread my arm out. "This is a good place to camp for them. They can reach Segges' field in one day if they ride hard. The alternative is to camp in the open. Here they can do as they will have done at Otterburn, they can live off the villagers but if I am wrong then we attack them from behind when they take the other road south and that they will not expect."

"It is well that you lead for I would have waited on the road to the east."

"And you may well be right. It is why I have yet to unpack the wagons. I have plans for them but only when I know for certain that they will come this way."

We spent a nervous night awaiting news from our scouts. I was awake before dawn. It had been a bitterly cold night and, despite our fires and our furs, we had not been warm. Up here, in the uplands, the covering of frozen snow was thicker than at Stockton. It would affect the battle. Gilles helped me to dress. "Will we fight this day, Earl?"

"Perhaps but we must be ready to in any case. Remember to keep lances and spears ready for me in case we do charge."

"Against so many knights? Would that not be suicide?"

"It depends upon the worth of our enemies. If they are as good as we are then yes but if they are not then their superior numbers will mean nothing. At least here, if we lose, our people at home will be able to prepare their defence."

"You think we may lose?"

"No, but we have rarely fought against such great odds. Perhaps I should have stayed behind my walls."

I had not heard him approach and almost jumped when Edward spoke, "Had you done that, Earl, then the door to Yorkshire would have been open. All your work and that of King Henry would have been undone. We are outnumbered but yours is the right decision, as ever!"

An hour or so later, when the sun was already up, Edgar the falconer galloped across the beck. His horse was lathered. "They come this way, lord. Aiden found one of their scouts. Before he died Aiden persuaded him to divulge their route. They march here and intend to camp in the village this night. They will reach here in four or five hours. Aiden and Edward follow them still."

I clapped my hand against my sword and turned to Edward, "Good! Then I want the wagons emptying. Take one to your men at the ford. It can become a wall behind which they can fight. The other should be placed across the bridge in Wolsingham. The servants and grooms can hold that. Gilles, tell Sir Edward's knight to gather their squires. The squires can defend the bridge and deny the enemy the crossing."

"Aye lord."

Sir Harold said, "And us lord?"

"We make the ford a death trap. Philip, Dick, I want your archers to bury spears in the bank of the ford and use that as a barrier. Your task is to hold it as long as you can. Wulfric. I want a second barrier close to the bridge. You and your men will prepare that. When all is done and we have eaten I will give you my plan." As they hurried off I turned to my former squires. "And we will create a little mischief at the ford."

After finding my saddlebags I led the three knights down to the ford. The water was knee-deep. When winter took hold and the rains came then it would be much deeper; passable but deeper. I took out the caltrops I had brought. "Spread them out across the ford. Put some under the water at the far side, Sir Harold and Sir Tristan. Sir John and I will do this side."

I had had Alf make me fifty of these deadly weapons. My horse would be glad that he no longer had to carry them. They were heavy. They were so designed that they always landed with one painful spike sticking up. They would maim a man or lame a horse. Whatever the result it would slow down our enemies as they crossed the ford and it would cause a bottleneck. I took the last ten or so and spread them on either side of the ford in case any knight thought to go around the trap. When we had finished we returned to our horses.

Fires were burning and the meat which our archers had hunted was being cooked. As the outside was cooked men sliced hunks from it. A man with a full stomach who was rested was more alert and better equipped to fight than a man who had marched in the cold all day and eaten oats. Not long after noon, my scouts rode in. Luckily we were at the ford and I shouted. "Ride down the beck a hundred paces and cross there. We have seeded the river with caltrops."

Soon they joined us. "They are five miles down the road. They are not turning at the crossroads. They come here to Wolsingham."

"You have done well, the three of you. Eat for we shall need your bows!"

With the squires guarding the bridge we had just sixty-five of us guarding the ford. We were forty paces back. The hard frozen ground meant that the enemy horses would not sink into the mud but if they were the slightest bit careless they might slip. Our sixty-six archers were spread out on the flanks using whatever cover they could manage to find. With their horses nearby they would be able to flee quickly enough and take up their position on the other side of the wagon and the River Wear. The mounted men in the middle were in three ranks of twenty men. As we knights were in the front rank as well as Wulfric and my most experienced men at arms, that was the force that would do the most damage.

We saw their scouts appear. They appeared over the brow of the road and skittered to a halt when they saw our spears and horses. Two watched us while the other two hurtled back down the road. It was tempting to loose arrows at them but it would have been a waste. My archers could be seen but not their true numbers.

We saw the banners appear over the skyline. It was now heading towards dusk and the light was fading. I wondered if they would camp and attack in the morning or risk an immediate attack. Their leaders gathered and then I saw their army fill the horizon behind them. There was a debate going on. It became heated for I saw arms waved and fingers pointed.

Wulfric laughed, "My lord, they have been beaten by you too many times. They are looking for the trap."

Eventually, two knights peeled off and led men to the east. They would try the other ford. While their leaders waited for the report they formed four lines of warriors. It looked like they had eighty mounted men there. Thirty others had headed east. That meant that the great mass of warriors whom we faced were on foot. From our right, we heard the whinnies of horses and the shouts as men died at the ford. There was a clash of steel. The skirmish lasted no more than the time it takes to ride around my castle and then twenty-two riders and two riderless horses came back.

Another debate ensued. This time it was brief and, with the sound of a trumpet, the six leaders pulled their horses to one side and the lines advanced. They had learned their lessons and they kept a healthy gap between the lines. Dick and Philip of Selby had measured the range. As soon as the first line trotted down the bank to the ford and were twenty paces from the water their sixty arrows, augmented by my three scouts, were released. They did not release high in the air to create a deadly arc; instead, they used a flat trajectory. They had more chance of a hit for the helmets were all open-faced. Eight men fell, mortally stricken, but horses were also struck. An arrow in the centre of a horse's head kills immediately and three riders were flung over the heads of their mounts.

The charging riders pulled up their shields to protect their faces. They could not see the water. As they splashed across some lost their footing on the loose and slippery stones and then others found the caltrops. Horses reared and as they did so their riders became easy targets. Arrows found parts of the body not protected by mail and they also struck the chests of rearing, wounded horses. Had we had more archers we would have slaughtered them all but, even so, none of their front rank made our shore. The second rank fared little better but the third made the other side having only lost eight men.

We were a hundred paces from them. They began to spread out into a longer line, "Charge!"

We hurtled at them. It was not a gallop but a canter and we stayed together. They had lost their unity when they spread out and we were a solid mass of horseflesh and metal. I pulled back my spear and, as we met their disordered line, I punched forward. The knight I hit was struck just over his sword hand. It tore through the metal of his armour and then through the soft gambeson. He was already falling over the back of his horse when the tip found flesh and I pushed a little harder and then twisted and pulled. The tip came away bloody.

Sir Edward on one side of me and Wulfric on the other had no enemies to fight for the archers had cleared the knights on either side of the one I had slain. I did not want to risk the water and I yelled, "Wheel!" We were just twenty paces from the beck. The second line moved apart to allow us to move through them and then they struck the remnants of the second and third lines. When the Scottish trumpet sounded the retreat we knew we had won the first part of this battle.

The Scots withdrew to the brow of the hill. The light was fading. Would they risk another attack? They turned and disappeared out of sight.

"Do you think they are going home, lord?"

"No, John. That would be a good ending but they have many more men than we do. They will camp. Wulfric, I want sentries watching the ford. Sir Tristan take your conroi and reinforce the ford on the Wear. They might try something there."

They both left. "Sir Harold and Sir John have your men strip their dead of anything of value, mail and weapons. Have the dead horses butchered and then place the Scottish dead by the beck. It will be another obstacle for them and it will remind them of their losses."

I dismounted and took off my helmet. It was not over but we had seeded their minds with doubts. I looked at the dead as they were piled by the river. Over twenty men at arms and knights had fallen I knew there were others dead in the river and on the other side. I was in no doubt that others had made it back but were wounded. One of Harold's men at arms had a bad wound and four others needed attention. It was a small loss. My archers combed the field seeking unbroken arrows. They would only be used when all the good arrows had been released. We wasted nothing.

We returned to the village. We had not bothered the people but now, as the smell of roasting horseflesh filled the air, a few of them ventured out. I called out to them. "Come and join us. There is plenty of meat. It is Scottish horse meat."

The smell was too tempting even for the timidest and they sat around our fires sharing the bounty.

I sought out the headman. "Do you hear much from the Bishop, headman?"

"No lord. At least not directly. His steward sends to us for timber and his hunters use the forests but we rarely see him."

"And are you bothered much by the Scots?"

"Aye lord. Never an army such as you faced today but there are thieves and robbers who try to take what we have." He smacked the sword at his side. "We defend what is ours."

I nodded, "They will come again tomorrow."

He smiled, "And you will send them packing for you are the Wolf of the North. Every Scot knows and fears your banner. Travellers who ply this road tell tales of your deeds. When we saw your banner we knew that we would be safe for we are English. The ones who need fear your ferocity are the Scots."

"Well, tomorrow, my friend, have your people keep indoors until it is over. It may not be quite as easy on the morrow."

I had each of my knights take a watch that night as did I. Perhaps I gave this Baron of Skipton too much credit. I had thought, with his superior numbers, he would have tried a night attack. He did not.

I had the last watch, the one before dawn, and I watched snow as it slowly fell. Within a short time, everything was covered in a thin blanket of white. I knew that the snow meant it would be warmer and the ground, which had been frozen hard, would now be thawed. It would not be the same when they attacked us this day. I began to change my plans. I smiled to myself as I walked our lines. In times past I would have had to ask the Earl of Gloucester, the King or the Count for permission to do so. Now I was Warlord I answered to no one.

By the time it was dawn and my men were roused, fed and armed I had my new plan. "Move all of the horses save Sir Harold's men at arms. I want the horses south of the river." While we ate I told my knights and leaders what I intended. I sent Edgar the falconer to keep Sir Tristan informed. My falconer would wait with Sir Tristan as a messenger. We woke the villagers and sent them across the river to safety. They offered to fight alongside us but it would not be right. They were not warriors. They were farmers.

I walked with Sir Edward and Wulfric to the beck. Some of our archers had stood guard there all night. I sniffed the air for the wind was, as it had been for some days, from the northeast. "Do you smell that?"

They both looked at me as though I was mad and Sir Edward said, "Woodsmoke?"

"Aye and that is all. If you stood downwind of our camp you would smell horsemeat and venison. They have had cold rations. From what Aiden said they have been using the villages they have taken to supply them. We denied them Wolsingham. We have a hungry army. They will be keen to get at us. They saw us butchering their horses. Forget their leaders and the knights; the ordinary warrior will try to cover this slippery morass of snow-covered mud to get at us. That is why we use Harold and his men to draw them on to us. When they cross the beck they will be desperate to get into the village and we use it as a castle. We have our men at arms between the huts with archers behind." I turned. "Come let us walk back and see what they shall see."

It became obvious which places would be attacked first and the three of us decided which men would go where.

With Sir Tristan's men at the ford along with many of Sir Edward's, we were down, largely to the men of Stockton, those I led and Sir John. They would have to do. The weapon which would break the Scots would be the war bow. The archers would be our third rank and they would kill as the Scots struggled to get at us.

Sir Harold mounted his men. He had fourteen and a squire. "Remember Harold that you flee as soon as the Scots leave the beck. Your purpose is twofold. To prevent them from seeing our defences and to draw them on. You ride towards the village and then along the river. Cross at the ford and then join us in the village on foot."

"Aye lord. I will not let you down."

They headed to the beck while we planted the broken spears we had collected from the battlefield as a barrier before us. I had all of the spears we had brought and we each had three of them. There were no squires to pass them forward. I had had to spread my knights out. We had used the ashes from the fires and reeds from the river bank to make a firmer footing for us. Whilst not dry it was not slippery. In a hand to hand combat that might make all the difference. Between each hut was a strongpoint held by one of my knights or a sergeant at arms. With me, I had ten of my men at arms for I had the road to defend. Philip of Selby and fourteen of his archers were behind us.

As we waited I knew the weakness of my strategy. If they ignored the wall of spears and attacked the huts they could hack their way through them and make our defence irrelevant. I counted on the fact that they would be angry at their treatment the day before and be keen to get at us. Rage which was blind often hid simple solutions.

All that we could see were the rumps of the fifteen horses before us. There were no archers in the woods although the Scots would be expecting them. There were no caltrops in the river. All that they saw was a thin line of men at arms. Suddenly I heard Sir Harold shout something and the line wheeled and came directly towards us. He did as I had asked and kept a straight line to keep our defences hidden. When they were twenty paces from us they wheeled. Even though they were not travelling quickly and all obeyed their orders one horse slipped and skidded a little. The hooves of the horses had transformed the white sheet of snow into a grey sloppy, slippery ice swamp.

As Sir Harold and his men headed east I saw the Scots. I frowned. There were no horsemen. This was just foot soldiers. I saw that they were led by a knight. I did not recognise his banner which was blue with a diagonal red cross. The Scots had interspersed their men at arms amongst the lightly armed Galwegians and mercenaries. I would have to worry about their horsemen later.

The conditions underfoot became apparent when the knight tried to run. He slipped. His men, many of whom were barefoot, fared a little better but, even so, their charge was little more than a fast walk. When they became unbalanced I watched as they waved their arms to recover. Philip of Selby said, "Now then lads, watch for targets. There will be plenty. If the Earl has no one to fight then we have done our job!"

We held the section across the road and this would be the point of their attack. It was also the closest to the Scots and we would be the first to engage. Philip of Selby launched the first arrow which whizzed over my head and plunged into the face of a man at arms. The man at arms was before the knight and he had slipped, as his arms had flailed his shield had dropped. Soon our archers were targeting individual Scots. Each one they aimed at was hit. Not one arrow was wasted. Of course, the men that they felled were a drop in the ocean. Philip and his men had hit but thirty out of the hundreds who came. The knight shouted, "Halt!" Followed by, "Shield wall!"

In the time it took to form the wall another twenty men had died or been wounded and I noticed arrows coming from our flanks. Soon our entire force of archers would be releasing arrows.

The Scots eventually had a wall of shields protecting those behind who had none. Philip said, "Right lads, release high in the sky. On my command! Now!"

This time fifteen arrows went straight up followed by another fifteen and then another. After five such showers, I saw that the heart had gone from the wedge. I could see gaps behind as the Scots closed with us. Philip and his archers would now concentrate on those behind the front ranks and it would be up to me and my men to hold the wall of shields until my archers had won the battle for us.

I held my first spear high for, as the Scots came close, they had to negotiate the planted spears. They watched their footing and the path they had to follow. A man at arms was ahead of the knight once more. He stared at me and I held his eyes. The moment they flicked to the ground to see where the next spear was my right hand darted out and the spearhead entered his eye. I pushed hard. Even had it not been a mortal wound he would have fallen. As he did so an arrow sped from behind me and, as it was at a range of fewer than ten feet, embedded itself in the right shoulder of the knight.

I pulled back my spear and hurled it overhand. It embedded itself in the knight's chest for his shield had fallen to the side. I picked up another and braced it against the ground as enraged men at arms and wild Galwegians ran at us. It was a costly mistake. Those who avoided the spears were struck by arrows released at a ridiculously close range. Even mail would not stand against them. When my last spear was shattered I drew my sword. We had been pushed back a little and I stepped forward into the gap which appeared. My men followed me. As I stepped forward I held up my shield to take the blow from the war hammer wielded in two hands by a huge warrior. I had taken such a blow before. It could break an arm and the secret was to angle the shield so that the force of the hammer was deflected. As it slid down the face of my shield my sword stabbed into his unprotected middle. I felt it grate along his spine as it came out of his back. The huge warrior fell backwards.

The effect of the arrows was now apparent and we no longer had a mass of men before us. This was the time to destroy their morale, "On! Charge!"

My men roared and we stepped forward. We did not run but we were an alarming sight. We all wore mail and wielded good swords and axes. They broke and ran. It was then that my archers had more targets than they had arrows. As the Scots turned their backs they died. The slippery ground meant that many were saved as they slipped before an arrow could hit them but when they slowly rose some died anyway.

I had thought we had won until Edgar the falconer galloped up. "Lord! The knights are attacking Sir Tristan. Sir Harold has gone to help."

"Philip keep after the men on foot. To horse!"

We moved back through the village. I could see that men had fallen. There was no time to see who. Gilles, get your horse. Squires join us."

We crossed the bridge to our already saddled horses. I could hear the battle to the east. I prayed we would be in time. I mounted Badger and, drawing my sword spurred him east. We had no time to form lines and to organise ourselves. We would arrive piecemeal. I saw a wild mêlée taking place as men at arms and knights from both sides were engaged in a furious fight to take the ford over the Wear. Arrows still fell upon the Scots which meant the wagon castle was still held but the mounted knights and men at arms swirled together in a wild mass of swords shields and horses. I spurred Badger and his powerful legs ate the virgin snow as he thundered to the mêlée.

I spied Sir Harold and his men as they fought to get through to his friend Sir Tristan. They were surrounded by the Scots. The men at arms whose backs were to me only heard Badger's hooves at the last moment. I did not slow him down. Three things hit the Scots at the same time, my shield, my horse and my sword. My blade found a back while my horse and my shield bowled over a man and his horse. Badger's hooves ended the man's life. I saw a knight prepare to stab Sir Harold in the back. Without breaking stride, I brought my sword around in an arc and smashed it across the back of the knight. He threw his arms in the air as his spine was shattered and he fell to the ground. I pulled back on Badger's reins and, as he raised his legs, his hooves smashed down on the man at arms to the left of Sir Harold.

My wild charge had cleared those behind us but Sir Tristan was still beleaguered. I heard a roar behind me as Wulfric charged into a knot of Scots. I turned and was splattered with their blood as he swung his war axe. More of my men at arms were behind, led by Sir Edward. Our rear was safe.

I spurred Badger who leapt forward. Sir Harold fell in at my side and I saw Gilles appear at my left. Beyond him, Wulfric was wielding his war axe like a scythe at harvest time. And then I saw Sir Tristan fall. His men at arms closed around him and I had a horrible vision of Rolf and his Swabians. This would not happen again. I saw Baron Skipton as he raised his sword in triumph. I kicked hard with my spurs and Badger hurtled towards them. I veered around the fallen men of Elton who were trying to protect Sir Tristan's body. Gilles, although inexperienced, was laying about him with his sword. He was fortunate that the men he fought had their backs to him. But it was Wulfric who carved us a path to the Baron. None could face his fury.

I put Badger between the Baron and Tristan's men. I punched at the Baron's shield with my own. Pulling Badger's reins to the left meant his head reared and he bit into the rump of the Baron's horse. It kicked and shied away. I stood in my saddle and brought my sword over towards Baron Skipton's head. He was so busy trying to get his skittish horse under control that his shield barely blocked my sword and it was driven into his helmet blinding him. My quick hands meant I pulled back and stabbed at his side. He tried to bring his shield down and succeeded only in driving my point into his thigh. Blood spurted. He pulled his horse's head around so that he could use his sword. I wheeled Badger to face him and stabbed him at his other side. He barely blocked it. I could see the blood was flowing freely from his leg and that it was a mortal wound but so long as he remained in the saddle his men would fight on. I pulled my hand back and feinted to stab in the same place. He tried to block me but he was slow. I changed it to a sweep and hacked off his head. His torso slipped from the saddle.

He had his men at arms behind him. Wulfric and Sir Edward slew two and then the others shouted as they threw down their weapons, "We yield! Mercy!"

It was as though we had stepped from a storm into a house. Everything stopped as the men at arms threw down their weapons. The other knights saw the disaster and turned to flee. They had to run the gauntlet of my archers and they did not pass the ford unscathed.

We had won but, once again, we had paid a terrible price. Sir Tristan lay in a circle of his own warriors and he lay still. The only thing worse than a battle won is a battle lost.

Chapter 20

"Wulfric secure the prisoners. Sir Edward see to your men at the ford."

"What about the men at arms and knights who fled, Lord?"

"Dick and his archers are pursuing the foot. They will catch any who are tardy. We do not have enough men to follow, Harold."

"Aye lord."

Edgar!"

I jumped from Badger's back and handed the reins to Gilles. I saw that three of Sir Tristan's men at arms lay dead and the rest all bore wounds; testimony to their fidelity. I saw that Sir Tristan had a blow to the head. There was a deep dent in the helmet which should not have been there. I took off my helmet and put my coif down so that I could put my ear to his mouth. He was breathing but it was shallow. Edgar dismounted and joined me.

"He breathes but he has a head wound."

Edgar pointed to the slashed mail across the shoulder. There was blood seeping from it. He had a second wound. "We must take off his mail and his helmet lord and see the damage."

"Let us take off the helmet first. If we have to we can cut the mail from him." The two of us carefully eased the helmet from his head. His skull protector was red with blood. We took it off and I saw a dent in his head that matched his helmet.

Edgar shook his head. "I am sorry, lord. This is beyond me."

I stood. "Gilles, fetch the wagon here. I want a bed building inside it."

Gilles shouted to the other squires, "Come, the Earl has a task for us."

I looked up and saw Wulfric and Sir Edward, "You two take command. We leave at dawn. Gather what you can."

"And the prisoners? Do we slit their throats?"

Wulfric was never subtle and the men at arms heard him. "Lord we beg for mercy! We surrendered!"

I shook my head, "Guard them for now. I will make my decision when we have seen to Sir Tristan." I looked at the men at arms, "Pray for him! You will live if he does!"

Edgar said, quietly, "Then they are dead men lord for that is a bad wound to the head."

I sighed, "In Constantinople, they have doctors who cut open the heads of men. Those men live, well, often they do. Sir Tristan breathes. So long as there is life then there is hope. Fetch hot water and I want the sharpest dagger you can find."

His men at arms raced off, eager to do something. I helped Edgar to cut away the offending mail and part of his gambeson. The wound was not deep but it was bloody. While we waited for the water Edgar took out his needle and gut.

I heard the creaking of the wagon as Gilles and the squires brought it over. "Lord, we have used the cloaks and clothes from the dead to make a soft interior."

"We need to ensure that he does move. Put in the spare quivers to make it solid."

The water arrived and while Edgar bathed and cleansed the shoulder I cleaned away the blood from Sir Tristan's head. I tugged his hair and saw that the bone inside moved with the hair. One of the men at arms handed me a dagger. It was the design the Italians called a stiletto. It had a long narrow blade and I knew that they were always sharp. I put the tip beneath the hairline while pulling the hair. Sir Tristan was between life and death and he did not stir. That was a mercy. I pushed into the skin and blood began to seep. I slipped the blade of the knife gently under the skin and began to make an incision so that I could examine the wound. It came apart like a ripe plum. I made a long cut up to the top of the damaged skull.

Looking up I said to the nearest man at arms, "Wash your hands and hold these flaps of skin apart so that I can see the damage." He came back and knelt next to me. "Keep your head back for I need the light." I peered in and saw the broken pieces of bone. They appeared to be loose. Even as the man at arms held the flap a piece fell out and I heard him gasp. "Fear not, your master is not harmed. Edgar, when you have finished stitching, look here."

A moment or two later and he joined me. "That is a proper mess, lord."

"Yet I spy hope. If I move away the broken bone and cover it with skin it may heal."

"You need something to replace the bone lord. Something solid."

"How about a piece of metal? Gold?"

"Aye lord, but where would you get such a piece of metal? It would have to fit perfectly."

"Wulfric, in my purse is a gold crown, take it out."

Wulfric did as I asked and handed it to me. I saw that it was just slightly smaller than the hole. It was almost the right shape. "Wulfric, take this coin. I want it beating thinner and to fit the hole you see."

"You will put the coin in his head, lord?" I nodded. He took the coin and crossed himself, "And this is magic, lord. I shall do my best."

I carefully removed the tiny pieces of bone with the tip of the dagger. Edgar said, "He is breathing easier, lord. There may be something to this."

I heard the banging as Wulfric hammered the coin. It would have been quicker had we a forge but he used brute force and a captured war hammer. He returned to us. "Put it in vinegar, Wulfric. It will purify it."

"Lord, it will sting!"

I smiled, "And I will not mind for if it stings him then he will be alive."

He handed me the cleaned coin and I placed it over the hole. "Now Edgar you must sew the skin with tiny stitches and it should be as tight as you can make it. We do not want the coin to move."

"Aye lord, I shall be a seamstress!"

It seemed to take an age but eventually the job was done. "Now cover him with blankets and try to give him some beer. We will risk moving him in the morning."

Edgar and I stood. I suddenly realised that we had many men around us. They began to cheer. I shook my head, "When Sir Tristan speaks then you can cheer us until then, we pray."

Sir Edward clapped me on the back, "I have seen many things, lord, but that today was the most astounding. When I tell my children, they will think I talk of Merlin and that it is fantastical!"

"Wait until the morrow. Well, how do we stand?"

"Dick and Philip of Selby chased the survivors. They stopped when they ran out of arrows. We have great amounts of booty and horses. We paid a heavy price, lord. Sir Tristan and I have few men at arms to take home."

"For that I am sorry." I looked over at the prisoners. We needed no more slaves and yet something stopped me from ordering their deaths. I walked over to them. "What is your name?"

The man who had surrendered said, "Robert of Settle, lord." He looked over to Sir Tristan, "Does the knight live?"

"He does but do not think that sympathy from those who tried to kill him will stand you in good stead. Why should I spare you?"

"Because, lord, our master is dead. We were not oathsworn but hired men. We followed him north when he quarrelled with King Henry. We do not wish to stay among the Scots. We wish to go back to England and serve another master. We are good soldiers."

Wulfric snorted, "If you were good soldiers then you would lie next to your master!"

I waved a hand to silence Wulfric. "If we took you on as men at arms I would need a binding oath."

"Lord, you cannot take on such men! It is wrong." Wulfric was incandescent with rage.

"Wulfric you are a fine warrior but you need to know when to keep your mouth shut. Sir Edward, would you be willing to have some of these as your men at arms?"

"If they swear an oath then, aye."

I nodded, "Tomorrow we head back to our valley. You shall swear an oath in my church. Your behaviour and conduct over the next day will determine if your wish is granted."

"We will behave, lord. You have my word."

Once again there were a huge number of dead animals which had to be butchered. The villagers did well. The headman asked if we would be taking the bones of the dead animals away. Gilles looked surprised when he did so. I smiled, "They will use them for soup and then burn them before grinding them up to enrich the soil. Of course, you may have them and we will not be taking any more of the dead animals with us. They are yours."

"Thank you, lord, if the winter is a hard one then that could be the difference between life and death."

Tristan's men at arms and squire kept a close watch on their master during the night. Edgar and I were summoned when he made a sound or if his breathing was erratic. I did not mind for it showed what they thought of their master. We had burned the enemy dead at sunset and the fires hissed and spat all night keeping the sentries warm. The following day we buried our own dead in the earth which had been burned. I had lost five men. Mark and Will's son my archers, Brian the Celt, Richard of York and Osric son of Dale had all died. They had died well but they were harder to replace than gold. We said our words and blessed them on their way to heaven. I knew not if they would go to heaven. They had not been shriven before we fought. I did not think the God I worshipped would turn away brave men.

When dawn broke we began the task of lifting Sir Tristan into the wagon. We did it painfully slowly but eventually, he was safely cocooned inside the wagon and we headed south. We had had no ransom nor would we be getting any but the men who had come south, especially the knights had coins and treasure aplenty. I noted that the coins were mainly Scottish but there were many French ones. I saw Louis' pudgy fingers in this Scottish pie. The other wagon was used to carry back the mail, swords, saddles and weaponry. We had to be frugal these days. King Henry would not come to pay for weapons. The Bishop of Durham would no longer be hiring us to fight for him. We were on our own.

It took all day and part of the night to reach home. We could have stayed at Norton or Hartburn but we were keen to push on and reach Stockton. Harold went with us although his men returned to their manor. His wife was in my castle; my sanctuary. I had sent Aiden and his falconers on ahead to warn Father Henry of the crisis. The priest and Tristan's wife, Lady Anne, were anxiously waiting as we headed through our gate.

"More light!" Alf and others brought torches and stood around the wagon as Father Henry climbed in to examine the wound.

I climbed next to him. "He had an indentation in his skull. I cut a flap of skin, removed the fragments of bone and replaced it with a piece of gold the same size." I saw his wife raise her hand to her mouth as tears sprang from her eyes. "I could not see what else to do."

Father Henry shook his head, "And you have done more than I would have risked. From what you have told me no man could have done more. It is not in the hands of God." He stood. "Carry Sir Tristan into the Church. We will stand vigil all night and pray for him. The Earl has done all that he can and it is now down to God."

I stood too. "You men at arms who followed the wrong leader. Go with Father Henry and Lady Anne. Let your prayers, this night, cry out to God. Your fate and that of Sir Tristan are entwined like the strands of a rope."

Robert of Settle nodded, "Aye lord. We shall. I believe that our prayers will save the young lord. And I for one wish to serve you."

John my steward looked anxious as he approached me. "Lord, there look to be empty saddles."

"There are, John. We left many brave men north of here but our land is safe for the winter. Let the people know that their continued freedom was bought with the blood of our warriors."

"Will Sir Tristan live, lord?"

"We have done all that men can do. He lives and he breathes. The rest is up to God." I was weary but I had one more thing to do. "Aiden, ride to Yarm and tell Sir Richard what has befallen his son."

He nodded and ran off. Wulfric was close by. "When he decided to side with Stephen of Blois Richard of Yarm gave up any rights, lord."

I nodded, "He is a father as am I. It will not hurt."

Wulfric nodded, "The boy fought well, lord. He and Sir Edward's men held up ten times their number. I know others who would have fled the field."

There was no greater praise. Wulfric approved.

John said, "Lord there are letters arrived from the Archbishop and the Bishop and..." he paused, "One with a royal seal. The King has written to you."

"Thank you. Have our ships returned yet from Anjou?"

"No lord."

"And our people prosper?"

He nodded. "We have had more families joining us." He saw my look, "They are families, lord and not spies. We sent all single men away as you ordered."

"Good, it may seem harsh, John but it is necessary."

I walked out of my gate and went to the church, I normally did this and spoke with my wife. Now I had even more reason to do so. The church was filled with the mumble of prayers. I knelt, not close to Tristan but by my wife's grave. I silently implored her to help in saving Tristan's life. The church felt suddenly warm. After a moment or two, I stood and listened to the prayers. The men we had captured were praying as hard as Lady Anne herself. I walked to my young knight and touched the side of his head where I had put the coin. "We need you, Sir Tristan, we need you, come back to us."

I turned to go. I saw the gratitude in Lady Anne's eyes and suddenly I heard a gasp from Father Henry. I turned back and saw that Sir Tristan had opened his eyes.

"Did we win, lord?" His voice was thin but clear. He lived!

"Praise the lord!"

His wife threw her arms around his neck. Father Henry poured some wine into his mouth. I nodded to the men at arms from Skipton and gestured for them to leave.

"Yes Tristan, we won and you had a great part in that victory. Father, can his men take him to more comfortable quarters? I think the lord has done his part."

"Aye Earl and you did yours too. Sir Tristan owes his life to you and Edgar as well as God."

I went out into the cold night. Robert of Settle and his men at arms waited for me. "Lord it is a sign from God that we were meant to serve you. We were penitent and God answered our prayers."

"Aye. Come to my castle and tomorrow we will see about finding you new masters." As I went, wearily, to my quarters the word my father had often used came to mind, *wyrd*. Had their prayers saved Sir Tristan? We had lost men at arms and yet our enemies had provided us with more than we had lost. This was hard to explain. I would sleep on the matter.

The sleep helped me make up my mind. I woke early. No one, save the sentries, stirred. I went down to my hall. Alice had left a jug of wine and a tray with cheese and cold meats. They were covered with a cloth. I ate as I thought.

I would divide the twenty men amongst my knights. Sir Edward and Sir Tristan would get the largest proportion for they had lost the most. After the previous night, I did not doubt their desire to serve but spreading them out would ensure their loyalty. With the problem of Sir Tristan and the men at arms out of the way, I finally read my three letters. The Bishop of Durham's was one of complaint. He did not approve of my men using his roads nor did he approve of his knights communicating with me. I was ordered to stop. I almost threw the parchment into the fire and then thought better of it. I could smell his clerk in all of this. The Scots were using their influence to drive a wedge between us. I put the letter on one side. There would come a time for a reckoning.

I read the Archbishop's letter too. I knew that it would be formal for we used spoken messages through trusted men to talk to each other. In the letter, he implored me to heal the rift between me and the King and to look to God for help. He urged me to continue to be a wall against the Scots. I smiled. There were spies in York too and the Archbishop was telling both the Scots and the King that he was doing his duty. I would ask Philip of Selby to visit his uncle. Archbishop Thurston needed to know the events in the north.

Finally, I read the letter from King Stephen. I read it three times. I took the three letters and locked them in the chest in my chambers. I ascended the stairs to the ramparts. Sven the Rus was the captain of the guard, "Good morrow, lord. It will be a stormy day I fear. The wind comes from my homeland. That brings with it more snow."

As we had travelled the last part of our journey I had noticed that there was less snow. A slight thaw was always worrying for a rise in temperature always brought more inclement weather.

"It is a good job we are well supplied."

"We are that. Wulfric said we had a great victory."

"We did. We had few knights but they all had the hearts of lions!"

He gestured to the standard which fluttered in the stiff, icy wind, "More like the heart of a wolf, lord. In my land, we have many packs of wolves and we respect them for they are wise creatures. I have often watched, as a boy, a pack moving. They are led by the old and the weak so that the whole pack moves at their pace. Then come the strongest wolves. They are ready to meet any danger. The main pack follows and at the rear comes the leader who watches for danger so that he can react quickly. I have watched you since I came here. I can see why you have the sign of the wolf for you are like wolves of the wild. You protect the whole pack and I for one am glad to be part of your pack."

It was the most I had ever heard Sven the Rus say. "I did not know that, Sven. I have hunted wolves before but never seen a pack move."

"It is another reason why men fear you, lord, for, like the wolf, you never know when you are beaten. A lion will run and hide when it begins to lose. I saw that in the east when our Emperor went on lion hunts. A wolf only stops fighting when his heart is torn from his body and even then, watch for the teeth."

We both turned as we saw the first faint glow from the east. There was a red glow that echoed Sven's prediction. A storm was coming.

Chapter 21

Sir Richard of Yarm and his wife arrived not long after first light. They must have travelled through the blizzard which whipped in with the dawn. They were both blue with the cold. Sven admitted them although I could see from his face that he was less than happy about it. My men of arms could not understand how Sir Richard's loyalty had shifted to Stephen of Blois.

I was well wrapped in a fur as both dropped to their knees in supplication. "Lord, we beg to see our son. Does he live?"

"Rise. Come into my hall. Aye, he lives. God saved him."

Tristan's mother burst into tears. He was her only son and her daughter lived far away in Barnard Castle. She wished her husband to be my ally still. My servants took them to Sir Tristan's chambers. Sir John and Sir Harold were in my Great Hall.

Sir Harold said, "My wife is anxious to return home, lord. She feels she has imposed upon your hospitality."

"You know that is not true, Harold. You can both stay as long as you wish."

"I know lord but you know how women are."

I remembered Adela, she would have been the same, "I would look at the weather before you decide if you will travel. There is a storm and although Hartburn is not far away it may be better to wait until it has abated. Sir Richard and his wise wife have only travelled from Yarm and they are blue with the cold."

He nodded, "At least that keeps us safe from our enemies."

"Perhaps." I turned to a servant, "Ask Wulfric, Dick and the Steward to join me. I have news."

I could see that they were intrigued but they knew me well enough to keep their counsel. I would tell them my news when all were present. My three men arrived and stood.

"I pray you to sit and take wine." When they all had a drink I began. "I have had a letter from Stephen the Usurper. I am invited to meet with him in York on the first Sunday of Advent. He assures me of my safety and the letter contains a safe-conduct for me and my men."

I took my goblet to drink.

Wulfric was the first to speak, "You need not go, lord. We can gain nothing from it. I heard from the captured men at arms that he has lost most of Wales. He cannot attack us for he would lose and he cannot afford another loss."

"Aye Wulfric but that may mean he wishes to broker a peace with us. This could be a good sign." My Steward was astute. He was not a warrior but he understood trade and negotiation.

"I would still not go, lord. Let him come here."

I smiled, "I think that my rather high handed treatment of him the last time may well have made that impossible. Like you Wulfric I am not certain what we have to gain from this but I am also aware that I am the only open supporter of the Empress who resides in England. I lived in the East long enough to understand that diplomacy is a complicated business. I wished your views but I intend to travel. I will meet with him. Sir Harold and Sir John, I will take only my men at arms and Philip of Selby's archers. If this is a lure to draw me away from my castle to allow an attack I will leave it well defended."

Dick said, "Earl, I think the weather is our protector. A man would be a fool if he attacked Stockton in the heart of winter and we know that Stephen of Blois is many things but a fool is not one of them."

"Just so. Wulfric we will take twenty men at arms. You choose them. It might be a good idea to use two of the new ones who have just joined us."

"Aye lord." He had stated his objections but he would now do all that he could to ensure the success of the mission. I knew I had been lucky in my choice of Sergeant At Arms.

There was a knock at my door. My servant opened it. "Lord, Sir Richard of Yarm begs admittance."

"Enter." I smiled for I wished the tone to be set. Wulfric and my knights resented Sir Richard's defection and I did not wish harsh words to be spoken. Once uttered they hung in the air like poisonous mist and we could do without such ill-feeling.

Sir Richard looked nervous. "Thank you, lord." I nodded, "I now know that it was you who saved my son's life. I owe you more than I can say and I recant my decision to abandon the cause of the Empress. I can see now that it was a mistake. Men make mistakes and then they try to rectify them. I would serve you again."

"Words are easy to say, Sir Richard. I understand whence your words come. You thought your son was dead and now he lives. Do not join me just because I helped God to save Sir Tristan. That had nothing to do with you. If your son had died would you have recanted?" He said nothing. "I am happy for you to serve me again for I value Yarm as an ally. You protect my land; however, I would not have you rush into such a decision. If you feel the same way then join us here for our Christmas feast at Yule. That is time enough."

"I do not need that time, Lord, my mind is set."

"But mine is not. I have spoken. This is how I will have it."

"As you wish, Earl." He backed out of the room.

Sir John asked, "Why not take him back now, Lord? We need his men at arms."

"Were you not listening to Dick? There will be no attack until the spring at the earliest. We do not need his men, yet. I thought I knew Sir Richard but his defection came as a shock to me. Sir Hugh Manningham did not defect for his land was far to the north and he has helped us since then. Without his message, we would have been attacked by Baron Skipton. Sir Richard has done nothing. I understand he is grateful for his son's life but I will meet with Stephen the Usurper and see what he has to say."

Sir Harold said, "Surely you do not think that Sir Richard means treachery?"

"I doubt it but I am not certain. I have become a more cautious man since King Henry died."

I decided to arrive before the first Sunday in Advent. I wished to speak privately with the Archbishop. I visited Sir Hugh at Barnard Castle and Sir Edward at Thornaby. They needed to be kept informed in case anything happened to me. Before I left our ships arrived with more men at arms, wine and other invaluable supplies. I briefly considered sailing to York but realised that it would be quicker to ride and I had other plans for the *'Adela'*.

"William, I wish you to winter in Anjou. It is safer for your ship. The Tees, oft times, freezes over. You can clean the hull on the Loir and sail as soon as Spring arrives." I smiled. "I suspect it will be more comfortable for you and your men. I would have you wait until I have returned from York. I may have a message for Sir Leofric."

He nodded, "He has a son, now, lord. He has named him Alfraed in your honour. He asks if you will be Godfather."

"I am touched. When you return I will send a small chest of gold for my Godson. I also have letters and presents for my son. You can visit him too."

"Aye lord."

The delay gave Alf, my steward and Ethelred time to prepare more trade goods. The voyage was an extra and our profits were growing. We might be an island surrounded by enemies but we did not have taxes to pay. We made hay while the sun shone. It may have been winter and snow might have covered the ground but we took care as we headed south. I took Alan of Osmotherley for he knew the vale as well as any. He knew whom he could trust. Philip of Selby also knew the land well. The return journey might be different for I had not replied to the usurper. I wanted none to know I was travelling.

We did not take warhorses but we went well-armed. Gilles had a new suit of mail made especially for him by Alf. The hauberk he had had was one we had taken from a dead Scot. It was too large. The new one fitted him closely. His chausses were new and they took some getting used to. His helmet was also new. It was round and had a nasal. The pointed helmets were found to be more fragile than the newer round ones and any benefit from the angle was offset by the fact that they had a tendency to split.

As we approached York I saw that they now flew Stephen of Blois' standard. I guessed it was in anticipation of his visit. It did not sit well with me. Our normal warm greeting from the sentries was noticeably absent. We were rebels. Our reputation meant that we would be afforded respect but that was all. The Captain of the Archbishop's guard, Ralph, met us. "Earl, you and your squire are to be housed in the Archbishop's palace. Your men will be housed in the warrior hall."

I saw Wulfric begin to glower, "We will be safe Wulfric. The Archbishop has given his word and besides the people of York would not like the wrath of my men at arms visited upon them, would they Captain?"

Ralph shook his head, "Your master will be safe, Wulfric. You have my word."

"Good for if not then I will have your head."

For many men that would be an idle boast but not Wulfric.

Once in the palace, I shed my mail. I knew I would be safe, however, I still kept my sword and dagger close by. When I slept that night then Gilles would sleep across the door of the chamber. He would be woken by the opening door if any tried to enter.

Archbishop Thurston greeted us, "I have sent for my nephew. I am anxious to speak with him, and you Earl. It will be a small supper. Just the four of us." He looked pointedly at Gilles. "Your squire can be discreet?"

I nodded, "I trust him with my life and I would trust him with yours, your grace."

"Good, then we can speak freely. These are parlous times, Earl. Now you must excuse me; we have a royal visit and that necessitates a great deal of work. The King brings with him a large number of barons and courtiers."

I was desperate to know why the usurper had summoned me but I did not wish to appear concerned. I spent the time with Gilles. We visited the church which had been destroyed by Danes and then rebuilt. It dwarfed my own church for this one was over a hundred paces long. It was a fine church and I felt peace when we emerged to wash before we ate.

The first part of the meal was spent in my account of the putative attack by the Baron of Skipton. Even the Archbishop raised his eyes when his nephew recounted the miracle of Tristan. "Your people are lucky in you as a leader Earl. It is one thing to destroy, kill and maim but to heal too... it is nothing short of unique."

I shrugged, "Thank my father who made sure I attended schools and read widely."

"This problem with Skipton is a worrying turn of events. I fear that there are rebels in the north who will see the chaos as a means of gaining land."

"Have you not enough lords of the manor to control the land? I cannot see myself able to keep the land south of mine safe." He nodded. "So why does Stephen wish to speak with me? I have not changed my position and he knows me well enough to know I never shall."

He looked at Gilles and Philip and then leaned forward, "I think he wishes to make peace with Matilda and Geoffrey."

That took me aback and then I remembered our summer campaign. Stephen no longer had allies in Normandy. He clung on to Blois but that was far from England. This began to make sense.

"I see. I cannot see why Empress Matilda would agree to a truce."

"Perhaps he can explain better than I for I am not sure myself. Those were the reasons he gave when he sent me his letter." He paused, "And I have to tell you that Robert de Brus will be with him. I spoke with Philip earlier and heard of the conflict. I pray there will be none here, inside my land."

"I cannot guarantee anything, your grace. I will keep my temper but my people have suffered too much from someone who must have a crooked back for nothing about him is straight."

Two days later the advance riders arrived to warn that King Stephen was just hours away. I took myself and my warriors to the market, for it was market day, and I wanted to be away from the main gate and the accolades which would be thrown the usurper's way. We had coins in our purses and there were goods we could not purchase at home. While my men bought things that could be used for war I remembered the things Adela had sought and bought. There were some fine pots I purchased. Alice would like them. The seller packed them in straw and we took them back to the palace. On the way, we found a pair of drivers who were willing to carry them north in their wagon. As with many such meetings it hearkened back to the past. Both had fought alongside me in the border wars. Both had been archers who had been wounded; neither could pull a bow. One had been in the service of Geoffrey of Piercebridge and the other came from Normanby. They were reliable. I chose those who served me carefully these days.

The trumpets and accolades told me that Stephen had arrived. Those who were close to him strutted around as though this was their own palace. I smiled when they stepped back at the appearance of my men and me. They had helped to carry the pots back to the palace. It amused my men too for we were viewed as barbarians. We ignored the courtiers and hangers-on as we stacked the pots close by our horses in the stable. I intended to leave as soon as the meeting was over. If I could avoid it I did not want to spend a night under the same roof as this man I hated.

One of the Archbishop's deacons found me. "Earl, his grace is in the Great Hall. You are summoned."

I sent Gilles for Wulfric. It often helped to have such an intimidating figure behind me. I trusted the Archbishop but that did not mean I trusted all who might be at the meeting. When I entered we were the last. I saw Stephen seated on the Archbishop's own throne. Such things were important to him. He had with him a number of knights amongst whom was Robert de Brus.

Stephen stood and smiled. He walked towards me with his hand held out. "Earl, the Archbishop has told us how you ended the rebellion of Skipton. We are indebted to you."

I gave a slight bow which allowed me to put my hands behind my back. I did not wish to shake his hand. "You are welcome, Count, it served my purpose for they came to take my castle first."

My use of his former title caused the flash of a frown across his face. He soon recovered his composure, "Then you will be happy that I have already appointed a new lord of the manor. This is Sir Edgar Mandeville and he is the new lord of the manor of Skipton."

I nodded at him. I did not like his face. He appeared to have a permanent sneer on it. "Then I hope Sir Edgar knows how to fight Scots for they will be a constant thorn in his side."

"Fear not, Earl, I will fight all enemies of my King and me."

It was a clear threat and I nodded so that he could see I understood it. Stephen said, "And now I need words alone with you, Cleveland. Your Grace, would you accompany us to your cloister where we can be a little more private."

Once outside and wrapped in furs he began, "I need you to take a message to my cousin in Anjou."

I nodded. "Surely you have those who could take a message to her yourself."

"We both know how highly she prizes both your words and your opinion. I would end this schism between us. We are now the last grandchildren of the Conqueror. We should not be fighting amongst ourselves."

"And I take it you do not wish the message to be written down?"

"You are astute. The Archbishop is here so that you know I will not go back on what I say." He paused. "I would have peace. I give up all claims to Normandy if the Empress will give up all claims to England. I go further. I will provide men to help her to conquer Normandy."

He stopped and looked at me as though he expected me to give him a round of applause. "You offer to give the Empress what we have within our grasp?" I shook my head, "Did you not hear that it is only the land around Rouen which holds out and the Earl of Gloucester will complete that work in the spring. Then the Empress can give thought to winkling you out of the throne."

He became angry, "It is a reasonable offer! Will you take it or not?"

"Of course, I will take it but she will think me the new court jester."

"Then that is all that I ask."

I knew from his tone that this was not over.

When we returned inside there was a look of anticipation on everyone's faces. There was an imperceptible nod from Stephen. Robert de Brus gave a slight bow and said, "With your permission, your majesty, I shall return to my manor. I have neglected it too long."

He had to come past me and I put my hand up to arrest him. "My Lord Guisborough, a word before you go." He was smaller than I was and he had to look up into my face. "Do not send spies into my land. The last time I destroyed your tower and enslaved your men. Next time I will destroy your manor and kill all that I find."

They thought they had trapped me for there was a clamour as voices were raised against me. I knew what I was doing. I was telling Stephen the Usurper that I was not afraid of him.

"Do you hear, your majesty? This is too much! This renegade should be punished!"

I put my hand on my sword, "And will that be you? Will you fight me?"

The Archbishop put his elderly frame between us. "Not in these holy grounds."

"Then let us go outside, De Brus. We have bad blood between us. Let us purge it now. Come outside and face me man to man."

I saw fear in his eyes.

Stephen said, "That is not the way we settle things."

"It used to be. There was a time when Champions settled matters such as this." I turned to Stephen the Usurper. "What say you and I fight for the throne of England. You are a warrior. Who knows you might defeat me and then all of England would be yours."

"You go too far."

"Then nominate a Champion. I will fight any!" I glared at them all defying them to accept the challenge. One by one they all dropped their gaze. "As I thought, not a backbone amongst you!" As Robert de Brus continued out I said, "Heed my words Guisborough. I do not use them lightly!"

When he had gone Stephen said, "Deliver my message, Cleveland, and then prepare your castle for if my offer is rejected then I will pull it down stone by stone!"

He and his entourage swept out. The Archbishop shook his head, "You are headstrong. Why can you not play the game?"

"Because this is not a game, your grace. It is men's lives and the words of a dead King. If we cannot uphold our oaths then we are as animals in the fields."

He left. I turned to leave with Wulfric, who was grinning all over his face and Gilles who looked bemused. As we stepped out Sir Edgar appeared, "And a word of warning for you, Earl of Cleveland. You have insulted my king and I will not bear it. If I find any wearing your livery south of the Tees then they die!"

I nodded. "We know where we stand then. Prepare your walls, Mandeville, for if you annoy me then I will destroy you and your castle. Unlike the words of de Brus that is not an idle threat. It will be backed by my sword."

Once we had gathered our belongings I sent Gilles to fetch the wagon and drivers. We had pots to take home. I suspected my visits to York would be far fewer in the future. I had worn out my welcome. Archbishop Thurston, wrapped in furs, came to speak with us as we waited for the carters. "Alfraed you always seem to choose the most difficult course."

"I am sorry, your grace but Stephen's offer is pitiable. He has lost Normandy already and he wishes the Empress to give up her claim for England! It is ludicrous."

"But if she wins in Normandy then what? Will she and her Angevin come to England? Would we have two rulers? That would be anarchy."

I went closer to the Archbishop so that only he could hear my words, "If the Empress came to England then I would hope that all true Englishmen, knights, men at arms, men of the church would rally behind the banner of the true heirs of King Henry."

"The country would suffer if there were civil war."

I shook my head, "Then speak those words to the man who has stolen the crown and not me. Farewell Archbishop Thurston. You are a good man and I hope we fight on the same side once more but you know where my loyalty lies."

"Aye, my son, that I do."

He returned back inside. He seemed smaller somehow. I saw the usurper and his cronies watching us from the doors of the palace. Philip of Selby said, "Robert de Brus and his men left in hurry. Did you upset him, lord?"

"Left?"

"Aye, they got their horses and galloped out of the north gate."

"Then he heeded my words. I suspect he and his men will go to make their castle stronger."

By the time the wagon came and we had packed it the afternoon was half spent. We would not make it home before dark. We rode through the gate by the church and along the Roman Road. Once through the old Roman defences, the houses became sparse and it was an empty land through which we travelled. The road was well travelled and the snow had long since gone. However, the wagon meant we did not travel as quickly as we might have hoped.

As darkness approached Wulfric said, "We cannot travel all night, lord. It is turning colder and if it freezes then the road will become dangerous."

"I know. Alan, take us to your old home. We will stay there."

"Aye lord."

The snow hid all signs of the fires where we had burned the bodies of the assassins a year ago. The gates were still open and the virgin snow showed that only animals had entered of late. A year of neglect had meant that the hall was no longer watertight and small flurries of snow could be seen in nooks and crannies. The walls were, however, sound and the gates could be closed. My men were industrious and once a fire had been lit in the hall and the animals stabled we all felt better. We ate communally in the Great Hall with no division of rank.

I saw Alan looking at the dark stain on the floor. That was where his mother and father had died. He was now a man at arms, the equal of any save Wulfric. Gilles too had grown much in the last year. He was thoughtful and he knew the cause of Alan's silence. He sat next to him and began talking. I knew not of what they spoke but whatever it was it took Alan's mind off the stain and he even smiled.

I stood and walked to the fire. Wulfric and Philip joined me. "My uncle is in a difficult position, lord. He is the second-highest priest in the land. His position means he has to support whoever is crowned."

"I know, Philip, and the fact that he has sent you to serve me shows his true colours but there will come a time when he has to choose. When the Empress returns that will be such a time."

"Before then, lord, we have the problem of this Stephen of Blois. With King David in the west as an enemy, Stephen has bound us to the south and east with enemies. De Brus will not be alone and that Mandeville looks like a nasty piece of work. I am now glad that we hired those men of Skipton for we will need many more soon enough."

The two carters, James and Matthew joined us. "Lord we have something to tell you but we know not how."

"Speak, you both know me and my word. I will respect whatever you have to tell me."

"After you hired us we were offered money not to do as you asked."

Matthew quickly added, "We did not take it."

"Who was it?"

"We are not certain but I believe it was one of the men at arms of the de Brus clan. He had a cloak over his livery."

"Was he upset when you refused?"

"No lord but I liked not the look on his face."

"Thank you for your honesty."

"Lord, when we get to your home we would join you there."

"Why? You both have a business in York, do you not?"

"There are many men with carts and wagons in York. Sometimes there is no business. Besides, we both come from the valley. It is our home. There would be work for carters there, would there not?"

"Of course."

"And although we cannot pull a bow these days we can wield a sword. We have heard how you fight the Scots still and we would join you."

"Then join us and welcome!"

They both seemed pleased and after they had left us Wulfric said, "If they knew we had hired a wagon then they might plan an ambush."

I nodded. "That was my thought too. They know our numbers. De Brus is not brave enough to attack our castle but he might risk an ambush where he can outnumber us. It would be a way to rid the land of me and my best warriors in one fell swoop. We must work out where that might be. At least forewarned is forearmed. We are but half a day from home."

"Lord, that is half a day in summer. It might be nearer a day in this weather."

"Then we trust to God, our swords and the skill of Philip's archers."

We warned the men of the dangers and set off before dawn. The hills to the east hid dawn for longer than normal. The weather had eased so that it was just a grey dawn that came filled with scudding clouds. The lack of rain and snow meant we had good visibility. Alan knew the land and he and Stephen the Grim rode ahead with two of Philip's archers. Our strategy was clear. We had to keep to the main road and look for any sign that others had used the road. Guisborough was just twenty miles away over the other side of the Roseberry. They would have reached home before we had arrived at Osmotherley. That was more than enough time to prepare warriors. Wulfric guessed they would have left their own home before we had. They would look to intercept us. The question was, where?

Wulfric said, "We could deceive them, lord, and make for Yarm and not Thornaby. It would take us further west. I am guessing that they will try to take us by Hilton. There are dips and hollows on the road there. The wagon may struggle."

"Aye, if we take the road from Crathorne to Yarm we would just have that one steep bank and then it would be downhill. It is worth the risk."

We did not reach Crathorne for, not far from Arncliffe, our scouts rode in. "Lord, look on the crest of the hill."

I looked northeast and saw the banners of De Brus on the hillside. There were no roads leading down but there were trackways. The enemy had seen us and began to descend. He had sent only horsemen. The numbers suggested they outnumbered us. They disappeared into the woods. There they would make better time as the branches would have kept the tracks clear of snow. "Philip, I want half of your men inside the wagon. Tie their horses to the rear. We use the wagon as a mobile castle. Wulfric, we surround the wagon with our men at arms. We cannot outrun them. Let us outwit them. Matthew, when we are attacked we stop."

"Aye lord."

"While we can we put as much distance between them as we can."

Had things been better between us I might have sent a rider to Richard of Yarm but I felt I could not trust him yet. It was better to fight with men you knew you could trust than rely on those with dubious loyalty.

It was the long slow slope that slowed us down. With the extra men in the wagon, we moved at a snail's pace. The men of De Brus burst from the woods. There were forty of them. "Halt!"

Philip shouted, "Archers dismount!"

We now had archers within and without the wagon. The ones in the wagon had their bows strung. They were ready to release as soon as the enemy closed within their range. We drew swords and prepared to meet them. We could have fought on foot but I knew that the enemy horses would baulk at the barrier of the wagon. I wondered if the leader of these men knew that. As they came I saw just one knight. These were men at arms. The livery was that of De Brus but not the standard. He had sent a lesser knight to do this deed.

Philip shouted, "Release!" and the ten archers in the wagon sent their shafts at the enemy. They aimed and five arrows found their targets. One horse slewed around and slid to the ground mortally wounded. One man at arms clutched his arm.

"Release!"

This time the archers behind the wagon released their arrows high in the air. These were blind strikes but they kept releasing. It meant that the men at arms had to put their shields up to prevent the arrows from hitting them. I suspect their mail was not the best. The closer they came to us the greater the impact of the arrows. I saw the knight take an arrow in the narrow gap between the brow of his helmet and his coif. He was thrown backwards over his saddle.

And then they were within sword range. As I had expected their horses turned rather than risk the wall of horses and wagon. The leading man at arms brought his sword around to hack at my body. I blocked it with my shield and sliced down with my own sword. He could not both strike and defend. My sword sliced through the mail and lopped off his arm below the elbow.

A spear clattered into the side of my helmet. The straps broke and my helmet fell from my head. Gilles' sword stabbed out and found a gap under the arm of the man at arms. He wheeled away. And then Wulfric went berserk. Perhaps it was the sight of my helmet flying from my head or the fact that it was my squire who had saved my life. Whatever the reason he gave a roar and spurred his horse into the heart of the whirling men at arms. He stood in the saddle and whirled his axe in a wide circle. Those who were slow to duck and dive out of the way were struck. Two men fell to the ground. One was mortally wounded. My other men at arms exploited the gap created by Wulfric and followed him into the heart of the enemy.

I spurred Rolf and rode at the man at arms who was levelling his spear to take a wild Wulfric in the back. He did not see me coming as he pulled back his arm to strike what would be a fatal blow. I rode across the rear of his horse and swung my sword horizontally across his cantle. My blade bit through his mail and into his flesh. He threw his arms into the air and the spear fell to the ground. A second enemy wheeled his horse to face me. He too had a spear and, seeing that my helmet had gone aimed his spear at my head. It was a mistake. I raised my shield, ducked behind it and arrowed my hand towards his middle. The spearhead slipped over my shield and rose up. He impaled himself upon my sword. Such was the collision that my hand was only stopped by his middle. It took all of my strength to keep hold of my sword.

As I recovered my blade I looked around and saw that the enemy were fleeing. We had broken them. I raised my sword in triumph and my men cheered. Then I heard Edgar, "My lord, it is Wulfric. He has fallen."

I looked around and saw that Wulfric lay on the ground. Blood was coming from his side. He opened his eyes, "I am sorry lord, I lost my temper, I fear, for the last time."

"Don't you dare die on me, Wulfric! I have to chastise you when you are well!"

And then his eyes closed.

Epilogue

Wulfric took until after Yule to recover. The wound was a deep one and had required over thirty stitches. I worried that his shield arm would not be as strong again but Wulfric, once he was up and about was confident that he would be as strong after as he was before.

The snows followed us home. The grey scudding clouds had given way to heavy snow-laden ones. We were lucky to get the *'Adela'* away before winter set in. I entrusted my message to Gilles. He would tell Leofric who would, in turn, tell the Empress. I impressed upon Gilles the need to make my views and position clear. I would have gone myself but I feared for the mischief which De Brus, Mandeville and the Scots might cause in my absence. Wulfric's wound decided me. We watched *'Adela'* disappear into a white storm of whirling snow. I did not envy him the journey but knew that once he had passed Dover then the weather would marginally improve and by the time he reached the Loire it would be like an English autumn.

It was not just the weather that made us an island. We were now totally surrounded by enemies. The Archbishop had made it quite clear to me that the Bishop of Durham was no longer neutral. Stephen the Usurper had allowed the Palatinate to pay less taxes in return for tightening their borders with us. Our only door to the outside world was the Tees and we were now left with one ship tied to our jetty. That would be our only escape. I knew that, realistically, I would never take that way out but for the women who stood by their knights it would be a way out. For the rest of us, we stood behind our walls and we watched as winter tightened its icy grip. We had survived one year of the reign of Stephen of Blois. Until now he had allowed us to live. I had spurned his offer of friendship and now it would be war, to the death. I was truly a Warlord and I was fighting, as my father had done, to preserve a way of life. The spirit of the Housecarl lived on in me and my men.

Glossary

Allaghia- a subdivision of a Bandon-about 400 hundred men (Byzantium)
Akolouthos - The commander of the Varangian Guard (Byzantium)
Al-Andalus- Spain
Angevin- the people of Anjou, mainly the ruling family
Bandon- Byzantine regiment of cavalry -normally 1500 men (Byzantium)
Battle- a formation in war (a modern battalion)
Booth Castle – Bewcastle north of Hadrian's Wall
Butts- targets for archers
Cadge- the frame upon which hunting birds are carried (by a codger- hence the phrase old codger being the old man who carries the frame)
Cadwaladr ap Gruffudd- Son of Gruffudd ap Cynan
chausses - mail leggings. (They were separate- imagine lady's stockings!)
Conroi- A group of knights fighting together
Demesne- estate
Destrier- war-horse
Doxy- prostitute
Fess- a horizontal line in heraldry
Galloglass- Irish mercenaries
Gambeson- a padded tunic worn underneath mail. When worn by an archer they came to the waist. It was more of a quilted jacket but I have used the term freely
Gonfanon- A standard used in Medieval times (Also known as a Gonfalon in Italy)
Gruffudd ap Cynan- King of Gwynedd until 1137
Hartness- the manor which became Hartlepool
Hautwesel- Haltwhistle
Kataphractos (pl. oi)- Armoured Byzantine horseman (Byzantium)
Kometes/Komes- General (Count) (Byzantium)

Kentarchos- Second in command of an Allaghia (Byzantium)
Kontos (pl. oi) - Lance (Byzantium)
Lusitania- Portugal
Mansio- staging houses along Roman Roads
Maredudd ap Bleddyn- King of Powys
Mêlée- a medieval fight between knights
Mummer- an actor from a medieval tableau
Musselmen- Muslims
Nithing- A man without honour (Saxon)
Nomismata- a gold coin equivalent to an aureus
Outremer- the kingdoms of the Holy Land
Owain ap Gruffudd- Son of Gruffudd ap Cynan and King of Gwynedd from 1137
Palfrey- a riding horse
Poitevin- the language of Aquitaine
Pyx- a box containing a holy relic (Shakespeare's Pax from Henry V)
Refuge- a safe area for squires and captives (tournaments)
Sauve qui peut – Every man for himself (French)
Serdica- Sofia (Byzantium)
Surcoat- a tunic worn over mail or armour
Sumpter- packhorse
Tagmata- Byzantine cavalry (Byzantium)
Turmachai -Commander of a Bandon of cavalry (Byzantium)
Ventail – a piece of mail that covered the neck and the lower face.
Wulfestun- Wolviston (Durham)

Maps and Illustrations

Stockton Castle

Historical note

The book is set during one of the most turbulent and complicated times in British history. Henry I of England and Normandy's eldest son William died. The king named his daughter, Empress Matilda as his heir. However, her husband, the Emperor of the Holy Roman Empire died and she remarried. Her new husband was Geoffrey of Anjou and she had children by him.

The language we now call English evolved over a long period. The Ancient Celtic language was changed through the addition of not only Latin words but many from the languages of the auxiliaries who served on the frontier. The Jutes invaded, bringing their words with them and then the Angles and the Saxons. Although I call the language the natives of England speak, Saxon, its name is now accepted as Old English. Most of the functional words in English are still Old English. When Sir Winston Churchill wrote his 'fight them on the beaches' speech the majority of the words he uses are Old English in origin. The Normans added many words to the English language and Old English became Middle English. If we had the ability to travel back in time then the Middle English of Chaucer would have appeared as a foreign language to us. It took until Shakespeare's time for it to become closer to the language we use today.

King Stephen did indeed come to the north before Easter 1136 where he negotiated a peace treaty with King David. The Scots gave up all that they had captured save Carlisle and in return, King David's son, Prince Henry, was allowed to keep his lands in Huntingdon. Alfraed's successful campaign is fiction.

Books used in the research:

- The Varangian Guard- 988-1453 Raffael D'Amato
- Saxon Viking and Norman- Terence Wise
- The Walls of Constantinople AD 324-1453-Stephen Turnbull

- Byzantine Armies- 886-1118- Ian Heath
- The Age of Charlemagne-David Nicolle
- The Normans- David Nicolle
- Norman Knight AD 950-1204- Christopher Gravett
- The Norman Conquest of the North- William A Kappelle
- The Knight in History- Francis Gies
- The Norman Achievement- Richard F Cassady
- Knights- Constance Brittain Bouchard
- Knight Templar 1120-1312 -Helen Nicholson

Griff Hosker February 2016

Other books by Griff Hosker

If you enjoyed reading this book, then why not read another one by the author?

Ancient History

The Sword of Cartimandua Series
(Germania and Britannia 50 A.D. – 128 A.D.)
Ulpius Felix- Roman Warrior (prequel)
The Sword of Cartimandua
The Horse Warriors
Invasion Caledonia
Roman Retreat
Revolt of the Red Witch
Druid's Gold
Trajan's Hunters
The Last Frontier
Hero of Rome
Roman Hawk
Roman Treachery
Roman Wall
Roman Courage

The Wolf Warrior series
(Britain in the late 6th Century)
Saxon Dawn
Saxon Revenge
Saxon England
Saxon Blood
Saxon Slayer
Saxon Slaughter
Saxon Bane
Saxon Fall: Rise of the Warlord
Saxon Throne
Saxon Sword

Medieval History

The Dragon Heart Series
Viking Slave
Viking Warrior
Viking Jarl
Viking Kingdom
Viking Wolf
Viking War
Viking Sword
Viking Wrath
Viking Raid
Viking Legend
Viking Vengeance
Viking Dragon
Viking Treasure
Viking Enemy
Viking Witch
Viking Blood
Viking Weregeld
Viking Storm
Viking Warband
Viking Shadow
Viking Legacy
Viking Clan
Viking Bravery

The Norman Genesis Series
Hrolf the Viking
Horseman
The Battle for a Home
Revenge of the Franks
The Land of the Northmen
Ragnvald Hrolfsson
Brothers in Blood
Lord of Rouen
Drekar in the Seine
Duke of Normandy
The Duke and the King

Danelaw
(England and Denmark in the 11th Century)
Dragon Sword
Oathsword
Bloodsword
Danish Sword

New World Series
Blood on the Blade
Across the Seas
The Savage Wilderness
The Bear and the Wolf
Erik The Navigator
Erik's Clan

The Vengeance Trail

The Reconquista Chronicles
Castilian Knight
El Campeador
The Lord of Valencia

The Aelfraed Series
(Britain and Byzantium 1050 A.D. - 1085 A.D.)
Housecarl
Outlaw
Varangian

The Anarchy Series England 1120-1180
English Knight
Knight of the Empress
Northern Knight
Baron of the North
Earl
King Henry's Champion
The King is Dead
Warlord of the North

Enemy at the Gate
The Fallen Crown
Warlord's War
Kingmaker
Henry II
Crusader
The Welsh Marches
Irish War
Poisonous Plots
The Princes' Revolt
Earl Marshal
The Perfect Knight

Border Knight
1182-1300
Sword for Hire
Return of the Knight
Baron's War
Magna Carta
Welsh Wars
Henry III
The Bloody Border
Baron's Crusade
Sentinel of the North
War in the West
Debt of Honour
The Blood of the Warlord
The Fettered King

Sir John Hawkwood Series
France and Italy 1339- 1387
Crécy: The Age of the Archer
Man At Arms
The White Company
Leader of Men
Tuscan Warlord

Lord Edward's Archer
Lord Edward's Archer

King in Waiting
An Archer's Crusade
Targets of Treachery
The Great Cause
Wallace's War

Struggle for a Crown
1360- 1485
Blood on the Crown
To Murder a King
The Throne
King Henry IV
The Road to Agincourt
St Crispin's Day
The Battle for France
The Last Knight
Queen's Knight

Tales from the Sword I
(Short stories from the Medieval period)

Tudor Warrior series
England and Scotland in the late 14th and early 15th century
Tudor Warrior
Tudor Spy

Conquistador
England and America in the 16th Century
Conquistador
The English Adventurer

Modern History

The Napoleonic Horseman Series
Chasseur à Cheval
Napoleon's Guard
British Light Dragoon
Soldier Spy

1808: The Road to Coruña
Talavera
The Lines of Torres Vedras
Bloody Badajoz
The Road to France
Waterloo

The Lucky Jack American Civil War series
Rebel Raiders
Confederate Rangers
The Road to Gettysburg

Soldier of the Queen series
Soldier of the Queen
Redcoat's Rifle

The British Ace Series
1914
1915 Fokker Scourge
1916 Angels over the Somme
1917 Eagles Fall
1918 We will remember them
From Arctic Snow to Desert Sand
Wings over Persia

Combined Operations series
1940-1945
Commando
Raider
Behind Enemy Lines
Dieppe
Toehold in Europe
Sword Beach
Breakout
The Battle for Antwerp
King Tiger
Beyond the Rhine
Korea
Korean Winter

Tales from the Sword II
(Short stories from the Modern period)

Other Books
Great Granny's Ghost (Aimed at 9-14-year-old young people)

For more information on all of the books then please visit the author's website at www.griffhosker.com where there is a link to contact him or visit his Facebook page: GriffHosker at Sword Books

Printed in Great Britain
by Amazon